New Cuba

Timing is Everything

FH Spector

Guardian   Florida

The Library of Congress has catalogued this novel as follows:
Name: Spector, FH, author
Title: New Life in New Cuba: a novel/FH Spector.
Florida: Guardian Books, [2024]
TXu 2-445-830

ISBN: 979-8-9904471-3-4 (Print)
ISBN: 979-8-9904471-4-1 (ebook)

FHSpector.com

Book cover designs by CC

New Life in New Cuba, Timing is Everything, is a fictional story. Names, characters, places, and incidents are the product of the author's imagination or are used fictitiously.
Any resemblance to actual events, locales, business establishments, or persons, living or dead, is entirely coincidental.

Books by FH Spector

New Cuba Series:

One day…

Table of Contents

Chapter 1

Back Home and Possibilities

"Hold on, Phoenix," said Carlos as he drove his pickup outside the airport perimeter road. The truck jostled on the rocky area surrounding the landing strips, but it was the ideal place for him to wait and watch as plane after plane made a smooth landing. "Any minute now," he told the pup as he parked facing the runways. He opened the door, and Phoenix followed him out.

Making his way to the front of the truck, he found a spot and leaned on the bumper, Phoenix lay at his feet. "Annny minute now," he reached down and patted her head. Carlos shot to standing and leaned back on the truck every time a plane approached. Phoenix matching Carlos; standing, sitting, standing, sitting. The gravel crunched as he tapped his feet and adjusted his position as plane after plane hit the tarmac. The screech of their massive tires is even louder than from inside the plane.

He'd missed Carmen more than he'd ever missed anyone. The days seemed to drag on and on as he ticked off the squares in the calendar with a giant X; one day closer to when Carmen comes home. Then he looked down at his watch and up as he spots the airbus make the approach. "That has to be her plane. Let's go." He opened the tailgate, and faster than he could command, Phoenix jumped in and sat.

Carmen's plane landed smoothly on the tarmac in New Cuba after a horrendously long flight from Fairbanks. after a horrendously long flight from Fairbanks.

Over the years, the airstrip had undergone many name changes, but now, a US state, the federal government settled on Havana International Airport.

Airport planners, architects, and contractors redesigned the terminals to be more efficient. They added gates complete with jetways. No more walking on the runway, and up and down treacherous aluminum stairs that were rolled into place. Even the gaping potholes in the runway asphalt were repaired.

Inside the terminal, professional designers created an inviting atmosphere with new paint colors, and stylish furniture added a touch of sophistication.

In one area, the history of Cuba's transition to New Cuba was portrayed by Cuban artists through paintings displayed on a long gallery wall. Every image a fragment of Cuba's historical struggle, accompanied by labels detailing the events.

Popular chain restaurants opened facilities to cater to those hungry and stuck with a layover, and several bars were added for the troubled or whoever desired a stronger relaxant, and last-minute gift shops in each terminal for the shopping addicted.

Carmen went on this trip with her oldest and dearest friends, Nina and Mary. They picked the destination out of their ceremonial coconut about two years before, and Carmen thought it was the perfect time to take a break.

Her partners, Pilar and Gabby, would take care of their establishment, and she hired extra help to ease any pressure, though worry still weighed her down.

It had been difficult to let go, and leaving her property to her friends was a big step. Besides all the help, Carlos was around the corner, so she put any worries in a sack for later. Their relationship was strong, and they relied on each other as though they'd been together much longer than they actually were.

Carmen ached all over to get to him and her pooch, Phoenix. She'd forgotten what it felt like to want to be with a man. To be consumed with thoughts of him, to feel his touch. One look from Carlos and she'd come undone. She'd spent a lot of time remembering those early days. The way he'd lean in the doorway, his eyes smoldering over her, heating her from the inside out. Unable to admit it then, how hard she fought the deep desire to leap onto him.

Her relationship with Carlos was in stark contrast to her previous relationship with her ex-husband. The marriage ended years earlier. Something that should never have started in the first place left her with three perfect children, and for that she was grateful. Carmen reveled in Carlos's caring and loving nature.

Once the fuselage door opened, Carmen grabbed her purse and exited the plane, almost sprinting down the jetway. She had to wait for her luggage to arrive, but that didn't deter her.

As soon as she got inside the terminal, she raced to the baggage area, past the duty-free shops that overflowed with various last-minute gifts a traveler may need; New Cuba flags, 'All I got was this stupid t-shirt shirts,' maracas painted with flags, and other assorted 'New Cuba' labeled chachkies.

The new airport sported an entire cigar shop dedicated to

selling the most luxurious brands of Cuban cigars. The aroma permeated that section of the port; a heady blend of leathery dry leaves and sweet smoke. It was no longer illegal to purchase Cuban cigars, and the state's tax revenue from the sale of cigars had skyrocketed.

Relieved to be home, she paced and tapped her feet while waiting to collect her luggage from the carousel. As bags slithered through the hole in the wall, she continued to think about the visits she'd had so many years before the last invasion.

Carmen remembered the lack of carousels and everyone's 'gusanos' littering the place like large, black construction trash bags.

The previous administration started calling Cubans who left the island 'gusanos,' worms for abandoning their homeland. And when they returned for a visit, the large black duffle bags were called 'gusanos.' She let out an audible guffaw at the memory of the ordeal.

In those days, blue security cellophane was used to wrap the bags. You scanned for the one with the white sheet of printer paper you'd written your name on with a big black Sharpie.

Carmen had to weave her way through the piles of seventy pound cheap, black duffle bags, praying hers didn't tear open when they threw it, or opened on purpose and robbed, for that matter.

Her mother had once brought an entire wheel of gouda for *her* mother, and a customs officer confiscated the treasure.

She thought it odd other people brought in food and medicine that wasn't taken. A pang of sadness crept in and her heart sank.

5

Nowadays it was different. Carmen spotted her suitcase coming through the rubber verticals that separated the baggage area from the rest of the terminal. She'd tied a large swath of neon pink tulle on the handle. The carousel squeaked and squawked around as she waited for her bag to be close enough to grab. Carmen had packed *just* enough and carried her heavy winter parka.

Carmen used all her strength to pull the bag off the conveyer, and the four spinners made it a breeze to maneuver the luggage through the crowd. "Excuse me, perdon," she said as she squeezed sideways through the crowd. Carmen could feel her insides urging her forward and the butterflies hurrying her out of the baggage area.

At the exit, the terminal doors opened, and the heat of the afternoon hit her like a punch in the face. She could smell the exhaust from the antique cars that were lined up to pick up passengers. And even though it was still February, Carmen compared the frozen white wilderness she'd just returned from to this hot, lush land of sun and palm trees.

Outside, next to the 'No Parking' sign, she spots the familiar pickup and Carlos, waving like a madman. She told him not to meet her inside because she wanted to see Phoenix as soon as she landed. He couldn't leave her in the car or bring her inside, so he'd agreed, and waited until she appeared at the door.

Carmen's smile said it all as she dashed through the crosswalk in front of the paused traffic. Behind Carlos, a barking Phoenix waggled in the truck bed, her whole body jerking.

6

Reaching the truck, Carmen pinched her cheeks to relieve the muscles that hurt from smiling. After letting go of her bag, she leapt onto Carlos, wrapping her legs around him and planting a kiss so deep that when the traffic light changed, no vehicle budged from their spot.

"I've missed you so much, and I hate it when you go away." Carlos squeezed her tight, almost becoming one person. He stuffed his nose into her hair and inhaled.

"I missed you too. But you know the girls and I need our adventures." Carmen hugged Carlos back just as hard, then planted another, more penetrating kiss as she tugged at his man-bun. Carlos's hair had turned almost all gray. Flecks of blond, brown, and even a few chestnut strands still held their color.

"I love when you do that." He smirked and set Carmen down so she could greet her pup.

"Hi my sweet girl." She petted and hugged Phoenix, who by now had jumped from the truck bed and was waiting her turn.

Carlos opened the passenger door and placed the luggage in the back of the truck. The dog jumped in and sat between the two, leaning her full weight on Carmen the entire way home, slathering her chin with sloppy kisses.

"So, is everything okay back at the hotel?"

"Yes. Stop worrying. All is good. You're booked through the summer, and most of the fall. The cooking and horticulture classes are going well, and the restaurant is about finished."

"Good, good." She exhaled, and Carlos caught the fleeting

sound of disbelief, so he let it go. It bothered him she seemed to always be waiting for something to happen, to destroy her world. She'd see for herself. He took her hand and kissed it, holding it close to his chest.

"So tell me, how was Alaska?"

"We talked every day, you know how it was. Cold, beautiful, wild. We loved it." Carmen chattered about an Inuit family that invited them for dinner on their last night there. "It wasn't for me. They eat a lot of fat, or fatty foods. I'm not even a fan of pork belly."

Carlos laughed at her yuck face. "Yeah, I remember Gabby trying to get you to try a piece. You spit it out all over the table."

"Well, it was no different, my friend. I stuck to the few vegetables at the table and told them I was a vegetarian. Nina loved it, and Mary just picked at it. They were mourning their daughter who'd gone missing."

"I've heard about that, saw something in the paper. It's terrible that no one is doing enough to help all those native women that have gone missing."

"I can't even imagine. Between the desolation of where they live, the cold, and how long it takes anyone to get to them...hopeless."

They continued driving through town after town on the Carretera Central, in silence. Carmen opened the window and inhaled the fresh, warm country air. Her nose thus far hadn't defrosted. She eyed every place they passed. There were still lush landscapes and rolling hills. Farmers still tending their cattle and crops. Though she'd already lived in New Cuba for a couple of years, she was still in awe of the speed of progress across the island.

Road signs advertised new planned communities, condominiums, and multi-use villages that were all the rage back on the mainland. She smiled, thinking how wonderful it was that Cuba would be current with the rest of the world, at the same time burdened because all the natural beauty would soon turn into another concrete jungle. Carmen saw the signs.

As they passed familiar spots, Phoenix whined for a stop to romp through a field, or sit at a café that offered treats for pups. Carmen pet her pooch's ears, snuggling into her kaleidoscopic fur. "Ahh, soapy and clean."

"She had her grooming appointment this morning. I know you like her to be clean and smell good." Every word out of Carlos sang right through her, waking the butterflies that hid in every corner of her soul. Phoenix let out an agreeable bark.

Carmen spotted the royal palms that lined her driveway long before they arrived. As they turned onto the gravel, her insides squirmed, urging her to jump out and run to get there faster. Happy to be home, and warm, she let herself out of the car the minute it went into park, and made a beeline for the stairs, crunching over the gravel. As she passed her Corvette, she slowed and slid her hand across the tailfin. "I'll see you in a bit, old girl."

At the front doors, her excitement fought with the sheer contentment coursing through her. Her body vibrated as she grabbed for the door handle. Behind her, a bounding Phoenix, and behind the dog, Carlos, calling out to wait for him. Of course she couldn't. He shook his head and laughed.

Carmen threw open the front doors to a small crowd that yelled, "Welcome Home!" Her friends and employees all cheering her homecoming. Pilar's girls rushed toward her, and she gave each one a powerful hug. "My gosh! I think you've all grown a foot since I've been gone." As she stepped inside, she closed her eyes and inhaled as deep as she could draw in air.

"How was it? I bet it was cold," asked Pilar.

"Oh, it was cold, but so worth it."

"How are Nina and Mary?" asked Gabby. "Did they have fun too?"

"They're good. Yes, they had a great time. We all did. They'll be visiting soon. Right now, I just need a long, hot shower."

"Of course. We can't wait to hear more about your trip. Come on girls, let's go home. We'll see Tia Carmen later."

The crowd dispersed, and Carmen went to her room to freshen up and gather her thoughts. An ecstatic Phoenix leapt onto the bed, tail in full wag. The dog purred as she held her face to Phoenix's forehead and nuzzled her. Neither noticed Carlos slipping into the room with a stealth only reserved for spies. He grabbed her from behind. "OH! You scared me." Carmen turned around, her eyes piercing.

He lowered onto the bed, kissing every exposed piece of her neck, then stopped and stared into her eyes. "I know you want to rest…" and without warning, she pulled him in for a breathless, husky kiss, and an embrace that others would only aspire to measure up. Carlos slid his hands around her back and down, pressing her into him, then back up again, then he stood and pulled her to standing.

Carmen turned him and shoved him out the door. "What time will you be home?" he peeked at her through the crack.

"Later tonight. I want to check things out here." Carmen closed the door with a sheepish grin, winking at him seductively. Carlos couldn't wait to be with her, but he had to be patient and let her do her thing. It was difficult when *her* thing clashed with *his* thing, (and not in a good way).

Carlos had taken a gunshot from Machado, and after being discharged from the hospital, Carmen took it upon herself and moved in with him. She thought it a sign, but insisted on keeping her room at the hotel as her personal space. He didn't mind. After all, she'd moved in and they were building a new life together. There were times he wished she'd see how he felt about her not being close by.

Carmen had been gone for two solid weeks. To both her and Carlos, it seemed like months. After her attorney and handyman's betrayals, she stayed at her hotel, waiting for another shoe to come flying out of the sky and hit her in the head. It never did. Even so, she struggled to ignore anything she saw as a sign.

She'd needed a vacation, and took that trip to Alaska she'd

planned with her girls Nina and Mary. The three flew back to Miami, and Carmen continued on to New Cuba, her new home.

After her shower, she stepped out onto the main floor, taking a few moments to greet her patrons, with Phoenix trailing her. She loved hearing how they were enjoying their stay, and it satisfied every part of her that wanted something she'd built herself. At the stairs, she jogged up the steps.

Strolling the top two floors, she checked on flower arrangements and made sure the rest of the guests were enjoying themselves. When she arrived at her spot on the third floor, she stretched her arms wide on the railing, like she had so many times before, surveying the floors below. She was home. Another deep inhale and exhale. Looking down at her pooch, the dog turned in a circle, then rolled over, waiting for a belly rub.

"Well, that's new." She squatted down and gave her girl a much desired tummy rub.

Later that evening, the partners met for a fun girls' night in the study. Pilar and Gabby reported no issues, relieving Carmen of the sack of troubles she carried the entire trip.

After pouring some pinot grigio into their glasses, Carmen filled them in about what Fairbanks was like in February. "It was negative 35° the entire time. I'm so grateful I brought thermals, but it was so worth it." She took a sip of wine, smacked her lips, and leaned back, sighing.

"I don't think I'd survive," said Pilar.

"Since insurance won't cover you to drive the Dalton Highway, we hired a tour company to take us to the Arctic Circle. On the way up, we got to stand under the Alaskan Pipeline. It was fascinating. Did you know you could see the pipeline from the road all the way up?"

"Can you imagine what it was like to build it in those conditions?" asked Gabby.

"Right? Anyway, the driver was Inuit and told stories about his dysfunctional family the entire ride up. He told us that *'Living in the wilderness year round can make people a little kookie,'* as an explanation for their weirdness. Plus, so much intermarriage. The whole thing grossed me out." Gabby and Pilar giggled when Carmen tried telling the stories in the driver's voice.

"Did you tell him that living in the hot Caribbean can make people a little kookie as well?" asked Gabby.

"Hilarious. I told him having an older generation Cuban mother will to make you kookie."

"That's for sure," said Pilar.

"We used the same driver to get us to the Chena Hot Springs. Nina and I looked forward to the hot water, but Mary was worried she'd freeze to death once she got out, so she waited in the falling snow. I can guarantee we were warmer. We put on our bikinis and glided into the steamy hot water. It was fantastic." She told them how from outside the spring, Mary threw them a snow ball that became a melting hot potato game between Nina and Carmen. "The water was the perfect temperature. I almost didn't want to get out."

Once the frigid temperatures chilled her to her core, Mary left the girls to their own devices and followed the signs to the warmth of the restaurant, ordering a warm cup of hot chocolate spiked with Kahlua at the bar.

"That driver was so accommodating. He took us to a real dog sledding farm. We got to sit on a sled while a musher took us for a ride. We obviously couldn't drive ourselves. But seriously, this woman must have had a side hustle as a comedian. Her stories about life in the arctic had us almost peeing around every turn." The one about the bear and the hard core naturalists running to the outhouse naked in the middle of the night was one of their favorites.

"I wonder what kind of degree you need to be a musher?" asked Gabby.

"Are you looking for a fourth job?" asked Pilar while Carmen laughed.

"So then, the tour driver invited us to dinner with his family. We got to witness the dysfunction first hand. Boy, was he on target with that statement."

Carmen answered Gabby about the food, and how it wasn't her taste. "Of course not! I didn't cook it," laughed Gabby, followed by the other two. "Don't worry, no more pork belly for you!"

"I wouldn't go there again. Once is plenty."

"Have you picked a new vacation spot yet?" asked Pilar.

"No. I think we're taking a short travel hiatus. This trip was exhausting."

By the end of the evening, the wine depleted, as well as the food. They said their goodnights, and Pilar and Gabby made their way home. Carmen and Phoenix stepped into the driveway and headed straight for her Corvette. "Let's go home, sweetie." The reverberation of the engine sent happy shudders deep inside and set her sexy butterflies free.

Pilar arrived home to sleeping children, and a sleep deprived Luis and Cristina whom she sent home with a short, "Gracias." Weary eyed, they waved and nodded, then hobbled down and across the street to their house. Over the last couple of years, the couple stepped in to help with the girls so their mother could continue her duties as marketing director for the hotel and the upcoming restaurant. Pilar listened for the clank of the iron gate in her front yard before she went back to her own chores.

In her kitchen, Pilar stood with her hands at her waist. "Looks like the girls made cookies." Pilar took one chocolate chip cookie and nibbled on it as she stowed the cleaned bowl and cookie sheet Cristina had left drying. She eyed the stemless wine glass and bottle of Cabernet on the table and smiled. "Cristina knows me so well." Pilar pulled the cork and poured the burgundy liquid into the glass, splashing a few drops on the table.

Before she could wipe up the spillage, her cell phone rang. It was Juan. Ever since Cristina and Luis's wedding, the two had become friends. He'd check on her if he learned she'd be out late, and she'd make him lunch from leftovers and drop it off at the station. Pilar noticed more and more that there were more and more leftovers. It had all become cozy and familiar.

Pilar answered on the second ring, and Juan could feel the warmth of her smile through the telephone. They talked for over an hour, and Pilar filled him in on Carmen's vacation.

"That sounds like quite an exciting trip," Juan said when Pilar had reached the end of the narrative.

While Pilar truly cared for Juan and felt herself growing closer to him, she decided not to involve her daughters. It was too soon. After all, Eduardo had only been gone a little over two years now. She didn't want her daughters, or anyone else for that matter, to get the wrong idea. Pilar would keep this friendship a secret.

Before Gabby reached the bedroom, she heard Jose snoring. It sounded like bears fighting over a peanut butter sandwich that was caught in both their mouths. It was hard not to laugh at the long snorts, followed by lip smacking, that ended in a slight whistle. She lovingly covered him before heading to the kitchen to write out some notes for the new restaurant. Her head throbbed with ideas for the menu.

Gabby remembered the day she told Jose she still wanted something more. Something for herself. Without a thought, he offered to build her the restaurant of her dreams, which she happily accepted.

The new restaurant Jose was building wouldn't be fancy. Gabby drove him crazy, stopping by at random times on random days, asking how much longer. He joked that if he allowed her, she'd have laid mortar to brick, and built it herself. Jose ended up drawing the line and barring her from seeing anything or asking when it would be done.

Gabby's time and energy were consumed with detail after detail from the day they began construction. She'd planned the layout, the kitchen, and the décor, right down to the napkins. She obsessed over the comfort of her patrons and ordered the most comfortable chairs she could find, no matter the cost. Now that the damn thing was almost complete, she could order linens and tableware.

Most of all, she perseverated over the variety of items she'd have on the menu, and went through multiple iterations of what she thought should *be* on the menu. As a chef, it was the most exciting part of planning a restaurant. Being in New Cuba, she wanted to keep Cuban cuisine in the forefront; the basis for all dishes.

Gabby decided it would be a seasonal restaurant with rotating selections, along with a few staples everyone would love.

She and the girls decided it would be a dining destination, freeing up breakfast and lunch for the hotel, and the hotel would no longer serve formal dinners in the evening, but simple grab-and-go for guests who didn't want to venture out after a long day of fun.

Carlos woke when he heard the vroom of the engine as it turned the corner. He leapt from the couch when he heard the clutch as Carmen set the car in park in the driveway. Quickening his pace, then slowing himself down, he opened the door.

She figured he might have been asleep. His hair was tousled and his eyes were tiny slits. Through the white t-shirt that hung snuggled over the top of his pants, and she noticed that the button on the top of his jeans was undone. "Were you sleeping?"

"No. I was waiting for you. Dinner's ready." She gave him a sideways squint, looking down, then rubbed her closed mouth over her teeth, biting the side of her lip. He looked in that direction and sprang to button up.

"And… what are we having?" She peeked around him, her mouth watered over the aroma steaming from the kitchen.

Carlos closed the door behind her. "You'll see." Hauling her close, he planted a kiss so deep her legs quivered. Peeling inches away, she stared into his hazel eyes, running her fingers through his hair, pulling it back.

"I'm starving…"

"Let's eat."

"That's not what I meant…" Carmen turned him and pushed him against the door, pressing herself into him.

Through knit brows and a smirk, he wrapped his arms around her and looked long into her face. "Oh…" Without warning, he swept her up in his arms and carried her away. "Phoenix, door."

Carmen looked over his shoulder and her pooch popped up and closed the front door. Laughing, "Did you teach her that? Good girl!"

"We've learned some new things while you were away." As he entered the bedroom, he closed the door behind him with his foot, leaving Phoenix in the hallway.

For the next two hours, Phoenix lay waiting for her humans to reappear, whining, walking around, and grunting at the sounds emanating from the room. She even fell hard against the door a few times to remind them she was still waiting.

Carmen emerged barefoot in a t-shirt and boxers, and hurried on tiptoe to the couch to snuggle the dog while Carlos served a candlelit dinner of shrimp and lobster creole over jasmine rice and maduros that demanded she come to the table. After a big smooch, she and Phoenix hopped over to their spot in the kitchen.

"My favorite!" Carmen said. She hopped up and down in her seat, fast clapping, and looking over her plate. "I remember my dad inviting clients over for a business dinner. They'd hired him to do a large addition to their home. He had my mother make fresh shrimp and lobster creole in a giant pot. It was impressive. I don't know how she was able to carry the pot. When she began serving, I kept saying, 'One more' to the tails, and my dad kicked me under the table."

"Sounds about right," he laughed, and she rolled her eyes. That first forkful had her humming. The sweetness of the bananas complemented the richness of the creole sauce and the fragrance of the rice. The perfect bite. Their conversation floated from one topic to another. She was home.

After her long travel day, and the crazy time change, exhaustion pressed on her and she couldn't help but excuse herself. Along with the warm meal, she had been satisfied in every way and was ready to sleep.

As she brushed her hair in the dresser mirror, she eyed the seashell necklace hanging from the side finial. She skimmed her index finger over it, gave a half smile, and crawled into bed.

Carmen recalled the day she found it on the beach at Haulover Inlet. How later, Carlos explained, it was a sign of a new journey, and he was right. A sign at a fortuitous crossroads. One she hadn't noticed. Contented, she slid under the covers. Phoenix cuddled right in and they both drifted into a deep slumber.

At breakfast the next morning, "Any luck on those keys we found?" Over a year earlier, some keys had fallen out of the fireplace flue in the study. They still hadn't figured out what they opened. They'd spent days trying every door, to no avail. The metal clanked around in Carlos's pocket when he walked, a subtle reminder.

"No. Frustrating, but I'm still looking. Someone hid them in the flue, for a reason. They must be important."

Carmen knew he was right. It was a sign. But she didn't want to pressure him to keep looking. "Well, don't knock yourself out about it. I had a friend tell me once that if you turn over a glass, you'll find what you're looking for."

"Did it work?"

"Think about it. Whatever is missing will eventually turn up. It's only a matter of time."

"But did you try it?"

"Turning over the glass? Yes. I did. And yes. It worked." She slapped his shoulder. Carlos laughed and tried to dodge the slap, shooting her a sideways glance and eyebrow raise.

After cleaning up, she jumped in her car and headed to work. She wanted to check on the staff, and was eager to find out about the progress on the restaurant, though she knew she wasn't allowed to ask. As she pulled in, more guests were arriving, while others were leaving. "Love all the action." Turnover was important. She parked her Corvette in the 'Owners' spot and let Phoenix out. The dog stayed at her side until she began walking, then trotted next to her as if she were getting a steak or something.

As Carmen looked up at the hotel sign, she remembered the first time she laid eyes on the place, and the utter disaster she'd brought back from beyond the grave. The splintered wood on the porch, the tree that grew in the pool. Somehow, she eliminated the 'haunted house' feeling she got every time she walked in.

At the front desk, Pilar was finding movie tickets for the couple in room 333. The Alonso's were from Puerto Rico and had been island hopping on their honeymoon.

"Honestly, if we'd seen this place, we would have had a destination wedding." The woman walked over to the gallery hall where a photo of Cristina and Luis's wedding hung under a sign that read, 'We invite you to book your next event at La Mariposa de Pinar del Rio.'

Carmen held her breath while she heard people refer to their hotel as a 'destination.' "Hopefully they spread the word and we'll get more event bookings," she told Pilar through her ear to ear smile.

"That would be great!"

"Have you checked out the restaurant?"

"You know we're not allowed to even ask," Pilar laughed.

At that very moment Pilar's phone rang, and she glanced down at it, flipped it over, and turned off the ringer in one swift movement. Her face heated to a bright ruby- red, and her smile hinted at her secret.

"Who was that?" asked Carmen, though she knew all the signs of a woman smitten.

"What... who...? Oh, no one." She scrunched her eyes and shook off the question.

"'No one' makes you smile like that? Come on."

"Juan." As soon as she said his name, she covered her face.

"Sergeant Rodriguez?"

"Yes. We've been...talking." Pilar uncovered herself, but failed at trying to conceal her smile, or shake the feelings that seem to grow where she thought nothing should be growing. "It's nothing." She looked away.

"Can you please talk to me? I promise, I won't judge."

"I'm not ready."

"Well, whenever you need me, I'm here."

"No. I'm not ready to be seeing anyone. I don't think it would be good for the girls."

"It's okay. You don't have to be ready. Just tell him. He'll understand."

"That's just it. We're only friends. Nothing more, so there's nothing to tell him."

"Then why the big toothy smile when you saw his name light up across your cell?"

"I…I feel…I don't know what I feel," she exhaled. "Or how I should feel. Or anything, for that matter. He's kind and sweet. So thoughtful." Pilar's brows were tightly knit until she looked down, relaxed, and smiled again. Her phone screen chimed with a voicemail. Another smile. She turned the phone over and looked up at Carmen. "What?"

"You seem…lighter, happier when you talk about him. Maybe stick to how you feel, and not what you *should* feel. You have nothing to be ashamed of."

"But, Eduardo…"

"You aren't betraying him. He's not here anymore. You are. Think about that. You're too young to spend the rest of your life in mourning. In life, timing is everything." Just then, Angela set herself behind the check-in desk and smiled, uncomfortably. She could feel the thickness of the tense moment, but opted to look down at her computer.

Pilar remained silent, thinking about what Carmen said, then she picked up her phone and files. "I have to go. I have a couple of calls to make. Someone wants a tour. She's interested in having her wedding here. The other is a Quincéañera."

Pilar left Carmen at the front desk and walked outside to listen to Juan's message. She laid her files on the railing, put the phone to her ear, and leaned on the porch railing. She turned back, looking through the doors at Carmen who was peering back through the doors at *her*. A knowing smirk played across Carmen's lips as she leaned her chin on her hand.

At the sound of his voice, Pilar looked up at the ceiling and smiled. Looking back at Carmen, she shook her head and beamed wide before rolling her eyes and retreating to the safety of her car.

Carmen thought of her own mother who'd widowed young, yet never remarried, dated, or had any companionship. It's the old Cuban way; mourn forever. She hoped her friend's worries of betrayal wouldn't stop her from moving on, find happiness, and not dismiss possibilities that came her way.

Walking into the dining room, Carmen began lifting the covers on the chafing dishes at the buffet. It was time to clean up the lunch offerings, since they looked like dried up something.

As she turned, she spotted someone at a table. Alone. Her herringbone gray hair style was not to be mistaken for anyone else. Carmen scanned the rest of her, down to her red soled shoes. Margot Sanchez. The realtor she'd taken the listing from when the house was for sale.

"Hello, Margot. Welcome. I hope you enjoyed your lunch."

"Ms. Coronado. It was fine. Your hotel is doing well. And I see you're adding a restaurant."

"Yes. Thank you. It will be open in a few days. Can I get you anything else?"

"No. I've seen enough. I may have a buyer. They're interested in purchasing hotels across the island."

"As I've said. The Mariposa is not for sale." Carmen stared Margot down. She couldn't believe her arrogance.

"Things may change. I'll leave my card. Just in case," said Margot in a slow, deliberate way. Then she glided away, leaving a waft of expensive, unpleasant perfume in her wake.

Carmen waved her hand in front of her nose, slid the card into her pocket, and followed her into the lobby. Margot stopped in front of the glass display case, eyeing the boxes that were locked inside. "Interesting display."

"Yes. Once in a while, we find another box and add it to the collection."

"Hmmm. And you…plot, where you found them?" She turned to look at Carmen. "Why?"

"Well, we don't know who they belonged to or why they were buried where they were. There's so many of them, and all are valuable. It's possible that one day, someone will come looking for their box, or an ancestor's box. It would be nice to return them to their rightful heirs."

"How…altruistic of you," Margot's contemptuous stare bore into Carmen's kindness, making her jut her head back. "Interesting you should display them…like this."

"What do you mean?"

"Look closer, Carmen. Some are more valuable than others. I bet some were buried deeper than you realize. Like secrets."

Chapter 2

Mourning Forever and Preoccupations

Before Margot left, she glanced up at the top floors, spying the people that sat in some of the spaces or leaned on the railing, looking down. She turned to the fountain and stared into the basin. Carmen waited, but Margot didn't say a word.

As she turned to leave, she paused in front of the azulejo mural. The caustic woman flipped her jet straight gray bob and headed for the door. Her heels clacked her robust footsteps on the marble floor and Carmen stared after her, glancing toward Angela, who'd witnessed the bitter woman's perplexing remark.

Both women watched through the windows as Margot got in her white Mercedes that was valeted outside the door. "Throw this card out for me will ya?" Carmen handed Angela, Margot's business card.

"Who was that?" asked Angela as Carmen walked back into the dining room.

"Nobody. She's nobody."

Angela stared down at the card and brushed the sides of her curly hair down behind her ears. After a moment, she slid the card into the folio she always carried around.

Jose left before breakfast that morning. He lovingly laid a soft kiss on Gabby's head, inhaling her scent before moving a safe distance, trying not to wake her.

Once on the road, he stopped to pick up a large Cuban coffee and guava pastry at the Cafecito y Dulce. The new chain restaurant was popping up everywhere, sending the sweet smell of sugar, molasses, and freshly baked pastry into the air, followed by the warmth of fresh brewed coffee.

Reminiscent of donut shop windows, the restaurant offered a variety of coffees and sweets, as well as scrambled egg sandwiches on Cuban bread with a selection of toppings, pressed or unpressed.

Their small sit down space had about eight tables for patrons, and a long narrow metal counter with stools. The grab-and-go window had its own attendant for people in a rush that couldn't stay awhile and partake in chatter that was no doubt filled with gossip. Metal bistro tables and chairs lined the outside walkway of the shop, decorated with small vases that held roses in a variety of colors.

These days, Jose's preoccupation with the future had him spacing out throughout the day. He was getting older and thought more and more about being a father someday. Anytime he'd spend with Carlos, he'd listen to stories about how *his* kids had grown up, and it made his desire for fatherhood grow.

Jose and Gabby had been busy with their businesses for so long, they hadn't noticed how many years they'd been together. How much time has just flown by? Though Carlos told him not to worry, it would happen '*when the time was right,*' he couldn't help but fret. This new restaurant for Gabby would keep her even more busy, and away from him, and the weight of it almost crushed him.

Then there was *his* career.

Juggling several jobs at once, and having lost his partner, Eduardo, focusing had become a challenge. He missed him dearly and still carried the burden of his own involvement in Eduardo's death. Jose tried to shake off the memory whenever it would sneak up on him.

Jose often regretted that visit to Guerrero, blaming him for the damage to Carmen's house, and without knowing, set him on a vengeful track toward Eduardo.

Guerrero's brutality. The way he killed Eduardo, right in front of his young daughter. While he didn't witness the attack himself, he could hear the blows to Eduardo's skull, the smell of blood that must have spattered everywhere. The only solace Jose had found was that Guerrero would spend the rest of his life in prison for Eduardo's murder. His partner's absence left him an enormous responsibility; provide employment for his crew.

Combining Jose's team with Eduardo's doubled the amount of employees he handled, and had to check on, so he had little extra time. Though he appointed supervisors at each site, the projects were still taking longer than he'd planned, and clients began pressuring him for completion dates.

Besides his business, he'd wanted to talk to Gabby about their future. He just couldn't find the right time. Between the sandwich shop and the hotel, and now planning the restaurant, Gabby blurred as she whizzed to and from the various places, planting fast hugs and quick kisses on him as she flew by, leaving no trace. Jose hoped this was all temporary.

Once the restaurant was up and running, they'd get back to their life. Still, the tiny fear that this new endeavor would steal away his Gabby even more weighed like an anchor over his heart.

Shoving aside the innumerable thoughts dragging him down, he collected his coffee and pastry, got back in his truck, and headed for the restaurant job site.

As he pulled into the hotel driveway, he smiled at all the commotion going on out front. Guest were arriving, while others milled around the front porch with their Cuban coffee cups and buffet plates. The wide plank porch begged for company, and the outside seating arrangements were inviting. Carmen had the wood planks sealed, and purchased wicker seating arrangements with custom cushions in a tropical motif.

He looked up at the sign, "La Mariposa de Pinar del Rio." Carmen, Gabby, and Pilar had been sitting in folding chairs on the driveway, waiting to toast with champagne the day he installed the sign. They'd been so excited, they didn't mind the blistering heat of the day. He was thankful he'd been such a big part of bringing the old place to the present.

Jose smiled as the people laughed and talked their way around the porch. Then he remembered the day Carmen had fallen through that very porch and an audible chuckle escaped his throat as he drove on through.

Jose had to pull her up and carry her to the sofa in the study. Her leg had scraped from top to bottom and blood trickled over the side of her thigh. Though it was not one of her finest moments, he recalled Carmen laughing about the ordeal whenever she tells the story.

Bearing right, past the parking area, he drove onto the new gravelly driveway section that would lead to the restaurant.

Two weeks ago, they completed the building itself, including a large ranch area that could accommodate about fifty guests in the outdoor pavilion.

Leaving his 1978 Chevy truck in front of the construction trailer, he grabbed his hard hat and gloves from the bench seat, and his coffee from the drink holder Gabby had installed. She thought it would be safer than holding a cup of hot liquid while driving and shifting on the tree column gear. He gave a half-smile as he caught sight of it and remembered their 'discussion' about adding it to the vintage truck. 'She was right,' he thought and smiled.

"Buenos dias!" he called to the workers.

"Hola!" they returned. No matter the heat of the day, or exhausting the task, it amazed Jose how jovial the workers maintained their composure.

Jose went to the foreman for an update on completion. "Hey George. How are we doing? Any idea when it'll be ready?" He knew Gabby was eager to get started, and when she smiled, his heart swooned. He also knew she was dying to find out when she could have the keys, but they agreed she wouldn't pester. Jose hadn't even allowed her to visit the site or have a peek.

"Hey boss. We're putting the finishing touches in the

kitchen. It'll take a couple of days. While that's being done, we're completing the parking area and driveway. We've also arranged for the landscaper to complete the installation per Carlos's plan, and then the cleaning crew will be in to make it spotless. I know you want to bring Gabby as soon as possible, so… plan on a week from Saturday."

"Ten days. Perfect. It'll give me time to arrange something special." His heart beat hard against his ribs at the news he'd soon get to bring Gabby to her new place. He got back in his truck and drove to the other two job sites.

Gabby awoke to an empty house. She sat up in bed and listened for the sounds of morning. All quiet, save the chirping birds outside the bedroom window. Leaning toward her nightstand, she grabbed her notebook and pencil, reading over her midnight notes. The ones she scribbled while half asleep.

Every time a thought entered her mind, she'd write it down. Good or bad. In the morning, she'd look them over and scratch out the ones that were all crazy talk, followed by a distinct, "What was I thinking?" and laughter. "Thank goodness I'm the only one who sees this. Yikes!"

After getting herself together, she threw some salted butter in a cast iron pan and flipped on the gas burner. She whipped some eggs hard against the side of the bowl, added a pinch of salt and pepper, then spilled the mixture into the sizzling pan. After slicing open a fresh piece of Cuban bread, she buttered and laid it on the flattop, pressing the lever over the bread until she heard the sear of the cream.

Once her eggs were done, she opened the press, laid her scrambled eggs on top, closed the bun, and pressed again. It was her favorite breakfast. Simple and flavorful. Using a pair of tongs, she set the sandwich on a paper plate, and sat at the table to review her calendar for the day, and shot off a quick text to Jose.

Missed you this morning.

Missed you too. Didn't want to wake you.

Quiet dinner at home tonight?

Sounds perfect.

Gabby ended her text with a heart emoji and stared at the screen as three dots blinked from the other end, then disappeared. When no other message came, she shrugged, and set her phone on the table, staring at it, then continued on with her scrambled eggs on freshly pressed Cuban bread, simple and comforting.

She was dying to ask when the restaurant would be ready, but reminded herself she'd promised not to be a nuisance. Every day she counted on yoga stretches to relieve the tension. Sometimes it worked, others it didn't.

Gabby imagined it would be ready soon and trusted Jose to tell her as soon as he could. On the inside, she was all flutters, and that had her moving about in a torrent of activity all day long, speeding from one thing to the next to keep herself distracted. The closer completion came, the more anxious she became.

Busying herself, she dropped by the sandwich shop to check on inventory and her employees. At Jose's urging, she hired Olivia, her new manager. She was a whiz at keeping detailed books and ordering supplies from vendors. The place almost ran itself.

The shop had three other employees, and Olivia rotated *their* assignments as needed, and kept Gabby in the loop every week.

Gabby slipped in through the back door of the sandwich shop, grabbed her chef's coat from the hook, and made her rounds to the diners, catching a smidge of gossip here, a little buzz there. Everyone's food was up to snuff, assuring Gabby that all was well. Satisfied, she returned to the back office, removed her chef's coat and hung it on the hook in the kitchen.

On to the hotel. She knew she couldn't see the restaurant from the driveway since it sat far in the back, centered beyond the massive gazebo. She did everything in her power to keep her distance until he'd hand her the keys. Inside, she found Carmen at the front desk. "What's shakin'?"

"Nothing much. A lot of reservations. I can't believe how well we're doing." Google-eyed, she peered up at Gabby, then blinked away the excitement, replacing it with a far-away stare.

"I can. We've put a lot of work into this. It shows, and people took notice. What's the matter?"

Carmen let out a long breath. "Can we talk about Pilar?"

"Yes! What is happening? She's been aloof, quiet. Are the girls okay?" Gabby asked, not knowing about the phone flip.

"The girls are fine. Rose is already thinking about her Quincéañera. It's less than a year away. She reminds me of Nina when she was turning fifteen. And it's Sergeant Rodriguez. Well, not, Sergeant Rodriguez."

Carmen told Gabby all about the phone call and how Pilar lit up at the sight of his name on her phone screen. She explained how Pilar couldn't help feeling guilty that she might be interested in someone else.

"Oh. The Cuban-women-mourn-forever thing."

"Exactly."

"I'm afraid this is something she'll have to work out for herself."

"I know, but I worry she'll decide to 'mourn forever,'" Carmen air quoted, "and she's far too young to spend the rest of her life alone."

Gabby shook her head in agreement. There wasn't much they could do to help Pilar. "Let's see how it goes and we'll help if she needs us." Carmen nodded, then Gabby bounced into the dining room, making the rounds at each table.

As she checked on the buffet, she'd lean in and take a sniff. She could always tell when something sat too long. She had stepped back from cooking and hired and trained cooks to make everything the same way. Though Jose accused her of being too controlling, she'd answer that consistency was the key to success.

Spot checking their work kept her satisfied they were doing as instructed. Between the sandwich shop and the hotel, she had little time for anything else. And when the restaurant opens, she wants everything else running itself so she can focus on the restaurant alone. Hiring new people to run these two areas of business freed her up so she could do just that.

Back in the lobby, "Hey Carmen. Have you been out to peek?" Gabby's insides squirmed to get into the place.

"No. I don't want to be a nuisance either. I'm sure they're almost done. Most of the big trucks left about two weeks ago. However, I saw.."

"What? What did you see? Tell me!" Gabby insisted, but Carmen stayed tight-lipped.

"I don't want to spoil anything for you or Jose." With that, she went on with her work, avoiding eye contact.

Gabby rubbed her hands together, stretched overhead, stretched to the back, then exhaled as she slumped over the taller section of the front desk. Laying her forehead on the cold granite, she cooled herself. Carmen laughed at her attempts at self-control. "It's almost done, sweetie. Find something to occupy your time."

"If only I could." Gabby nodded, turned, and walked out the front door. Back at her house, she pulled out her notebook and began outlining menus, grand opening brochures, and setting appointments with liquor vendors. She was more than ready to get back into full restaurant mode. She'd picked up an organizer and began filing everything in its rightful spot.

Carmen went back to work, confirming reservations and tending guests' requests.

She hired Angela as a concierge, though ended up having to jump in whenever the demands were too outlandish, or they made Angela uncomfortable, and there were plenty of those instances to go around.

Angela was in her early twenties and took herself too seriously. She wore her curly brown hair in a tight bun. Carmen wasn't sure how long it was because Angela never wore it down.

For her interview, she'd dressed in a powder blue suit with a white silk shirt that hung blousy over the waistband. Her heels were of a respectable height, ensuring she could get from one place to another in a decent amount of time, unlike the other applicants in their five-inch ankle snappers.

Angela's nails were trim, in a nude polish, and her makeup, subtle. No long, fake nails and eyelashes like most of the other applicants. And while Carmen found the use of Spanglish a quaint practice, the mix of Spanish and English was unprofessional, so those applicants didn't make it past round one of interviews.

Angela carried herself well, confident and formidable, as though she had been in the field for many years. During the interview, she impressed Carmen with tales of her travel life. Her parents had taken her all over the world, and she'd seen first-hand what a good concierge looked like, as opposed to a bad one. She knew how to kowtow to guests and show her frustrations in private.

Once she'd gone to college, she'd changed courses multiple

times, always landing back on hospitality.

Carmen liked that she'd been so drawn to the field, hired her on the spot, and so far, she was doing an excellent job. She found Angela to have a good sense of humor, like all the other employees and friends that came and went throughout the day. Angela fit right in.

Recently, Carmen realized Angela had taken notice of Diego. They were around the same age, both single. Angela was certain he used pomade to tame his pompadour, and it suited him well.

Diego's trim beard only enhanced his strong jawline, and the way he clenched his muscled jaw sent ripples through his beard and shivers down her back. Angela exerted great effort to hide her growing affection for him. Even going so far as to snub him.

One day, Carmen caught her staring at Diego's arms flexing when he moved one of the enormous potted palms, and she couldn't help herself. She leaned in and whispered, "Close your mouth, dear." Then laughed at Angela's beet red reaction as she shuffled and picked up the stack of papers she'd been sorting, running to the office, and closing the door with a bang.

Diego noticed her charging away, and looked over at Carmen, who smiled and shrugged, then went back to work. He didn't realize the outburst had been all about him, but he stared after her none the less. Carmen watched as he didn't break the focus on Angela's retreat, and she smiled a delicious smile all schemers possess. The only thing missing from that smile was a handlebar mustache she could twist at the ends.

Diego had a kind face. His piercing, golden hazel eyes would laser-focus, blocking out anyone else in the room, listening to whomever was speaking. Every morning, he'd press his maintenance uniform with sharp creases at the front of his slacks. He looked professional. He always had a kind word, and a helpful nature that seemed to endear him to Angela that much more.

Despite her previous experience with her old handyman, Richard, Carmen grew to trust Diego with their hotel, giving him the extra room to live on the grounds. Another sign she'd grown and was ready to trust people again.

Jose made sure he was ready to take on the role of Maintenance Manager, with one employee to help when needed, and he met the challenge head on, earning his place in their close-knit group.

Around four o'clock, a few days after Pilar's phone flip, Sergeant Rodriguez stopped by to see Carmen. It was unexpected, and knowing how Pilar was feeling put her on guard. "Hi, Carmen. How's everything going?" The police officer had removed his hat and slowly turned it in his hands as he spoke, thumbing the stitching on the edge.

"Busy. Really busy." Carmen thought if she expressed how very busy she was, he wouldn't try to talk to her about Pilar. She couldn't help but notice the sergeant was fidgety as he stood in front of the desk.

"Good. Good." After too long a pause. "I'm…ugh. I'm

wondering if you've noticed anything…about Pilar. Anything different?"

"No. I haven't. Is everything alright?

"Oh, yes. Yes. I left her a message a few days ago, and she hasn't returned my call."

"Well, she's probably busy with the girls." Carmen thought it odd he didn't stop by when she was working. He had to know her shift ended at three, so he must have waited for her to leave.

"Okay. I'll try her again. Thank you." The sergeant left, replacing his hat as he walked through the front entrance. It was the only thing he had to combat the blazing sun that blinded him as he crunched over the gravel to his squad car, shaking his low hanging head.

The engine roared to life. He drove down the long driveway, making a left on the Carretera Central. The sun caught his rear window and flashed oncoming cars, temporarily blinding their drivers.

Juan couldn't stop thinking about Pilar and fought the urge to turn around and go to her house. Instead, he looked out the window at people going about their daily routines. She wouldn't like him just showing up. He'd have to wait until Pilar got in touch with *him*. He'd wait as long as it would take. She was worth it.

From the night he first saw her, he became so drawn to her that any idle time was spent thinking about Pilar. He wasn't about to come on too strong, or push her until she was ready. Juan will never forget the night he first laid eyes on her.

Pilar's husband, Eduardo, lay murdered on the side of the road near the wall in Guantanamo. One look at her and Juan froze. He wouldn't forget her wailing for her husband, nor the tears that engulfed her. From where he stood, he could feel the crushing weight of her pain in his own chest.

That night, Juan swore if he had the chance, he'd make sure she never hurt that way again. He took off his hat as he headed toward Pilar, when her friend Carmen and Pilar's young daughter appeared and knelt at her side. He turned away and replaced his hat, but didn't forget her.

Back at the station, he passed other officers as he went straight for his chair. He recognized the brown paper bag before he reached his desk. She had beautiful penmanship, and wrote his name on it with a swirly 'J' and a long, curly swoop at the end of the 'n.' He gave a half smile, half chuckle.

Inside, and still warm, he opened a container of arroz con pollo that had everyone in the precinct turn into prairie dogs, popping their heads up from their cubicle dens to peer around, searching for the source.

"Back off, she's all mine," laughed Juan. Using his foot, he grabbed one of the wheeled legs of his office chair, spinning it closer behind him so he could sit for dinner. As he inhaled the savory aroma of onions and garlic, and chicken and jasmine rice, he dug in, and within minutes, he'd devoured the dish. He leaned back, patting his stomach, and sighing.

"Any left?" asked the new rookie.

"Not a chance." He looked at the bag again, admiring the writing, imagining there was more to it that just some handwriting on a bag. At least, he hoped.

Outside the windows, the sidewalks burned with people rushing about, going in and out of doors that flashed the last rays of the setting sun. Juan felt content and imagined Pilar cooking, having enough left over to bring to him the next day.

Returning his gaze to the tabletop, he realized he'd been eating with one of Pilar's kitchen forks out of one of her Tupperware containers. He scrunched his eyebrows as he turned the fork and knife in his hand, then gathered the mess and returned it to the brown paper bag. Any other day, she'd drop off food in disposables. This was a first.

At eight the next morning, Pilar arrived at the hotel, ready for work. As she walked toward the front desk, she noticed her brown bag next to a small white bag. Her name, printed on it, nothing fancy. She put her hand to her stomach. Something about it stirred her, though she couldn't figure out why.

"Juan was here," said a chipper Carmen, almost singing. She couldn't help but notice the way Pilar was standing, examining the bag from a distance like it would explode.

"I can see that."

"Are you feeling okay?"

"I think so."

"The bag will not bite. He brought me one too. It's just pastry. He's saying thank you for whatever was in the brown bag."

"I know, and I'm nervous and I don't know why."

"Butterflies?"

"Yes. Many. Many butterflies. Along with other stuff. Maybe breakfast."

"Okay, come on. Have some coffee with your pastry. Angela is around. She'll take care of the front desk."

In the kitchen, the two friends shared coffee while the cheese and guava pastries flaked away when plucked up from the plate. Carmen waited for Pilar to speak but gave up after a long silence. "What's the problem?"

"I don't know. It's terrifying to think about pursuing a relationship with...*anyone*." Tears stung at Pilar's eyes and she blinked away, attempting to stop them from flowing. Then she started picking at the pastry, watching the flakes fall to the plate in front of her.

"But why? I'm not seeing the problem. Help me see it."

"Carmen. You, of all people. I know what you've been through in your life. I have children to consider. What if he turns out to be some lunatic? When I think of everything your ex-husband did, what he did *do*...to *you*. I think I'd rather just be alone. The prospect of that happening to me is horrifying." Pilar turned every shade of red on the rainbow.

"You can't compare my experiences with this. He's a totally different person. He seems very nice, and caring. His feelings for you are obvious, and I think your feelings for him are obvious, too."

"I'm afraid."

"I understand. But that shouldn't stop you. Okay, you have your kids to consider. So, don't involve them until you're sure."

"No. I can't. I just can't get involved with anyone." Pilar wiped the tears away and shook her head.

"Okay, I won't say anything. Hey. How did it go with that bride you were calling the other day?"

Pilar didn't answer. Only stared down at the flakes of pastry, pieces of guava and cheese that littered her plate.

Carmen stopped pushing. She realized Pilar was not ready to talk about whatever was bothering her. It was all she could do to get Pilar thinking about something other than Juan Rodriguez. "Did you see that couple that came in on Thursday? They were all over each other. I almost had to turn the hose on them by the pool. There were kids there!" She waited, but her tactics were not working. "Then someone complained that they were humping on the balcony, though, when I went to check, I saw nothing."

"Really?" Pilar didn't laugh.

"Yes. Really. Pilar, that was funny. Talk to me."

"I don't even know where to start." Pilar started crying, then bit into the guava pastry, letting the flakes crumble down the sides of her mouth, melding with her tears, and onto her black blouse. She took a sip of coffee and swallowed hard. "I miss him so much."

"I can't even imagine."

"How do I go on? How? I try so hard not to have the girls

watch me crumble, and I've been pretty good at keeping it contained." Pilar gave in and tears streamed down her face. Carmen handed her a napkin.

"But?"

"But this man. I'm so confused." Pilar covered her face with both hands, then spread her fingers, peeking out at Carmen, waiting for a reaction. But Carmen only laughed. "Why are you laughing?" she uncovered her face.

"Because I think deep down you already know. You just can't bring yourself to say it. What are you afraid of? That people might not agree with your timetable? That someone might talk? Oooooo…" Carmen made spooky fingers. "Who cares? It's your life. Eduardo has been gone for two years. It's okay."

"I don't think the girls are ready."

Carmen held Pilar's forearm. "The girls? Or you? Listen, do whatever you like at your pace. But talk to Juan, so he understands where you're coming from. I promise he won't run away."

"Sure. But will I?"

Chapter 3

Not Sergeant Rodriguez and Public Sex

Pilar considered Carmen's advice. She had to think of what to say to Juan without bursting into tears. She realized that extending him an olive branch with her personal kitchen utensils was a silly move, but it was the most she could offer. He returned the set, washed and dried. How she loved a man who did the dishes. Pilar smiled. She hadn't felt that way in a long time; like a smitten teenager.

Just then, a woman came from the back patio, dragging her child behind her. "There's a couple practically having sex in the pool!" she screamed. "Someone do something!"

Pilar turned red and radioed Carmen, then tried calming the hysterical mother. "I apologize. We'll take care of the situation immediately. Please be our guest in the dining room while we sort out the problem." Pilar helped the woman and her child into the dining room, offering them plates and drinks.

Meanwhile, Angela headed for the pool area, meeting up with Carmen on the way there.

"I'll take care of this, Angela." Carmen was so incensed, she struggled not to scream.

Angela hadn't dealt with anything like this before and was eager to see how the owner would handle it. As soon as she was outside, the heat of the summer sun had her sweating through her top, leaving pit stains on her light yellow blouse. Angela lifted her arms and ruffled her blouse to shake out the heat.

"Excuse me. Excuse me," Carmen said, her voice escalating when she realized they weren't listening. The woman had her bikini bottom down, and the strings of her top floated in the water next to her. She was straddling the man she was with and grinding away in the pool. "May I please have a word with you in my office?" The other guests gawked at the scene playing out at the edge of the pool.

"Is everything okay?" asked the woman as she dismounted and turned to face Carmen, her breasts exposed, yet she was unbothered.

"Angela will bring you in."

The woman walked out of the pool topless, pulling her bikini back up, and the man's speedo strained against the hardness of his boner. The couple exchanged confused glances. Speechless, Angela averted her gaze and handed them each a pool towel, and lead them to the hotel's main office where a fuming Carmen stood impassive.

Carmen had a few minutes to debate what she'd say without offending the offenders. "I understand you're on vacation, but this is a family establishment. Your behavior in the public areas has been brought to my attention for the third time now."

"So? The man snapped, his erection trying to peek out the bottom of the swimsuit. "People expect debauchery in Cuba."

Carmen fought to keep from looking down. Like an automobile accident you couldn't look away from. "What? Where did you hear that?"

"Listen, it's the very definition of Cuba."

"I don't know what dictionary you're consulting. If you're

referring to events that took place in the 1940s and 50s, that's ancient history. *New* Cuba is a respectable travel destination. Gone are the days of public wantonness. Would you behave this way on the mainland? If you are not happy with our guidelines, we'd be more than happy to find you other arrangements."

"No. We'll find our own accommodations. Cancel the rest of our stay," said the woman, staring at Carmen. Then she dropped the towel that covered her bare breasts, turned and left the office, slamming the door behind them.

"That was intense. Is she going to walk to their room naked?" asked Angela.

Carmen paced. "I know she'll make a spectacle of herself. The conversation went better than I imagined. I'm sure the incident will give us a lousy review. They'll have trouble staying anywhere with that behavior, but I'm glad they're gone. It's embarrassing to have strangers complain people are having sex in the public spaces of your property." Carmen's cheeks went from a light rosy color to beet red at the mention of public sex.

"Did you see the bruises on her wrists and legs? What was that about?"

"Perhaps sex injuries? Maybe they were hanging from a ceiling somewhere," said a serious Carmen. Angela stifled a laugh as she exited the office, turning back once, shooting her a manicured eyebrow waggle and a half smile that prompted Carmen to break down and cackle.

The couple departed with no more trouble. Angela went to their room with a chambermaid to find the whole place turned upside down. Dresser drawers on the floor, towels in the tub with the water running, and one of them left a nasty pile in the toilet. "Pigs," said Angela before calling in a second chamber maid to help, then reported the scene to Carmen.

"I swear, some people."

"So gross." Angela was so disgusted by the couple, her whole body shuddered.

Carmen laughed, thinking, *Wait until she has kids. She'll know what gross is.'*

Later that evening, Carmen sat in the kitchen while Carlos put the finishing touches on dinner. From the box of smoked salts, he chose the black salt and sprinkled it over their salad, then grated some fresh parmesan cheese. "I love that you love to cook." She was eyeing his backside again, a favorite pastime. The way his arms flexed, and the way his eyes would sparkle when he'd caught her ogling him. "You'll never believe what happened today." Carmen went on telling him about the public sex problem, guffawing the entire time.

"What? Is public sex at the hotel frowned upon? Well, I'm glad you said something before…" he broke from his straight-faced comment when he couldn't hold back the laughter any longer.

"Hilarious, mister. We have families staying there. Can't have indecency going on. Plus, that guy thinks he flew into 1940s Cuba. I think he expected gangsters, thugs, and whorehouses."

"Well, I heard Cuba was something else back then. But that's all over. Time changes everything, and New Cuba has a wholesome image now. One we all need to build up and protect."

"Yeah, yeah, yeah. Blah, blah, blah. I'm still on board. Save your breath." After living in New Cuba for a couple of years, she was hooked. It's where she'd belonged all along and couldn't see herself living anywhere else. She had both feet planted right where she'd stepped the first time.

Carlos served dinner. A simple steak Milanese with a shredded cabbage, cucumber and tomato salad, dressed with white vinegar and a good Spanish olive oil, from Spain. The sprinkling of black salt over the top added extra zing. Carmen remembered one of her Tias shredding cabbage, razor thin, with an ancient knife, sharpened on a stone, that belonged to *her* mother. The aunt didn't have a mandolin available in those days. Another round of melancholy.

"What is it?" asked Carlos.

"Same old stuff. It creeps in and my heart aches. Sometimes I think it's over the stupidest things." Carmen rubbed her chest, then looked up at Carlos. She held in the threatening tear and smiled.

Reaching over, he stroked the back of her hand with his thumb. His love and warmth traveled up Carmen's arm and straight to where she hurt, like a salve.

Carmen had shared stories of her family visits, describing them as the best times of her life. Whenever something would hit, tears would threaten, and the inevitable sadness followed. It was the only family she knew. Though they were not part of her every day, she felt their love and concern, no matter how far away she was. They mattered.

Her father's sisters were the polar opposite. They lived not too far away in Hialeah and were horrible people. Whenever they visited her parents in North Miami, her sister would take her by the hand and they'd run out the back door to the neighbor's house, avoiding their vicious stings and utter disdain, calling them dirty or garbage. What eight- and ten-year-old wants to hear that?

Once, they'd been told that his crazy sister didn't consider them her nieces because they, quote "Didn't come from *her* sister, and who knows who their father is." Basically calling their mother a whore.

Carmen could not be mistaken for anyone else's child; in looks, attitude, and demeanor, she was *his* child. Over the years, she'd kept her distance, and assumed they'd all passed since they were much older than her mother. Carmen's sister Sara was to inherit a house from the younger of his two remaining siblings, but somehow, they amended the woman's will and removed and forgot about Sara.

Wednesday morning brought a round of rain. Being late April, it was to be expected. They had already prepared for the possibility of a hurricane, with the season being just around the corner. During Hurricane Florinda, they learned how to better handle the extensive property in a more efficient way. No storm would catch them off guard.

While Carmen and Pilar went over the guest book and reservations for the next week, they talked about the restaurant opening when Jose came in through the back doors. "Hello pretty ladies."

"Hi, Jose. How's the...everything going?" asked Pilar.

"Nice catch. You didn't ask," he laughed. "It's done. I'm connecting the propane tomorrow with Alex, and the cleanup crew is coming afterward. I'll bring Gabby in on Saturday." If Jose smiled any wider, the ends of his mouth would meet at the back of his head.

"Who's Alex?" asked Pilar.

"Gabby hired him as a sous chef. He's between jobs and asked if he could help move things along. I hired him to help these last few days until he starts with Gabby. Speaking of which, I'd like to do something special for her. Ideas?" The man couldn't contain his own excitement, waving his arms wide, then back again.

"Yes! We'd love to help," said Carmen, and the three conspired to surprise Gabby at her new restaurant.

The next girls' night meeting started off with the usual. Debrief the staff, address any recent issues, hire or fire someone (the latter never happened).

Once they excused the staff, the three partners could relax and talk about everything else. How well the hotel was doing and how soon the restaurant would be ready.

An uncomfortable, yet comical, conversation regarded posting a guest behavior sign somewhere. They didn't want a repeat of the whole 'sex-in-public' thing, though the incident supplied many, many jokes and one-liners. After this, they'd always share a knowing glance at suspicious check-ins. "I swear. You should have seen this guy. The speedo was tiny and couldn't hold in...the entire...stiff package. And the woman. Holy cow! Not in the least bit modest. She walked back to her room topless."

Gabby couldn't stop laughing, and Pilar covered her heating face and shook her head. "Stop," she said.

"About the restaurant, Gabby. When it's ready, we'd like to help. Just say the word and we're there," said Carmen.

"Well, word. Jose says I can see it Saturday, and start getting ready for opening." Her excitement overflowed into bouncing and hand clapping. These days, she had so many notes for the restaurant, she carried them around with her in a Pendaflex expansion file that was busting at the seams. "I've already ordered the linens, table settings, and tables and chairs," she counted off. "Everything should be here by this Sunday."

She prattled off her list like an auctioneer, and her eyes shifted like wild beams of light, darting between her partners.

"Sounds like you have it all under control," said Pilar. "I've laid out a date for your soft opening, with full advertising hitting the area and internet the following week." She opened her laptop to show the girls her ad campaign for the restaurant.

In warm tones, a swooping upscale video showed Gabby in

her pressed white chef's coat and toque as she cooked behind flames that shot several feet in the air, while a famous Cuban singer provided a voiceover, a favor Gabby called in. Her sultry voice was seductive.

"That's amazing!" said Gabby. "When did you get that footage?"

"I have my ways, never you mind."

"Pilar, this is wonderful," said Carmen.

"The campaign will include a link to the hotel as well, and vice versa. I think that way we all benefit."

"Perfect." Gabby and Carmen agreed. The excitement was building.

Saturday morning finally arrived. Gabby hadn't slept a wink that night. She'd already steam pressed her chef's coat and toque, and hung them on a wood hanger. *This* set was the first one she'd ever had, a gift from her mother when she graduated from the Auguste Escoffier School of Culinary Arts, with honors. Her mother had her name embroidered on the top left of both pieces, 'Chef Gabriella Chappell.'

Gabby ran her fingers over the Navy stitching. Her eyes welled. She missed her mother and hoped her accomplishments filled her mother with pride. Gabby imagined her mother floating just above her, an adoring smile lighting up her face. She backed away from the garments and tilted her head as she looked at the pieces that were packed away for so long.

At that moment, it occurred to her that her following from her restaurant days would get wind of this new venture, and things could spiral again. She had no intention of living that 'gotta-git-it' lifestyle again. There was so much more to this life in New Cuba, and she had every intention of living it the way she wanted.

Taking a deep breath, she grabbed the hanger and walked her uniform out to her '73 VW van and hung it on the hook behind the driver's seat.

Gabby purchased the restored vehicle right after Jose offered to build the restaurant. She gave up her little white car for something roomier, and this fit her style to a T. She loved the blue and white contrast, and the shiny chrome striping.

When she was out driving, people could hear the putter of the engine and recognized her coming from a mile away, flashing a wide smile and waving from the window as she passed, trumpeting the old horn. She would imagine her mother sitting in the passenger seat, holding her chef's uniform.

The previous owner had even updated the roof rack and the ladder on the side, staining the steps in an authentic light shade, then sealing to protect it against the intense rays of the Caribbean sun. The van appeared almost new.

Back in the house, she found Jose in the kitchen with no shirt and the top button of his jeans undone, drinking a large cup of Cuban coffee. He carried that twelve pack well, and all she could think was, *'Damn, he looks good shirtless.'* All her melancholy dissipated. "Well, hello there." Gabby went right over and ran her fingers down his midsection, counting the rungs of muscles that made up the washboard that was his stomach.

"Hello. What have you been up to this morning?"

"Just getting myself ready. I'm still getting to see the restaurant today, right?"

"Yesss." He dragged out the s's as he pulled her in close. Then he kissed her deep, dipping her back, like the sailor in that famous picture. She loved that and laughed like a giddy schoolgirl. "I'm going to change, then we'll head out."

Gabby was almost shedding skin while she waited for him. She shook out her arms, shook out her legs. Jogged in place. Went into a downward dog to calm herself, but still had trouble containing her excitement. After too long a while, Jose came out (it had only been about ten minutes). He laughed. "What are you doing?"

"Trying to relax." Gabby kneeled, taking a happy baby pose, then shifted back to sit on her knees as she looked up at him, her eyes begging to be taken to the restaurant, but she remained tight-lipped.

"Okay. Let's go." Jose offered his hand, and she popped up from her pose, sliding her feet into her black Dansko clogs, and followed him out the door, bouncing like a new puppy. He relished every twitch and every little jump of excitement she gave at the mere mention of getting to see her new restaurant.

Luis and Cristina had now been married for almost two years. They were inseparable. He'd moved into her house, and kept his as a guest house for when her children visited, or any of their friends needed a place to house their own visiting relatives. He still farmed his small grove of fruits and vegetables, along with his wife's help.

The neighbors loved watching them work their tiny plantations together, sharing tools and the occasional kiss, and no one heard them bickering anymore. There was a lot of hand-holding and arm swinging, and they clung to each other like their life depended on it.

Cristina would fuss over his meals, making sure he was eating right, and drinking enough water. The cardiac scare of a couple of years ago had turned out to be dehydration and not a cardiac event, but the idea of something happening to him made her keep her guard up.

About eight years older than she, he still moved around like a much younger man. Sometimes, she could hear his fast steps as he came up behind her and she'd call out, "Don't you dare grab my ass old man." And Luis would chuckle.

Unlike Cristina, Luis didn't fuss. He just did whatever he thought he needed to do for her without even asking, more matter-of-factly. If she had no say in the decision making, she'd pause, reminding herself that he was being caring and kind, in his own bossy way. It was hard to break out of the old habit of wanting to choke the life out of him. Plus, it was important to set a good example for their charges.

They loved babysitting Pilar's girls whenever she needed. In fact, the girls called them Mima and Pipo. A long held Cuban tradition of calling grandparents and great-grandparents these loving nicknames was alive and well in New Cuba. The couple relished how the girls considered them their grandparents.

The girls never knew Eduardo's parents since they passed away years before the last invasion. And when Pilar married Eduardo and moved to New Cuba, her parents disowned her. They'd never met the girls, and in a small way, Luis and Cristina made Pilar feel like there were parental angels floating around her.

"Good morning," said Cristina, opening the gate to Pilar's yard. "I brought coconut cookies for the girls."

Pilar took the container, peeled back the plastic lid, and inhaled the sugary coconut scent of Cristina's cookies. "You should sell these. You'd make a fortune."

"I'm too old to try all that now. Besides, I'm busy with my yard and your girls. When would I have time?"

Pilar set the container on the kitchen counter as Cristina pulled out a chair and fell into it, almost tipping it over. She was out of breath and sweating.

"Are you alright? You don't look so good." Pilar said.

"Si, si. I'm just so tired. It's the heat."

"Are you sure? Your ankles are swollen. When was your last checkup?"

"Oh, I don't know. I'm fine. Stop worrying. It's all old people's stuff, anyway."

Pilar didn't push. She'd talk to Luis, so he would get her checked out. "Okay. But you shouldn't be outside in this heat."

"I wanted to talk to you when the girls were busy. What's going on with you?"

"What do you mean?" Pilar said as she got up and went to the sink, turning her back on Cristina.

"You seem distracted. What's on your mind?" After a quiet pause, "And I think I know what it is. I just want to hear it from you."

Pilar knew she couldn't keep it hidden any longer. People were noticing. She turned from the sink to look at Cristina, exhaled, then sat, this time, hard. She rubbed her face, covering her eyes, then peeked out at Cristina, who tilted her head and raised her eyebrows. "Well?"

"Okay. I think I'm feeling something I shouldn't be feeling."

"Who said you shouldn't be feeling your feelings?"

Pilar hesitated a little too long. "Me," she exhaled hard.

"I see the look on your face when Juan's around. When you talk to him, or he calls or sends messages. You keep feeding the man. What are you feeling?"

"I don't know. Shame."

"Why? Eduardo is gone. He wouldn't want you to be alone, or sad, hanging on to his memory. You're not betraying him, and you're far too young to mourn forever."

"How long did you wait… when your first husband passed?"

"Too long. He died when I was about your age. It's not that I didn't have any suitors. There were plenty of interested men. But I was stupid. In my day, a woman mourned forever, and there was a stigma. Times have changed. I thought Luis and I had missed our chance when I married Pedro, and he married Caridad."

"Wait, you and Luis?" Pilar almost fell out of her chair.

"Shocking, I know. He was friends with my brother Rafael. In fact, Luis was always at our house." Cristina smiled at the memory. "We'd sneak in a kiss here and there, nothing more. Those early days were tumultuous. My parents were strict. Courting only happened on Thursdays and Sundays, and only in the living room, sitting on opposite sides of the sofa with my parents across from us, staring. That was the old way." Leaning forward, Cristina wiped her brow with a napkin and laughed at the image.

"Really? I never knew. Sounds… awkward."

"It was the custom. We knew no other way. My mother had eyes on me at all times, or so she thought. And my father would stare at a suitor as though they were there to steal something. I guess, in a way, they were."

"How did you know you were in love with Pedro?"

"Love? No, that was an arranged marriage. My parents would bring a few suitors by, ones they approved of, of course. Whichever they felt most comfortable with would be the one they'd pick for me and my sisters."

"And Luis?"

"Luis? No. That was… something… else." Cristina had that far-away look, like something she'd lost. "Our timing was never right. My mother saw it on my face the day he walked into the house for the first time. Like a thunderbolt split the house in two. We just stared at each other. Then every time Rafael told her that Luis was coming over, she'd watch me bolt to the window and wait until he showed up. He pretended not to see me, acting aloof, until my mother relaxed."

"Then why didn't they choose him as a suitor? It was obvious there was something there between you. Wouldn't they want you to be happy?"

"That's just not the way it worked. Besides, Luis's parents sent him out of the country on the Peter Pan Flights. He returned when he'd finished law school. He kept telling everyone that he wasn't staying in Cuba. My parents weren't about to let me move out of the country."

"That's so sad."

"Still, I hung on every word when he spoke, smiling, like an idiot," she laughed and rolled her eyes. "And by the way, if you see me doing it now, you'll let me know, si?"

Pilar laughed, "Of course."

"That's how I know what I'm looking at when you think of Juan."

Pilar smiled and looked down. Cristina continued, "So, I married Pedro, Luis married Caridad, and they moved to the U.S. and made their life there. I made my life here. Luis came back when Caridad passed and stayed. They never had children. Just wasn't in the cards."

"You were always fighting with him."

"I know. I think it was all that pent up anger that we'd missed

60

our chance. But it's all in the past now and we couldn't be happier." She smiled and shook off the agitation she'd buried.

Sensing the lighter mood, she took her hand. "Pilar. Listen to me. Don't waste your time worrying about what people will think, like I did. Listen to your gut, it's usually right. I know you're being extra careful with the girls, but Juan is a wonderful man. The girls will be fine."

"Okay. Thank you for listening and sharing that story. I hate to cut you short, but need to go. I'm due at the restaurant. Thanks for staying with the girls. They're playing in Rose's room."

"Oh, today is the big day, I heard. Exciting. I'll see you later. Please think about what I said before it's too late."

Chapter 4

A New Restaurant and An Ambulance Ride

Jose walked Gabby out to his truck and blindfolded her, grazing his lips along her neck. "What's this now? Why do I need to be blindfolded? I want to see!" Gabby sounded like a petulant child. Jose wanted to tease her as much as he could get away with.

"We're going straight there. Just let me do this my way." Jose planned to stretch out the anticipation as long as he could.

"Ugh." Gabby sat in Jose's truck with her hands knitted together on her lap. She inhaled and exhaled deep, counting the seconds in her head, *'one Mississippi, two Mississippi, three Mississippi.'* She could swear he was driving slower on purpose.

By the time they reached the hotel, she had counted to three hundred three Mississippi and could feel herself unraveling. "How much longer?" she bounced like a child arriving at Disneyland.

"We're on the driveway." Jose laughed, and stopped the car in front of the restaurant, got out, and opened her door. He held her right hand in his, and ran his left hand down her back, placing at just the right spot below her belt line, making her shiver.

"I hope you're enjoying this."

"Well. I am. Nothing gets me going more than watching you squirm." Taking her hand, he guided her to the front of the truck, asked her to close her eyes, and removed the blindfold. "Okay. Open them."

Gabby opened her eyes and drew in a deep breath, covering her mouth. At the top front of the building, a large pink neon sign read, 'Gabby's' in swishy cursive lettering. He'd convinced her to give it her name. Simple and understated, and he was right.

"We centered the restaurant so it would look like part of the estate, and Carlos designed the landscaping as a continuance of the gardens. The winding paths that come off the sides complement the aerial view."

Jose opened the iPad he brought with him and showed Gabby the updated video. "Pilar will upload to the website tomorrow." He pressed play, and just like the original stream, it started at the main road, swooped up and over the entire property. The hotel, then the conservatory surrounded by gardens and banana plantations, the pool, and the ceiba tree. At the end of the dragonfly's head, a winding path wove into the new structure, simulating a flower.

Anchored in the center was the new restaurant. It had six oval shaped petals around the perimeter, patios. "I think you can use each of these petals as you see fit. Outside seating? Maybe for private parties?"

Gabby gasped. "That's amazing. I don't know what to say."

From where she stood, she could see the top floor of the building had a large covered area with plants, surrounded by an ornate wrought-iron fence. "Is that rooftop for sitting?" she pointed.

"Yes. What you do think?" Jose waited for her reaction as she took in the structure.

"I think I can't believe how perfect this is. It's beautiful, I love it." Gabby covered her mouth and cried. Her fingers trembling, she turned to Jose and wrapped her arms around him.

Jose kissed her, then continued. "I thought the mansard style would complement the conservatory since they're across from each other. Those iron pieces came from one of the estates in Havana that was torn down to make that high rise on the Paseo del Prado. The building was in such disrepair they couldn't save it, so the new owners sold off any parts they weren't going to use, and I grabbed a few. You'll see them throughout."

"That's a great idea." Gabby froze in her spot, her knees weak. She squatted.

Jose pointed to a large covered area to the right of the entry, and Gabby stood back up. "The outdoor seating area there can accommodate about fifty people. The rooftop, another twenty-five." Jose turned her to face him. "Are you ready for the inside tour?"

"Yes! Yes!"

Taking her hand, they walked to the doors. Jose ordered extra-large, custom iron handles that made up a capital letter 'G' when the door was closed. Gabby ran her shaky fingers over the letter, stopped and turned to Jose. "Thank you. This is more than I ever dreamed."

"You deserve so much more, babe. Let's go inside." With that, he opened the doors.

"Surprise!" yelled Carmen, Carlos, and Pilar, along with the rest of the staff. Behind them stood a long, raw edge wood bar with stools and a brass foot rail. On the back wall, enough glass shelves to hold at least two hundred bottles. And above those, a backlit wood sign pronouncing, 'Welcome to Gabby's Place.'

On a nearby table there was a cake with a topper that read 'Gabby's' in hot pink cursive lettering matching the one at the front of the restaurant. Next to that, a large box with a big pink bow on top. Gabby hugged each of her friends, her eyes wide as she looked around the inside. Jose paid special attention when she described what she liked best about her old restaurants, and he'd incorporated a little something special from each at Gabby's.

After snapping a few pictures and enjoying a slice of cake, the employees went back to work, and the partners stayed behind with Jose to open the large box.

"This is from Pilar, Carlos and myself," said Carmen.

"Oh, you didn't have to do that." Gabby beamed as she opened the box and found a large leather roll up bag brandishing a Kultro seal. Gabby gasped, then unbuckled the ties, and unrolled the expensive gift, revealing a brand new set of knives. "Oh. This is too much."

"You deserve it. We can't wait to watch you use them," said Pilar.

"You shouldn't have, but thank you. I love them."

"Can we continue the tour?" asked Jose. Speaking as fast as a hawker, and walking just as fast, he pointed. "The kitchen has state-of-the-art equipment. The Amerikooler walk in cooler came highly recommended. I had the twelve foot one installed. Over here, a seventy-two inch Lang griddle. I hope that's a good size. You have two Hoshizaki ice machines. One makes crescent cubes, and the other top hat cubes. I figured it's hot here and everyone will want ice. You have a Doyon gas heat and convection oven, quadruple deck..."

"Okay. Stop. This is too much. You're very excited."

"Yes. I've been just as excited as you, worse even, waiting for the day I can show you your new restaurant."

The others followed Gabby and Jose through the restaurant tour, snickering at his exuberance. The love he has for Gabby gushing out of him.

"Alright. Let me just walk around and look, please."

"Okay. Okay. I'll just wait by the bar," he breathed out. Carlos clapped him on the back and led him away, followed by Carmen and Pilar.

At the bar, Jose shook his hands and rocked back and forth as he heard Gabby coming out of the kitchen. His hands were dripping with sweat.

"Are you ready?" whispered Carlos.

"Yes," breathed Jose. "Yes," he breathed again.

"It's... I have no words," said Gabby as she stepped back into the bar area. Next to her friends were five champagne glasses and a bottle of Dom Perignon in an ice bucket. Jose stood several feet away, opposite the group. He'd changed into a tailored black suit, a white French cuff shirt with cuff links, and dress shoes. He'd slicked his hair back early that morning, and was looking spiffy.

Gabby looked back at her friends, scrunching her eyebrows

and tilting her head. Carmen nudged her over to Jose, when suddenly, he dropped to one knee as she approached.

"Gabriella Chappell. You are the love of my life. My days are full of joy because you make them so. I can't stand a single day without you. Will you marry me?"

In one graceful swing, Jose held out a ring box, flipping it open to reveal a two carat, heart-shaped diamond ring with baguettes flanking the sides. There were so many facets catching the light, it glimmered on every wall.

Gabby stared down into his eyes, her mouth hung open. "Yes! Yes!"

Jose picked her up and swung her around, kissing her long and deep, dipping her back like he had earlier that morning. She could feel his tongue down to her toes, tingling them awake. Then, a loud pop of the champagne bottle brought them back to the present as he slipped the ring on her finger.

"Did you guys know?"

"We knew, but no one else does," said Pilar.

"Yes," said Carmen. "We were sworn to secrecy. I'm so happy we could be here for your special moment. The restaurant is amazing. I can't wait to see what you've planned for the menu."

"Oh, I have to get to work," said Gabby, and she turned.

"Slow down for a minute. We just got engaged. Let's enjoy that for a few minutes before you jump in with both feet." Jose was excited for her, but he'd waited until now to propose and wanted his time.

Maria drove by several times a week, craning her head to watch the progress of the building. She didn't know what they were doing until she saw the Gabby's sign being hoisted onto the front of what she assumed would be a restaurant. She smacked the steering wheel with her palm.

She had grown angrier since the last time Carlos snubbed her. Maria knew that woman moved in with him. Into the home that should have been hers. More and more, she was consumed with thoughts of him, and how to make Carmen go away. Now that Guerrero would spend the rest of his life in prison, she didn't need to worry about what *he* would do, but she needed help.

Her thoughts floated toward Lucrecia, Guerrero's now *ex-*wife. She had his parents' remains removed and sold the property. Maria had seen her around town, dressed in a way that said, *'I do not know how to style myself, but I made a few bucks and this is the best I can do.'* Maybe she could think of a way to get her to help. She knew what Lucrecia was up to. She could use that and *make* her get Carlos to see her and help get rid of Carmen.

Maria waited down the road from Carlos's house until she saw them pull up in the Corvette. He got out, went around, and opened her door, helping her out. He was a gentleman, her gentleman. Maria had convinced herself that Carlos pitied Carmen, and that's why he let her move in, but that he would one day find his way back to *her.* She'd have him, or no one else would. Once they went inside, she backed up and went in the opposite direction, toward town.

"That was so sweet watching Jose keep it together to propose to Gabby," said Carmen when Carlos opened her car door. "I've never seen her smile so wide." He took her hand, and they walked inside.

"He was so nervous. He must have called me twelve times last night," laughed Carlos.

"Well, it was about time. How long have they been together? Her clock is ticking louder and louder."

"Over ten years. And I think his metaphorical clock is louder than hers."

The following week had been hectic, to say the least. Gabby spent much of her time preparing menus, ordering supplies, and dealing with vendors. She hadn't had time to think of her engagement or setting dates for anything. The only thing she could focus on was her new restaurant.

Saturday rolled around and their friends were hosting an engagement party in the hotel's dining room. A week passed since she'd done her hair, and her nails were a disaster from organizing her new kitchen. "This ring is so beautiful. I have to find time to get my nails done," she said as she looked down at it in front of the long mirror where she'd dressed.

"Gabby!"

"Coming!" she called from their bedroom.

"You look beautiful. We need to get to our engagement party. Everyone is waiting."

Gabby wanted to look her best. Not like she'd been working non-stop since she accepted his proposal. She'd curled her hair into ringlets, and finished applying a respectable amount of makeup. Her white vintage Dior cocktail dress was a perfect fit for her body. Its portrait collar accentuated her neckline and shoulders, giving her a classic Cuban bride look.

Gabby projected elegance and refinement. Her three inch white sling backs flexed her calves when she walked. "I'm ready," she said as she emerged, clinging to her gold clutch.

Jose pulled a hand from a pocket of his black suit and put two fingers to his mouth. "Wow. Maybe we stay here?"

After she finished giggling, they walked out to the waiting, enclosed, horse-drawn carriage. Jose wanted every event of their nuptials to be romantic, so he'd arranged for them to be carried to the venue in style. Gabby climbed in and nuzzled into the red velvet upholstery. It was summer, and she was thankful the carriage was air-conditioned.

When they pulled up to the hotel, the valet opened the carriage door, and out stepped Jose. He'd polished his patent leather dress shoes to a high, mirror-like shine. Gabby got up, and he extended a hand to his future bride, and as she took hold, she stared into his eyes. *'I must be dreaming,'* she thought. "You clean up nice, mister."

Taking care to not fall and flash everyone, she stepped out of the carriage, squeezing her knees together.

"Are you okay?" asked Jose. "You seem a bit... tense."

Gabby leaned over and whispered in his ear, "I didn't like the panty lines showing through my dress."

Jose stopped cold, just outside the carriage. "Do you mean..?"

"Yes. Now let's go."

"How am I supposed to control myself for the rest of the evening?"

"You'll figure it out."

At the stairs, Diego was first to greet them. He'd dressed in oatmeal linen slacks and white guayabera. Next to him, Angela wore a beige square neck puff dress with black polka dots and sky high heels. The two looked as though they'd dressed in the same closet.

Angela leaned in and looked up at Diego as the couple passed them. Diego looked down at her and smiled, then took her hand and followed them inside.

In the lobby, friends and neighbors stood ready to toast their engagement. The gathering included all their local friends, and the ambiance warmed the couple. Everyone wore chic outfits and held champagne flutes as the couple entered the space.

Once the guests found their seats in the dining room, dinner was served. Carmen and Pilar planned the entire evening; a four course dinner prepared by a chef friend of Gabby's, followed by dessert, then dancing.

Gabby asked Carmen to be matron-of-honor, and Pilar to officiate. Jose asked Carlos to be his best man. The obvious choice would have been Eduardo.

Since his death, Jose and Carlos had become great friends, often helping each other with projects or meeting up for a cold brew. The conversation often turned to 'The Girls.' It seems they had their own code for handling the ever so independent women in their lives and making sure Pilar was alright. When it came time for speeches, Carmen and Carlos had prepared a touching tribute to the pair.

As Pilar walked to her chair, she noticed a change in the seating arrangements and her pace slowed while she tried to remain calm. Her hands were moist, so she smoothed her skirt, trying to dry them. Every two steps, she glanced back over her shoulder, and her eyes darted around the room. No one seems to notice but her.

There, next to her seat, stood Juan, holding out her chair. Her legs went numb at the sight of his smile and kind eyes. It was as though he'd been waiting there all night. She looked up at him and smiled. "Thank you." Her cheeks seared, thinking about how she hadn't returned his calls, and her hands shook.

When she sat, he unfolded her napkin and glided it onto her lap. Her A-line blue cocktail dress had a stiff crinoline that covered Carmen and Pilar, coercing itself into Juan's space. Pilar tried to gather it closer so he could sit more comfortably, knocking the napkin onto the floor.

"It's okay, I'll get," said Juan as he backed up his chair and dove under the table (and her skirt) to find it on the floor.

After turning every shade of red, she gave a quick nod before looking to her left at Carmen and shooting her a wide-eyed gawp.

Carmen raised her eyebrows, smiled, and said in a low voice, "It's okay. I promise, he won't bite you…" then she whispered, "…unless you want him to." Pilar couldn't look in his direction for some time after that comment.

Before long, Pilar had a couple of glasses of wine, and it helped her relax. She and Juan slipped into their cozy, familiar conversation, and she stopped looking over her shoulder, though she hadn't realized. Pilar didn't bring up her absence, and Juan didn't either. He was thankful Carmen found a place for him next to Pilar.

Juan was careful not to push. He worried he'd scare her away if he moved too fast. But several months of her bringing food, or the two talking for hours on the phone, or sending messages back and forth had him hoping she would soon find a way forward…with him.

Pilar's daughters were home with a sitter. A blessing in disguise. This was an adult only evening. She was glad Carmen convinced her to step out for the night and not worry about what the girls were wearing or what they were doing. She needed that break.

It was hectic, the world of a single mother of three girls. Now, without Eduardo, she was getting used to doing everything herself.

Carmen turned toward Carlos, leaned in, and giggled. He looked down at her and said, "It looks like your meddling might work out."

"I know. He's perfect for her. She's just stubborn." Carmen's heart filled with glee at seeing them together.

"Stubborn, or still mourning? I hope you're right. No one likes to be set up like that."

"I'm not setting anyone up. They were both attending. They both needed a seat. So what if they were sitting next to each other?"

Carlos gave her a kiss and laughed before looking across the table and out the window at the light blue Nissan approaching the front of the hotel. He'd seen Maria driving down his street a few times. He was certain she was aware he wasn't interested, yet she kept showing up.

"Let me go!" shouted Maria as she stumbled up the steps, waving her tiny red purse. In the foyer she almost fell, as her ankles twisted this way and that, off her narrow too high chrome heels.

"Where is she?" she continued to shout.

"Ma'am, can I help you?" asked Angela, who'd hurried from the table to intercept, followed by Diego.

"Carmmeenn!" Maria shouted as her knees gave and she passed out in Diego's arms.

"Whew, she's really drunk," said Diego as he held her up and carried her out over his shoulder. "Can you smell it? Call her an Uber."

"Yes. I can smell it. Oh! She's not wearing any underwear," whispered Angela. She threw her napkin over Maria's behind. The move shielded her naughty bits and giving her some privacy.

"I didn't need to know that." Diego set her down on a rocking chair on the front porch, where she remained passed out. When the Uber arrived, Diego picked her up, slid her into the back seat, and gave the driver her identification. "Please take her home. Here's her license."

After they left, Angela turned to Diego and asked who she was and why she'd done that. "Ask Carmen when no one is around."

Diego took Angela's hand and helped her up the stairs, placing a light hand on her back. Once they reached their seats, he pulled out her chair and waited for her to sit. As they finished their meal, they joked about the half-naked drunk woman that tried to crash the party.

From where Carmen sat, she smiled while watching how Angela and Diego were getting closer and closer. A sign of things to come.

"Take it easy, Cupid. Stop matchmaking everyone you see. Let them come upon it themselves."

Carmen looked at him and widened her eyes, then looked away. "We'll see." She was proud of how fast Angela and Diego handled the situation, and with such finesse.

Maria's outburst didn't garner any attention, and the guests had all gone back to their conversations even before she was taken outside.

Carmen looked at Carlos and sighed. He took her hand and gave her a quick peck on the cheek.

After dinner, the guests made their way out to the garden, where a live band played all kinds of music. There was salsa, merengue, contemporary, and even jazz. Even after sundown, the night held on to the day's heat, and the smell of rain filled the air.

Carlos twirled and dipped Carmen across the dance floor. He'd roll her in his arms, and she'd lean back and laugh. After a quick spin, he ran his hand from the side of her hip, caressing up past her obliques, along the side of her breast, up her arm, and then flipped her to face him. Carmen's body tingled in all the right places. She pulled him in for a kiss and led him to a high top table, joining Pilar and Juan. "Hey. Why aren't you two dancing?"

"Carmen. I'm not really... up for a dance." Pilar's eyes were so wide Carmen thought they'd fall out, and Carmen stared right back in the same manner. Juan and Carlos looked at each other as if to say, *What's with these two?*

She leaned in and whispered, "It's okay. It's just a dance." Then Carlos led Carmen to greet the other guests, saving Pilar from any further embarrassment.

Meanwhile, Pilar and Juan stayed at the tall cocktail table, watching the crowd dance. She gripped her wine glass with both hands, not knowing what to do with them.

With all his heart, Juan wanted to ask her to dance, but he worried she'd retreat into her shell even further. Pilar pointed out Luis and Cristina, waltzing across the floor. He could tell how much she loved the old couple. "I've known those two all my life," said Juan.

"Oh?" Pilar was not about to tell him she knew the story.

"Yes. Cristina was married to my cousin's grandfather, Pedro. I heard rumors about she and Luis, you know, when they were young. Not sure if any of it is true, but it's out there. I grew close to Cristina after her husband was found murdered. I didn't know him that well, but I felt so bad for her."

"Like me?"

"What do you mean?" Juan took a sip of wine, looking at Pilar over the rim.

"Eduardo was murdered. So you feel bad for me? That's what this is?" Her gaze angry and piercing, Pilar grabbed her clutch and stormed away, tears flowed unfettered, dragging her mascara with them.

Juan set his wine glass down and it tipped over as he banged into the table when he went after her, weaving through the crowd of slow dancers. "Pilar, it's not the same thing. Wait." Pilar and Juan trudged past Luis and Cristina. Carmen caught sight and took Carlos's hand and followed.

During the slow songs, Gabby and Jose swayed back and forth, melded together like there was no one else in the space. They even missed the other two couples race off. Once in a while, they'd look around at all the partygoers, committing the evening to memory until they spotted their favorite newlyweds.

"Look, there's Luis and Cristina. They look so cute, don't they?" said Gabby.

"It's a shame it took them so long to get together."

"Yes, but look how happy they are now," she said as she watched Luis take Cristina by the hand and lead her away. "Let's go over there." Luis and Cristina sat at a bench in the corner, his hand covering hers, his face pinched.

"Pilar, wait!" yelled Carmen, with Carlos trailing right behind them. Juan followed Pilar into the main office, followed by Carmen and Carlos. "What happened?" asked Carmen. Carlos closed the door behind them. Pilar heard the click of the doorknob pin.

Pilar turned, out of breath, "I knew I shouldn't have let myself get close!" she glared at Juan, then Carmen. By now, Pilar's face was wet, blotchy, and red. Her makeup had run, and she sobbed uncontrollably. "He's not interested in me. He pities me!" she pointed at him.

"What?" Carmen jerked her head at Juan. "What is she saying?"

"Pilar misunderstood what I was saying. I'd been telling her about how I've known Luis and Cristina my whole life. I told her I felt bad for Cristina when her husband died, and now she thinks that's why I'm interested in…*her*."

"Is it?" Carmen moved over to Pilar and put her arm over her shoulder.

"Of course not! I… I think I'm in love with you, Pilar. I'm not trying to pressure you, but I can't stop thinking about you. I can't sleep, and the only time I can eat is when you send me food. It has nothing to do with your husband's murder. You have to believe that," Juan pleaded, hands in prayer. "Please."

Pilar turned away, hugging Carmen, sobbing harder than she had before.

Carmen studied Juan, then looked over at Carlos, who nodded. "Pilar. Listen. I think he's telling the truth."

"Please go, Juan," said Pilar, muffled by Carmen's shoulder.

Carmen and Carlos looked at Juan. The room went silent. Juan's arms dropped. Then Pilar heard the click of the door and she spun. Juan had left the room. She backed away from Carmen and sat on the sofa, pulling her knees to her chest and wrapping her arms around them. Her flouncy skirt taking up all the area on the couch.

"I'll go talk to him," said Carlos, and he left quietly. Carmen sat next to her and handed her a box of tissues. "Talk to me, please."

Pilar wiped her face. "How could he love me?"

"You're quite loveable, my dear."

Pilar laughed at Carmen's tone. "Seriously. Why? I have so much baggage. There must be something wrong with him."

"No. I think you're looking for reasons to turn him away. Also, just so you know, I don't think it will work. He's been worried about you, asking why you don't answer him, and even stopped by to find out why you're ghosting him. He's hung out waiting on you for two years with no pressure."

Pilar looked at Carmen and stopped crying. Straightening her shoulders. "I'm going home."

"Okay, but think about why you reacted the way you did. Why you can't understand why he loves you." The two got up from the sofa and Pilar wiped her tears. "I'll walk you."

Carlos caught up with Juan at the fountain at the center of the hotel. The soft melody of the trickling water soothed his sore heart. "Juan, wait. I'm sorry. She's been through so much."

"I can't even imagine. How could she even think…" he opened his arms, questioning, his eyes pleading.

"Give her time. Let Carmen talk to her."

Juan nodded subtly and headed for the front doors, then turned back. "You know. I'll wait forever for her if I have to."

Carlos nodded. He knew how Juan felt. It wasn't long ago that he'd lost hope Carmen would come around. He walked toward the office as Carmen and Pilar headed right for him. "Are you alright, Pilar?"

"I'm fine. Thanks." She said in a tense voice and walked past him with no eye contact.

Carlos went right for Carmen and hugged her tight. "I'm sure she'll be alright. Just give her time." Carlos told Carmen what Juan had expressed, and that he believed every word.

"I'll go talk to her tomorrow. He seems like a great guy. It would be a shame if she didn't at least give him a chance." The two held hands and headed back for the party.

As Gabby and Jose approached Luis and Cristina, he turned to Gabby. "She doesn't look so good."

"Hi. How are you two doing?" asked the bride to be.

"We're just resting. How are you two doing?" asked Luis.

"Excited. It's going to be an exceptional year," answered Jose. "Can we get you anything? Some water?"

Before Luis could answer, Cristina tilted toward him, and her body went limp. Jose lurched forward to catch her before she hit the floor. "Call an ambulance!"

Chapter 5

Hospital Visits and Evil Plans

Maria's head pounded her awake at four the next morning on the front porch of her extra small, two-bedroom house. She was still in her clothes from the night before, and the front of her feet were no longer in her shoes. The ankle strap on her skinny chrome heels was the only thing holding them on her legs.

Pulling her leg up, she unclasped the buckle of her left shoe and let it drop to the floor, followed by the flop of her leg. Her foot landed on the dusty concrete with a slap. She bent to grab the right shoe buckle, and blood rushed to her face, blurring her vision.

The world spun around her and she threw herself back in the rocker, her body sliding down. Stifling the need to vomit, she closed her eyes, and the tears ran.

When had she become this unwanted person? It seemed the entire neighborhood was at the celebration, except for *her.* She blamed Carmen. Blamed Carlos. She had no one, and it was their fault. Maria rubbed her eyes, pressing her palms like she wanted them to sink into her brain.

Carmen and Carlos stayed at the hospital with Luis through the night. Cristina had slipped into a coma, and the doctors were running tests. "You two should go home. There's nothing you can do here." Behind him, the machines bleep, bleep, ting pounded in his ears.

"Luis, why don't you let us take you home?" asked Carlos. "You need to rest so that when she's awake, you'll have the energy to take care of her." His eyes hooded with concern.

"Carmen, stay with her," Luis insisted. "Carlos." Luis led Carlos outside the room and closed the door. He stopped a moment and looked back through the window at Carmen standing by Cristina's bedside, holding her hand, then turned back to Carlos, "Don't wait like I did," he stared him down.

"What do you mean?"

"I waited too long to come back to Cristina." Luis looked back into the room. "Now look. We haven't had enough time. Don't wait like I did," Luis sobbed.

Carlos had heard rumors, but dismissed the idea, seeing how much they despised each other. He put a hand on Luis's shoulder. "Okay. I understand. Let me take you home to rest a little."

"I'm not leaving her side," he answered, short and gruff.

The men went back in the room and Carmen took one look at Luis, then placed her arm around his shoulder. "We'll bring you a change of clothes and a few things from home," her voice, comforting. She knew his stubbornness would win out, so she wasn't about to fight him. Carlos stood in front of them and couldn't help but notice they had the same stubborn attitude. *Unmovable*, he shook his head.

The two drove home in silence. About three minutes into the drive, Carmen slid over the bench seat and wriggled in next to Carlos, who threw is arm around her.

"I hope she comes out of this fast," said Carmen when they reached the hotel. "I'm going to change, then run over and get some things from their house and head back to the hospital." Her face was wan as she stared up at Carlos.

"You might have Pilar take things over and *you* watch the girls. I'm sure she's worried sick."

"You're right. I'll call her."

Carlos was right. Pilar answered the phone in tears while Carmen tried to calm her. She laid out the plan, then headed to her house with a duffle bag of comforts for Luis and Cristina.

"Do you think she'll be alright?" asked Pilar. Her face was gaunt and her eyes bloodshot from crying. Carmen didn't answer, just walked her to her car. Pilar turned. "I didn't say anything to the girls. Let's wait."

"Don't worry. You go. If you need anything, just let me know." Carmen crossed her arms as Pilar backed out of the driveway.

Pilar's hands shook on the drive to the hospital. At the next light, she caught sight of the small duffle bag Carmen packed for Luis in the rearview mirror. She smothered her rising anguish because she didn't want to show up at the hospital hysterical. Pilar needed to be strong for them.

At the hospital, she found a spot not too far from the entrance and parked the car. She walked around to the back seat to grab the pack, when a warped reflection in the glass behind her caused her to lurch around and back against the car. "HUH! Juan. You scared me."

"I'm sorry. I was stopping by to check on Cristina and I saw you pull into the parking lot." At the mention of Cristina's name, Pilar couldn't hold back any longer and cracked, dropping the bag on the floor along with her purse.

She raised her hands to cover her face, then Juan pulled her close, hugging her to his chest. "I'm sorry."

Pilar didn't know how long she'd stood there with her face buried, but as she pulled away, his tear soaked shirt reported it had been a while. "Oh, my God. I'm so sorry. I... I..." she cried and wiped at the mascara stains she left behind. "I'll clean your shirt."

Juan pulled her back in. "It's okay, and unnecessary. I'm here." Without hesitation, she wrapped her arms around him. "I'm sorry about the other night. I may have overreacted."

Juan didn't let on that he agreed. He just smiled and said, "Let's go to the café for a few minutes, then we'll go upstairs."

She pulled away and looked up at him. "That's a good idea. Thank you."

Juan looked down at her and waited. "Ready?"
"Yes, yes." Pilar wiped her eyes as he picked up the duffle and handed her the purse that had fallen on top of it. He placed his hand on the small of her back and led her through the automatic front doors of the hospital in Pinar del Río, and straight to the cafeteria.

As they walked, she could feel the warmth of his hand on her and the sweet scent that was all man. He didn't wear cologne.

'Something else,' she thought and inhaled as quietly as she could.

Per usual, always the gentleman. He pulled out her seat, placing the bag on the chair next to her. He took her drink order and as he walked away; she grasped his wrist, and he turned. "Thank you." Her eyes said it all, and his heart swelled. He placed his hand over hers and nodded before walking away.

Pilar covered her mouth and nose with her hands as she stared after him. She could almost glean the scent that remained where she touched his arm. She remembered she'd been crying and quickly tried wiping the mascara stains that she was certain stained her undereye.

Juan returned within minutes with three coffees. Sitting across from her, he listened to stories about Luis and Cristina. The countless times they'd jumped in to help when Eduardo was murdered, and how the girls see them as grandparents. They had become even closer, and she couldn't imagine a world without them.

The rush of emotion was a runaway train. Pilar couldn't hold back stories about her own parents and expressed how grateful she was that she had Luis and Cristina. "I never thought my parents would disown me, but I wouldn't let Eduardo go." Pilar told Juan she regretted nothing.

At this, Juan adjusted his seat, offering condolences again. "Thank you, but really, it's unnecessary." She hesitated. But it appeared a door had opened, and she thought it might be a good time to let him know where she stands. "He's been gone about two years now." She waited, half expecting him to say it was too soon to be dating someone, the other half expecting him to get up and leave.

After too long a silence, and coffee just about gone, "I understand, and I hear you. I'm not going anywhere." Juan had bought a cup of coffee for Luis, which Pilar had slid close to her. "Last night..." She smiled, looking up at him, and touched his hand.

"No. It's alright," he stopped her. There was no need to say anything else. Their coffees were gone, and it came time to make their way to Cristina's room.

Pilar stood, took a deep breath, and nodded. Juan grabbed the bag she'd brought. "I'm ready," she said, and he walked next to her the entire way, carrying the extra bag.

There were many people in the elevator, and Juan stepped into the right rear corner of the lift. Pilar watched him make room for her, and she sidestepped the other passengers to get to him. He wrapped his arm around her and drew her close. For the first time, he felt she wasn't fighting him, and she leaned in.

When they arrived in the room, Luis was asleep in the recliner next to Cristina's bed. His hand was holding hers while they slept. Pilar stifled a gasp and found a seat across from Luis. She stared at Cristina, lying in the hospital bed. Her complexion ashen.

Juan set the duffle bag on the table in the corner of the room, then stood behind Pilar, setting his hand on her shoulder every now and again. Sometimes, she'd place her hand on his and tap. He wasn't sure if she was shooing him away, so he stopped trying to comfort her.

Whispers woke Luis. "Pilar. Sergeant Rodriguez, hello."

"Please Luis, call me Juan." He took the coffee cup from the table and handed it to him.

"Okay." He nodded, then paused and looked from one to the other and covered his face in anguish, tears dripping onto his slacks.

Pilar leapt from her seat and knelt next to him. "I'm so sorry, Luis. What have the doctors said?"

"They don't know if she'll wake up. I'm not leaving here without her. She's so stubborn! I wish she would just wake up," Luis said in a strained voice, almost angry, through bitter tears.

Juan stood near the door. He could feel himself wanting to take Pilar to a place where nothing could ever hurt her again. An impossible task. His heart raced as he thought about what their future might look like. He'd never married or had children of his own. His thoughts drifted from one thing to another until she interrupted his reverie.

"I'm sure she'll wake up soon. Isn't that right, Juan?" asked Pilar. Juan jumped with a start and walked over and stood behind Pilar.

"Yes. Yes, she will. You'll see."

After a few minutes, Luis had calmed himself, and drank the now tepid drink.

Pilar and Juan stayed for about an hour. Luis had fallen asleep again, and Cristina still had not awakened.

Outside the hospital, Pilar thanked Juan for keeping her company on her visit. He walked her to her car, opened the door, and made sure she was alright to drive home. He watched her back out of the parking spot and wave goodbye through the window.

At the next light, Pilar flipped down her visor and looked at her reflection. Her brows pinched, straining from worry. *'Ugh, I can't remember the last time I had my eyebrows done. I'm sure he noticed.'* She rubbed her eyes until a loud honk surprised her and she hit the gas. Her concerns weren't just for Cristina, but for Luis in a world without her.

Carmen's hair looked like a basket filled with flowers the girls had picked from the garden, and her fingernails (and then some) were each a different color. Pilar pulled into the driveway as Carmen finished tying the last braid on Daisy. "Okay Daisy. You're all set. You go play with your sisters and let me talk to mom."

Carmen stood and saw Pilar hold the steering wheel with both hands, leaning her forehead on them after she turned off the car, and waited, hoping she'd returned with some positive news.

Pilar got out of the car and dragged herself to the porch. As she approached the rocker next to Carmen, she squatted into it, exhaling like a slowly deflating balloon. Carmen mimicked the movement.

Tossing her handbag on the table between them, she looked over at Carmen, her eyes bloodshot, and her mascara, a blacktop road that stretched down her cheek, winding its way to her chin;

she'd been unsuccessful at cleaning up her eyes. "It's not looking too good for Cristina. Luis is a mess. Says he won't leave her in the hospital."

"That can't be good for him."

"It's not. There's nothing we can do. He's decided." Pilar let out a chortle mixed with a sob. "Luis was mad at her for being so stubborn and not waking up." She rolled her eyes and looked at Carmen.

"Of course he did." Taking Pilar's hand, "Listen, I know the scene well. All we can do is to be here when they need us."

Pilar nodded. She'd been gone several hours and needed to get dinner started, so Carmen got up to leave. She hadn't gone five steps. "Juan was there."

"Oh?" said Carmen, turning back.

Pilar turned around. "I may have overreacted."

"Ya think?" Carmen let her sarcasm fly, and Pilar chortled at her remark, then caught her up on the chance encounter.

"Well, it sounds like it went well, considering," said Carmen.

"Considering what?"

"That, and I say this with love, you're a basket case. Stop overthinking everything. Let things just happen. Trust me, I know. You'll be much happier." And with her lesson, Carmen stood, revved up her car, and drove herself home.

Carmen walked in the door, already talking. "I don't know what I would do if something happened to you," she hugged Carlos so hard she choked the air right out of him.

"Let's not talk about that. Don't even think it," he said. Reminders of his wife tried to force their way in. Her cancer metastasized fast, and like a rocket, he couldn't do a thing to stop it. Carlos shut his eyes tight. "Come on, let's sit out back. I'll grab some wine."

They cuddled on the patio sofa, and as usual, their conversation flowed from one topic to the next in its usual cadence, skirting the obvious worry about their favorite older couple. Phoenix distracted them with her prancing out to the field, retrieving her tennis ball, and dropping it at Carlos's feet for another toss. "Where's the flying saucer, Phoenix?" asked Carlos.

"Flying saucer?"

"Just watch. Phoenix, saucer." The dog took off like a bolt of lightning, returning with a frisbee.

"New tricks. I see."

"Watch this. Get it, girl." With a flick of the wrist, Carlos backhanded the red disc across the field and Phoenix jumped to catch it, mid-air.

"That's amazing! I guess you *did* teach her some new tricks." Carmen sat right on the deck and snuggled her pooch.

A few days later, Luis called Pilar from the hospital. "She's awake!" he yelled into the phone. His excitement overflowed through the tiny holes of her cell phone speaker. Pilar turned to Carmen, and they both left the hotel in Carmen's car while Luis was still talking.

"That's fantastic! We're on our way." Pilar hung up, then

turned to Carmen. "Thank goodness the girls are in school and I didn't need a sitter."

Cristina was sitting up in the bed. The steady beep-beep of the monitors was no match for Luis's energy. When the friends came into the room, he bolted from the recliner to welcome them, his dentures on full display. Cristina rolled her eyes at his exuberance as Pilar went straight to the bed for a relieved hug.

"I see our patient has her color back. What happened?" asked Carmen.

Luis looked at Cristina, who shrugged and nodded. "The doctor diagnosed her with adult, onset diabetes. Her blood sugar dropped so low she had a mini seizure and a minor stroke."

"I'm fine. Look." Cristina lifted her arms, waved her hands around, shook her head and blinked her eyes.

"Her body shut down when she passed out. The doctor said it was lucky, and it gave her a chance to heal before the stroke could do too much damage."

Carmen covered her mouth and closed her eyes. Pilar wiped a tear that escaped without her even noticing. "She's okay now, girls. We're going home tomorrow. They have her on the right meds, and bonus, she's married to a doctor." Luis held his hands wide open while tilting his head, overjoyed and smiling, ear to ear.

"Even so. Take it easy for a while. Don't overexert yourself." Pilar sounded like she was Cristina's mother.

"Yes, yes. I know. Now go. I don't need everyone hovering."

The patient made strong shooing motions and jerked her head toward the door.

Carmen laughed at how quickly the 'old Cristina' came out when provoked. "Let's go, Pilar."

Crisis averted, the friends did as asked and left the hospital, laughing at how quickly old people's forceful personalities can win out.

Maria sat at a small bistro table on the sidewalk outside the Cafecito y Dulce. She watched people coming and going about their lives. None stopped to greet her, or notice she was even there. One person asked if they could have the chair opposite her. "No. I'm not alone. I'm waiting for someone. Leave it there." The man raised his hands in surrender at her curt tone and walked away.

After waiting several hours, she spots Lucrecia and calls her over, offering her a chair. The older woman wore mismatched clothes; a light blue blouse with yellow buttons and a flouncy green skirt intended for someone much younger. The glass in her black-framed glasses was thick, and Maria wondered how she could see out of them. Gray strands of curls set off the blackness of her frizzy hair, held in place with two pink plastic berets. The kind meant for a child. The only item not cheap, was a vintage Chanel red frame purse with kiss-lock closure.

"What do you want?"

"We need to talk."

"I have nothing to say to you, and I don't want to be seen with someone like you."

"Me? What about you? Everyone knows what you did, what you're up to."

"Quiet," Lucrecia sneered, looking over her shoulder.

Maria took her foot and slid the other metal chair away from the table. People spun at the loud scraping noise it made across the concrete, then returned to their conversations.

"What is it? What do you know?" Lucrecia's eyes widened.

"People are talking."

"What people? You know nothing, stupid puta!" Lucrecia shoved her chair back and stood.

Maria hated being called a whore. She leaned forward. "This business with those people on the other side of the wall." Maria's voice remained calm, and she leaned back. Squaring her shoulders, she laid her hands flat on the table. After tilting her head, she raised her eyebrows and nodded.

Lucrecia pulled out the chair and sat, slamming her purse on the table. "What do you want, Maria?"

"That woman has made a fool of me. You know who I'm talking about."

"I know who you're talking about, but what concern is it of mine?"

"You know those people. There has to be a way you can get them to help me."

Lucrecia looked her over. Maria's low cut, see-through top,

and heavy makeup screamed pathetic. The woman seemed so desperate, Lucrecia thought she could use *her*. After a long pause, "We need that property."

"What do you mean? Who? What property?"

"The house, or hotel. Whatever you want to call it. We need her out and we need the property."

"Why? What's so important about that place?"

"None of your business. It came from high up the chain. We need that property."

"If I can help you, will you help me get even, Lucrecia? I've been watching them for two years. Two years. It's not right and you know it. That woman stole Carlos from me. There has to be someone that can help me." Maria choked back the sobs, holding her breath.

"Please. You never had Carlos, and you know it. You're useless. Why don't you look into *her*? See if there's something there you can use to get rid of her."

"No. You *will* help me."

Lucrecia got up, scraping the chair once again. "Stop this before you go too far."

"Help me or I will report what I know to the right people."

"Obsession is a disease, Maria. You should get that checked, along with..." Lucrecia didn't finish the sentence. She looked down and raised a single brow, then stepped from the sidewalk onto the asphalt as she headed for her car. Though she didn't look back, she thought, *I'm through with Maria. She's going to regret threatening me.*

The following week, Carlos and Carmen were out shopping and stopped at the Cafecito y Dulce for a quick break. They didn't notice Lucrecia talking with a man at a corner table, but *she* noticed them. She stared as Carmen threw her head back, laughing, and Carlos touched her arm. "Did you hear what I said?" the man asked Lucrecia.

"Yes. I heard you," she answered without breaking eye contact with the couple at the far away table. The man with her tracked her eyeline but couldn't make out where she was looking.

"We're all set then?"

"Yes. Bring them in." With that confirmation, the man left the café. Lucrecia continued to watch Carmen. Something about this woman irked her.

Chapter 6

A Family Visit and Difficult Grandparents

Pilar drove the five-mile-per-hour speed limit into the school drop off lane and her little garden of girls slipped out the sliding van door. They skipped to their respective teachers, turned and gave a cheerful wave and a smile. Her heart swelled at the sight of them, flooding her with warmth and gratitude.

The girls weren't too keen on the belted jumper uniforms, especially Rose. Suddenly, a lot of things were no longer cool because she'd outgrown them. But then Pilar sewed a navy satin bow to the waist, and just like that, their dislike of the garments vanished, and they'd turn with a flourish to show it off. On other uniforms, she attached some lace or tulle to the bottom to give the mandatory attire a little something special.

She couldn't help thinking about Eduardo and her heart went from swelled to wrenched. Pilar rubbed at her temples as if she'd be able to erase the pain. She needed to enjoy these times without thinking how much her husband would miss. Worse, how much the girls would miss. The monotonous swing of emotions was exhausting.

Just then, her phone chimed a new message.

Good morning. Did the girls get off to school alright?

97

Pilar stared down at it. Her face hurt from smiling. The fact Juan would check in on her every morning gave her warm tremors. She looked out the car window and pursed her lips, wiggling them across her teeth, then smile took on a life of its own, stretching wide. She knew she was smitten, and the guilt was killing her.

Reaching over, she slid the phone into her open purse. Pilar could feel herself giving in and she exhaled. The long list of chores and things to do at work would keep her mind from wandering or answering his text.

At nine that morning, she stood on the front porch of the hotel, waiting for the couple interesting in having their wedding at the hotel. As the BMW pulled in, the valet opened the door for the bride to be.

"Hello. Welcome to La Mariposa. I'm Pilar," she extended her hand.

"Hi. Bianca. Thank you for meeting with me so quickly."

"Of course. Right this way. Is your fiancé coming?"

"No. He's on call. He told me to handle it however I see fit, and that's just what I'm going to do." The woman had a soft midwestern accent. Her blue eyes danced when Pilar showed her a digital presentation of all the other events they'd had, and how they were a full-service venue. "Well, that makes it so much easier."

Pilar gave the blonde a tour of the hotel and the grounds, describing what they had to offer, and why a wedding at their establishment would stand out from any other on the island.

After several hours, Bianca handed Pilar a check that would cover half the six-figure affair. Pilar couldn't wait to tell Carmen.

"That's exciting! When will they get here? I can't wait to meet them," said Carmen. Carlos's family hadn't visited in over two years, and it was time they met Carmen. The few times Carlos traveled to visit his kids, he'd gone alone since the hotel was consuming all of Carmen's time. Besides, Carlos wasn't ready to bring his kids into their life.

"Saturday. Listen, I didn't tell them Machado shot me." At Carlos's confession, she shifted her head back.

"What? Why not? They're your kids," she shrugged. Obviously, this was something that's worried him, and he'd waited until now to mention it.

"I'd planned to tell them once I healed, but you and I were just starting out and I didn't want to complicate things. They would have jumped on a plane. Besides, they'd visited a few days before Ofelia died. I told them they didn't need to come back for the funeral. It wasn't necessary. That's why you hadn't seen them."

"I just can't believe you'd keep that from them."

"Really? You think you're able to judge why I kept something from them?"

"No. But I wasn't in the hospital. I didn't almost die."

"Well, it doesn't matter now. It was a long time ago. They don't need to know." His stern voice and an intense stare told Carmen she should just drop it.

"I understand, and I won't say anything."

"I'll get Luis's house keys. They can stay there."

"Well, I'm excited to meet them. I'll plan something at the

hotel. A pool party? Oh, I'll order from Gabby's and let her design the menu. You know how she loves to do that." Carmen's excitement warmed Carlos to his core and the mood in their home transformed.

"Perfect, my love." He pulled her close, wrapping his muscled arms around her, and kissed and bit her neck until he felt her shiver.

Pilar was shuffling papers at the front desk when Carmen appeared from the back of the house. "Good morning," she sang.

"What's all that about?" asked Pilar.

"Carlos's kids and grandkids are coming next Saturday. I'm excited to meet them. See another side of him with his family." Carmen beamed, and leaned her whole body on the cold granite counter, welcoming the chill, her elbows supporting her bounce.

Pilar smiled right through Carmen. "Are you listening to me?" she asked.

"Yes!" Pilar snapped up.

"Okay. What's going on? You've been spacing out, and it's not like you."

Pilar pulled her phone from her bag, swiped up, opened her messages to the thread from Juan, and flipped it around for Carmen to see. The phone landed with a clunk as it came to a stop.

"Why aren't you answering him? He's just being friendly and caring."

"I'm scared." Tears soaked Pilar's cheeks. Her head hurt

from thinking so hard about all the reasons she couldn't pursue a relationship. Not just with Juan, but with anyone. She curled her upper body forward, tucking her chin, and pressing her palms into her eyes.

"I can't imagine what you're going through. Do you like him? If you don't, just tell him, or that you're not ready. I can see it all over your face at the mere mention of the man, and so can everyone else."

"You're exaggerating."

"No. I'm not." Just then, Angela was walking by. "Watch. Angela, may I see you for a moment?"

Angela walked over. "Of course, boss, what's up?"

"Watch." Carmen pointed at Pilar, who by now had scrunched up her brow so tight it hurt her forehead. "Juan."

Pilar lit up like a New York City street. Her blush went to all parts of her face and down her neck. Angela's head jerked back at the sight. Then Pilar covered herself again with such cachinnation it made both Carmen and Angela cackle along with her.

"Thank you, Angela."

"Sure. No problem." Angela walked away smiling, and half confused, but still giggling.

"See."

Pilar uncovered her face and looked at Carmen. "When I told him I wasn't ready, he said he'd wait." Then her smile was back with a vengeance. She shook her head. "I know. It's all me."

"Yes. It is. I'll be at Gabby's if you need me." Carmen turned and seemed to float away.

As soon as she opened the back door, the mouth-watering aromas of food streaming from the restaurant filled the air. Gabby's was ready to open, and they'd been trying out the new dishes she'd planned.

Before she could grasp the large metal "G" handle on the front doors, one sous chef came bursting out, almost running her over. "Oh, sorry, Ms. Carmen."

"It's ok. Gabby inside?"

"Yea. Good luck," he said with a strong hint of bitterness, and rolled his eyes.

Carmen eyed the young chef, squinting at his snide remark. She tracked him as he got into his car, slammed the door and peeled out of the driveway, leaving tracks in the white gravel.

"Gabby?" she called as she entered. A bustle of activity buzzed around her. Servers were preparing tables. The bartender consulted her clipboard as she took inventory and aligned many bottles of spirits. Several others cleaned and prepped for the grand opening. The place was spotless and smelled of bleach.

Carmen found Gabby in the kitchen, barking orders at several other sous chefs. One dropped his metal spatula with a clank, and with a shaky hand retrieved it, then ran to the sink scrubbing it with soap and a metal pad. The other threw his towel over his shoulder and went back to work, seemingly unaffected by Gabby's tirade.

"Hey. Got a minute?"

Gabby turned around, annoyed, and bit her bottom lip, her nostrils flaring. "Sure." She slammed her towel down on the metal prep table and trudged to the walk-in cooler. The creak of her black clogs on the sticky floor was an omen to the chefs that Gabby was on the move.

Gabby closed the thick metal door after her friend stepped inside. Carmen heard the suction of the gasket seal them in the cavern, and she inhaled a deep breath, then opened and closed her fists. "What's up?" asked Gabby.

"Take a breath. You're very tense. What's going on?" Carmen stuffed her hands into her jeans pockets as her eyes darted around the enclosure. She didn't feel the cold or notice the crates of vegetables and assorted meats, just the fact that there were no windows and only one way out.

"I'm just busy and I can't get the crew to move faster. We open in two days." Gabby rubbed her face, pressing her palms into her eyes, and paced the length of the freezer.

"How can I help?"

"If only."

"Come with me." Carmen hooked her arm through Gabby's and led her out of the freezer and then through the back door. She walked her around to the front of the restaurant on the new walkway in complete silence.

"Look at me," she turned her. "You are a fantastic chef. You're respected by your peers and admired by all. The menu looks great and so does your new restaurant." At this, Carmen turned her toward the façade. "Take a deep breath and let's go inside." After walking her through the front doors, "And your employees are working very hard to please you," she waved around.

Gabby exhaled long and hard and looked around the dining room. Every single employee hustled through their checklist at break-neck speed. No unnecessary conversations, no dilly-dallying. Gabby turned to Carmen. "Thank you. I think I need to apologize."

"I think so. Maybe call the one that ran for the hills."

"Alex." Gabby nodded, then gave Carmen a hug and walked to the bar, calling her staff over. In a soft tone, she apologized and thanked them for their patience and hard work. Later, she did the same in the kitchen.

When she called Alex, he wouldn't accept her apology, and hung up before she could convince him to come back. Gabby treated him unfairly after everything he'd done to help finish the place, and there was nothing she could say to win him over.

Given Gabby's current state, Carmen waited until the next morning to request a menu for Saturday's visitors, which Gabby was more than happy to provide. "I hope they like me," Carmen worried.

"What's not to like? Besides, you make him happier than he's ever been. Trust me on that." Gabby had known Carlos for over twelve years now, and knew just about everything there was to know.

"You never know. Can't be all things to all people."

"I think you worry too much. How about I put together

some Cuban sandwiches, pan con bistec with the shoestring potatoes, and some tamales?"

"Oh, I love those steak sandwiches with the potato sticks. That all sounds great! Thank you."

With the menu all set, Carmen went to Luis's old house and straightened everything. She washed all the linens and prepared the kitchen with both Cuban and American coffee. Then she brought in some dry good snacks she knew most kids liked, and set wine and beer in the fridge, and on the wine rack, next to the fancier rum and gin spirits that were already there.

Before their arrival, she'd have fresh flowers on the kitchen table and in the bedrooms. It felt as if her own family were coming for a visit. She stood in each room with her hands on her waist, smiling.

Back at the house she shared with Carlos, she filled him in on the plans she'd put in motion for his family's visit. He warmed at the idea that she was excited to meet them, and that she'd gone through so much trouble to prepare. When she wasn't looking, he swept her up and carried her to their bedroom, leaving Phoenix in the hallway, whining her complaint about being shut out of the room, again.

It was about two in the afternoon when Gabby looked around her new restaurant. Everything was ready. After the morning's meltdown, she decided the crew needed a break, and sent everyone home to rest. One more day until the grand opening, and she wanted everyone rested and ready.

Gabby's staff cheered as they grabbed their belongings and headed for the door. She was glad to see them excited for a break, and they deserved it after the last couple of weeks of her crazy. They laughed and pointed at each other over some private jokes they shared, and Gabby just loved the camaraderie.

After they all left, she took a private tour of the restaurant. Everything was in place. Perfect. Gabby realized *she* needed a breath as well, and after looking it all over, she hung her chef's coat and toque on the hook, pulled out her keys, and headed for the door. She turned for one last look, committing it all to memory, walked out, and locked up the doors.

Outside, Gabby took two steps back and stared at the 'G' door handle. She nodded and closed her eyes, inviting gratitude to wash over her. A quick text to Jose and she'd be off.

Hey. I'm coming home early. See you there?

Yes!

After an intense hello, Gabby came clean about her meltdown at the restaurant. "I'm sure the staff thinks I'm crazy. Luckily, Carmen stopped me from making it worse. Oh, and Alex quit today."

"That's a shame. He was restless to get cooking and even

helped me with the appliance connections. Maybe he'll realize you were just nervous about the launch and come back," said Jose.

"He was furious. I doubt it."

The couple spent the rest of the afternoon and evening together, cuddled up in bed, watching movies, reading, and ordering in. There'd be no cooking or cleaning up.

Luis and Cristina had been home from the hospital for about a week. Too proud, they'd declined anyone's help, and Pilar had filled their refrigerator with food they could reheat, anyway. She'd followed the guidelines for diabetic cooking and hoped Cristina would stick to it. She knew the old woman had a stubborn streak that rivaled her teenager's.

"Stop fussing, coño!" Cristina was growing tired of Luis hovering in a panic every time she moved. "I'm fine, damn it!"

"I'm not about to let anything happen to you again," Luis argued.

Cristina grabbed her cell phone and called Pilar. "I need you to come take this old man out of here. He's driving me crazy."

"On my way," said Pilar. Luckily, their house was across the street, and all she had to do was walk over. "Come on Luis. I need help with the girls. Let's go."

Cristina mouthed a 'thank you' from behind Luis, who did as he was told, though he grumbled as he walked next to her.

"You have to let her rest. She knows what she can handle."

"Does she? Cristina didn't bother getting checked. I could have lost her."

"But you didn't. Come on and help me with the girls. I have to make dinner. You keep an eye on them."

The rest of the evening was quiet. At dinner time, Pilar and Luis packed up the food and the girls and headed back to his house. They found Cristina asleep in her chair in the living room.

"See. She's resting."

Luis went over to wake her for dinner. His eyes squinted at the rising and falling of her chest, and he exhaled. "Mi amor. Time for dinner." Cristina woke with a grunt, pulled herself to standing and gave him a hug. Rose, Daisy, and Lily gave her a gentle hug before taking her hand and leading her to the table. This, she would never argue with.

After dinner, Pilar and the girls packed up their offering and headed home under the soft street lights. Pilar delighted at their chattering. Today, their diatribe had something to do with Rose's impending Quincéañera. Pilar let them debate the topic, listening for potential ideas that would help her with planning.

The next morning, Pilar dropped her girls at school, as usual, and drove straight to the hotel. In the silence of her car, she thought about Luis and Cristina. It took them a long time to find each other again, and now they were inseparable. She couldn't help but draw a comparison with her situation with Juan.

At the check-in desk, Pilar stared at her cell. She'd spent the better part of the day pulling it from her pocket and returning it to her pocket, stopping when laughter caught her attention.

Angela and Diego strolled in from the dining room. They'd been talking and laughing about something Pilar was not privy to. Her eavesdropping didn't squash the deep longing she felt. She watched them with an almost resentful gawk; how relaxed they talked and moved about, free from worry and fear.

Then her cell phone rang. The vibration startled her. Yanking the phone from her pocket, the screen lit up with an automated emergency alert from the principal of the girls' school. All the color drained from her face. Her legs seem to wobble out from beneath her, and her heart pounded to get out.

Pilar grabbed her bag and ran out the door, slamming it behind her. Angela and Diego both turned and ran after her. "Pilar, is everything alright?" Diego yelled, but Pilar didn't hear him as she sped away.

Chapter 7

An Explosion and A Surprise Invitation

Angela and Diego looked at each other and pulled out their respective phones.

"Carmen, something's happened. Pilar got an alert, said, 'Oh my God,' and sped out of here. We don't know what happened."

"Thanks for calling me, Angela. I'll call her." Carmen slid out of bed and into her clothes before she could tell Carlos what had happened. She rang Pilar several times and her phone went right to voicemail.

Angela and Diego waited at the front desk. While Angela rubbed her arms, Diego paced with his hands on his waist.

Minutes later, Carmen arrived at the hotel, sprinting up the steps. "Has she called?"

"No," said Angela as she rushed forward. "Her face…"

"Terrified?"

"Yes, but…more than that." Carmen asked Angela and Diego to keep it to themselves. Gabby was opening her restaurant the next day and couldn't afford the distraction.

Before Carmen could give it any thought, her cell rang. "Pilar? What happened?" she said in a loud voice, looking up at Angela and Diego.

"The school is on lockdown. There's been a bomb threat. They told us not to use our cell phones and to leave the area.

Carmen could hear the panic through the outrage in her shaky voice through the receiver.

"Come back here. We'll wait together."

"I have no other choice. They aren't letting parents take their kids."

"The girls are safe. We have to remain positive. Just come back."

Within a few minutes, Pilar pulled into the driveway, and Carmen ran down to meet her car. "What did you see?"

"There's police and SWAT everywhere. I don't know what to do." She cried as she got out of the car and walked back up the steps with Carmen. The noon sun blazed high in the cloudless sky. Not even a breeze blew through the trees to ease the heat.

"We're going to wait right here."

Before they got up the stairs, a loud explosion shook the ground. They turned to see a large plume of black smoke rise in the air from the direction of the school. Pilar screamed, and they ran towards Pilar's car. "I'll drive," said Carmen.

"Hurry!" yelled Pilar. When she tried to talk, she hyperventilated, and Carmen could hear her saying 'No, no, no.'

"Calm down and breathe. This will not help the girls." Carmen turned the van right on the main road, heading straight for the school. Fire rescue vehicles and ambulances blew past her.

"Oh, no!" cried Pilar. She covered her mouth while her insides seemed to compress tighter and tighter. They could smell smoke and gas in the air as the closer they got to the school.

Guests flooded the ground floor, asking for answers. Angela and Diego assured them of their safety and they could go back to their vacations. The two looked at each other, not sure if the assurance they gave would be of any help.

Once the guests walked away, Angela turned to Diego and whispered. "It's hard to say that when I don't know if it's true."

The two stood at the check-in desk for a while, waiting for the next big thing, but nothing came. After some time, Diego reached over and took Angela's hand. "Everything will be fine. You'll see." Angela looked down at his hand on hers, then up into his eyes. He towered over her. She stood close enough to count the light tan freckles that dotted his nose and cheeks.

Now that everything seemed calm, Diego broke the intimate moment and turned to leave. She caught his musky scent, sending flutters through her chest and down her body to all the right places.

Diego whistled a tune as he turned the corner, not knowing that Angela was watching his work pants pockets dance as he marched away.

A chaotic scene was unfolding as Pilar and Carmen neared the school. One building was emptied as teachers led the uniformed students across the street. Giant red, orange, and yellow flames shot up from the back of the building. Black smoked billowed from windows, and the screams of children emanated from inside. The odor was a wicked blend of fuel, flames, and something no one could place.

Parents ran around screaming for their kids, while police and SWAT swarmed the area, guns drawn. The fire department battled the blaze from every angle, shooting hundreds of gallons of water at the burning building.

Pilar got out of the car and froze. Covering her mouth, she dropped to her knees. Carmen ran over and helped her stand. "We have to find the girls." She dragged Pilar with her.

The two dodged throngs of people while calling out for her daughters. There were parents running in every direction. Carmen and Pilar couldn't tell which way to go. The police began pushing parents back from the building, fearing another explosion.

Carmen and Pilar couldn't make out any voices above the police sirens and the screams of desperate parents. Carmen looked around. Everyone was pulling their shirts over their eyes and noses. The sting of the ash filling her nostrils. She told Pilar to cover her face as well. Looking across, plumes of black smoke billowed from shattered windows, obscuring the front of the school.

"What was that?" Gabby asked Jessy, the bartender.

"Sounded like an explosion," said Jessy.

Gabby walked out the front doors and could see the plume of smoke in the distance. "Now what?" she said to no one. She walked back inside and continued working until a scream from the servers' station got her attention. "What is it?"

"There's been an explosion at the school!"

"What? My God! Pilar's girls!" Gabby ran out the doors and into her car, peeling out toward the school.

As she arrived on the scene, she drove her VW van onto a grassy field a block from the school. Running toward the ruckus, she spots Pilar's empty car and knew her friend was there looking for her daughters.

Gabby began calling out for Pilar, but couldn't hear her own voice above the din. She could feel her heart pounding in her ears as she jumped to see over the crowd. The closer she got to the building, the more the police pushed her back. "My nieces are in there!" she yelled as tears stung.

"I understand, but it's not safe. We're doing what we can. Please back up!"

Through the pandemonium, a wail caught her attention. It was Pilar, her knees ground into the grass in front of the school walkway. Gabby's eyes filled with salty tears and she covered her mouth. Carmen was standing next to her, screaming at an officer. On a full run, Gabby darted toward them, zig-zagging through the crowd.

"I'm here, I'm here," she said, out of breath and dropped to her knees, and hugged Pilar. "What's happening?"

"The doors are chained from the inside, and only one of the custodians has the key. They can't find him." Pilar told Gabby through unrelenting sobs.

"Yet another reason bars on the windows aren't a good idea," said Gabby.

Luis and Cristina heard the explosion and immediately locked the doors and headed to the center of the house with their emergency bag. Of course, not everyone reacted this way, only the older generations who had lived through revolutions. The familiar sound put them on notice that something was coming.

He'd made a comfortable space for himself and Cristina until the storm, or whatever it was, was over. They each had a comfortable recliner they could sleep in, food, water, and any necessary medications. Luis knew how to prepare for hurricanes. This was no different.

After hearing a knock at the door, the two quieted down and waited. "Luis, Cristina? It's Carlos. Are you okay?"

The couple looked at each other, then left their shelter and opened the door. "Carlos? What is it?"

"I came to make sure you two were alright after the explosion at the school."

"The explosion was at the school? Oh, no! Are the girls alright?" Luis said with a frantic Cristina, hobbling up behind him. She looked over his shoulder and toward Pilar's house to see if her car was in the driveway.

"Yes. Everyone is alright. There were no fatalities from the explosion."

"Was it those bastards behind the wall?" Cristina's feelings about the Marxists that were removed from the state have never wavered. "They should move them to La Isla de la Juventud." The large island still had the abandoned Presidio Modelo. A prison used during the 1950s revolution. "Let them have it, and that way they won't cause any more trouble here."

"Wait, no fatalities from the explosion? *Was* there a fatality?" asked Luis.

"Why would they chain the doors?" asked Gabby.

"It's a safety thing. If they lock and chain the doors from the inside, it deters anyone from just walking in and shooting up the place." Carmen knew the protocol from the many times her teacher friend Mary talked about lockdown protocols.

Without warning, shots rang out, reverberating through the crowd, causing everyone to scream and drop to the floor.

The gunfire came from inside the building, followed by a loud banging. All at once, the front doors flew open and out poured the students that couldn't be evacuated earlier, engulfed in gray smoke. In the center of the swarm, Juan, carrying Lily, with Rose and Daisy at his side, jogging toward the crowd, followed by several teachers and several classes of students.

"There!" yelled Carmen.

Pilar looked up and stood from her kneeling position on the ground. Her face was red and wet, and Gabby's arm was around her shoulder. Upon seeing her, Rose ran straight for her mother, followed by Daisy and Lily, still holding on to Juan.

Pilar hugged Rose and Daisy tight to her body. As soon as Juan was close enough, he handed Lily to her mother. His uniform bore evidence of how much the child had cried. Pilar took hold of her daughter, swaying back and forth while the other two held on to her waist. She looked up at Juan, tears spilling down her face.

Carmen and Gabby stood close by, wiping away the worry that had shed across their cheeks. Pilar looked at Juan and her girls, then at Carmen and Gabby. Carmen nodded. It was the right time.

"Girls. This is my friend, Officer Rodriguez, um, Juan." The girls looked at their mother and then Juan, and smiled. Then Lily turned and smiled at him, and whispered in her mother's ear.

"Okay, Lily." Pilar looked up at the officer, "Juan. Please join us for dinner…tonight…at our house?"

"That sounds wonderful. I wouldn't miss it." He tipped his hat and smiled. His eyes melted to hers until he was called back to the scene. The three girls stared at the pair, who seem to have floated away together, and smiled knowingly at each other.

Carmen and Gabby looked at each other with a knowing stare, and restrained their laughter.

Pilar carried Lily while Rose and Daisy held hands and walked next to her. After belting Lily in the booster seat, she turned to Rose and Daisy and squeezed them tight, releasing all the fear that consumed her over the last few hours.

After a long while, every child left with their parents. The fire department took the lead sergeants through the building to find the point of origin. There was no evidence of an incendiary device, though it couldn't be ruled out. They still questioned the whereabouts of the missing custodian, and an investigation would follow.

It had been a long day, and all Juan could think about was the dinner invitation to Pilar's. He had to go home and shower and change, since he didn't want to smell like smoke the first time he went into her house. Forcing himself to focus, he finished his on-site paperwork in his squad car, hit send on the computer, closed the laptop, and headed home.

At almost six o'clock that night, Carmen and Gabby arrived at the hotel and headed for the restaurant. She'd ran out, leaving her crew in charge of preparations for the grand opening, and now she went into full on panic that she wouldn't be ready for the opening. She expected a mess and her anxiety twisted at her insides.

Flinging the door open, she looked around, and everything was pristine. The employees all stood around, waiting for further instructions. There was nothing left to do.

The dinner tables and the flatware were primed and ready. Understated centerpieces were positioned on each table, to not take away from her plating ideas. The glasses at the bar glimmered, and every bottle label faced forward, ready to be imbibed.

In the kitchen, the chefs completed their prep work and all the food containers were labeled and properly stored. The ice machines had fresh ice, and the staff had even pressed all the uniforms and linens.

"Huh. Wow. I don't know what to say. Everything looks perfect, ready. I have the best crew ever!" Gabby's voice cracked as she spoke.

Carmen stood behind her, covering her mouth, and when Gabby turned to look at her, she rolled her eyes. "I told you not to worry." With that, Carmen turned on her heel and left.

"You have all made me so proud. Thank you for holding down the fort. Now go home! See you tomorrow."

Her staff each hugged her on the way out of the restaurant. She turned to face the bar, set her hands in prayer, then looked up and said a quick thank you to her guardian angel.

Carmen arrived back home to a waiting Carlos. She'd left instructions to put dinner in the oven when she ran out that morning. Hopefully, it wasn't all dried out. She'd made a lasagna from an old childhood recipe.

"That smells great," said Carmen. She remembered learning the recipe from a neighbor that was teaching some girls on her street in North Miami how to cook. Just a few days earlier, she'd had news that the woman had passed away in her sleep. Carmen nodded, thinking of only the good times, and made the lasagna in her honor. The aroma of garlic and onions, mozzarella, and a savory Bolognese seeped from the oven.

"I waited to put it into the oven. I figured you'd be home about now. How are the girls?"

"I think they're okay. Sergeant Rodriguez pulled them from the building. You should have seen how he and Pilar looked at each other. It was a… tender moment."

"Butt out, Matchmaker."

Carmen answered him with her chin high. "I matched nothing. She invited him to dinner tonight. At her house. I hope she doesn't back out." Carmen laughed as she took the lasagna out of the oven, then arranged garlic bread slices on a foiled cookie sheet, and set them to toast. "The lasagna will rest while these bake."

"I'm just saying you don't want things to backfire on you. Be careful."

"Open the wine, please." She handed him a bottle of Cabernet and the cork pull. "Nina and Mary will be here in the morning. I have them set up at the hotel. They're so excited about the restaurant, they've been saving calories." Carmen laughed and rolled her eyes.

"We're all excited. I'm sure it will be a great opening. Gabby must be a walking bundle of raw nerves."

"She'll be okay. She sent the staff home, then locked up and did the same."

The evening ended early when the last drop of wine splashed into their glasses. Carlos tossed the empty bottle into the recycling bin on his way to the shower.

Carmen took Phoenix out back for her personal stuff. Gone are the days where the dog would disappear and Carmen would go into a full on panic if she didn't come right back. She remembered the anxiety it caused and now thanked her lucky stars that those days were over.

Pilar drove the girls straight home. The relief almost too much to bear. They all talked at the same time on the drive home as their ordeal turned into utter excitement. She was thankful for the resiliency of children. It took nothing for them to bounce right back like nothing happened.

She pulled into the driveway, taking her time to get out of the car. The three girls jumped out, "In the shower, please. Scrub that smoky smell away," called Pilar. Inside the front door, she paused. "What have I done?"

Chapter 8

A Lovely Dinner and Announcements

Pilar checked her fridge for something she could throw together and at least make a good impression. She knew she was a wonderful cook, but this one mattered more than she was ready to admit. Her refrigerator was ripe with leftovers.

She began setting out containers of chicken and rice, palomilla steak with rice and beans, and maduros. Always maduros. Sweet fried bananas are delicious with everything. She found a container of ropa vieja that was enough for the group, and she tapped her fingers on her chin, mulling over the containers on the table.

After lining them up, she paced back and forth, trying to decide which he'd like the best. In the end she went with the palomilla. She'd serve the thinly cut top sirloin with jasmine rice and black beans. The steak would marinate in lots of garlic, lime juice and a little salt, and in a separate bowl, she set aside sliced onions.

After showering away the earlier trauma, she tried finding something to wear that wasn't so… 'mommy.' She trembled, trying on different outfits, tossing them aside one by one. "Too small, too large, too frumpy".

At one point, she thought she'd made a horrible mistake and should *'call... no...text him, and cancel.'* And at that precise moment, her phone chimed. She held her breath, then looked down. Juan.

I'll be there in about fifteen minutes and I'm bringing a bottle

of cabernet. I hope that's okay.

Of course. That would be lovely.

She hit send before she realized what she'd done. Then another chime. This one came from Carmen.

Don't you dare cancel on him.

Yes, mother, I won't.

Good. Can't wait to hear about it tomorrow.

At last, something fit just right. She got dressed, looked herself over in the mirror, and tilted her head from side to side, turning her body to see all angles. Since Eduardo's death, she'd lost her appetite and her former stocky frame. The only thing that fit her smaller dimensions was an old dress she found in the back of the closet.

The last time she'd worn the frock was before she had Rose. "This is so outdated." She looked like a 1950s all-American housewife in the light blue gingham dress. The cap sleeve top had buttons and collar like a shirt, then puffed out to a full skirt from the shirtwaist.

On her way to the kitchen, she peeked at the girls, who'd dressed and were busy doing crafts in Rose's room. "Okay girls. We're having company tonight. I expect everyone to behave."

"Yes, Mommy," they sang in unison, mocking Pilar and batting their eyelashes.

"Hilarious." Pilar knew Rose had put the other two up to the sarcasm; she was now a full-blown teenager, with all the attitude she could muster. Pilar went into the kitchen and tied on her apron. She began preparing dinner, all the while reminding herself that it was a simple dinner of leftovers, and nothing special, nothing more. *'No big deal.'*

Before she knew it, the loud scrape of the metal gate caught her attention. Over the years, she'd paced the front path enough to know Juan would be at the door in precisely twenty-two steps.

Pilar didn't want to seem anxious, so she waited for him to knock before heading for the door, and busied herself with adjusting the silverware on the table, her hands trembling.

"Coming." Pilar stood in front of the door, pressing down her apron and the skirt, trying to make it flatten out a bit. Then she checked her face in the tiny mirror that hung by the casing and blew out her nervousness. After straightening her back and shoulders, she whispered several reminders, "It's just dinner. Nothing more." She unlocked the door and reached for the security chain.

Juan heard the metal scrape of the chain across the track on the other side. He paced in place, straightening his guayabera, forcing himself to still, though the bouquet gave away his secret.

When the door opened, Pilar and Juan didn't speak. They just stared at one another until the pitter patter of running feet came up behind Pilar and she rolled her eyes up. "Hi, Sergeant Rodriguez!" they sang in unison once again.

"Girls. Please. Juan, please, come in." She gave them a tight smile, then moved aside so he could step across the threshold.

"Thank you, um…these are for you." The bouquet had an intentional mix of lilies, roses, and daisies set off by variegated ivy and babies' breath. Pilar took the bouquet, her hand grazing his, sent sparks up her arms, chased by goosebumps that radiated everywhere.

Lily took his hand and led him to the living room. He warmed at the idea that Pilar's daughters had welcomed him into their home. "Do you want to see my drawing?" She asked.

Pilar took the bouquet and went to the kitchen to set them in water, all the while lending an ear, eavesdropping on her daughters' conversations.

Juan sat on the sofa next to Lily as she handed him a drawing she'd made earlier. Pilar came in and lowered herself into the club chair across from them. "She drew that when we got home from school earlier."

"This is mommy, Rose, and Daisy. This is me, and this is you carrying me."

Pilar's eyes welled up at the scene, and she put two fingers to her trembling lips. Juan held the drawing, nodded and smiled at the child, then looked over at Pilar. She could see tiny water drops swimming in his eyes.

"I made it for you so you can remember that you're my hero." Her tiny voice was heavy with gratitude.

Pilar covered her mouth, swallowing the giant knot in her throat. Juan thanked Lily for the kind gesture and told her he'd keep it forever, holding it tight to his chest.

Daisy and Rose patiently waited their turn. They'd made him a badge from tinfoil, cardboard and hot glue. It said, 'Sgt. Rodriguez, #1 Hero.' At this, neither Pilar nor Juan could hold back the flood. The girls gave *him* a hug and Pilar some tissue.

"Let's eat," said Pilar.

"Mom, sit here. Sergeant Rodriguez, you sit here next to mom. We're going to sit on this side." Pilar listened as Rose directed everyone to their seat. She'd sat her mother at the head of the table, and Juan to her mother's right, facing the three girls.

"Thank you, Rose. Your home is beautiful Pilar."

"Thank you. Ed-," she stopped herself. "We've lived here since annexation. I think it's ready for a coat of paint or something." Pilar looked around and thought, *'Maybe changing something here will help me move on.'*

"Well, I'm always happy to help. If you want, pick out a color and I'll grab the supplies. It'll be a fun project." He smiled at the girls, then looked over at Pilar.

Once again, Pilar was shaking. She stood from the table to serve from the stove, and Juan shot to standing. Startled, she the girls all looked at him, and each other, as if something had gone wrong.

Juan looked down at the six eyes that tracked his movements. "What?" he laughed. "My parents taught me to stand when a lady stands." He smiled, then sat back down.

"It's okay, you don't have…"

At this, the three girls looked at each other, then scootched their seats back, scraping the terrazzo floor, and stood staring at him with enormous eyes, giggling. Pilar froze in her spot, staring.

Juan shot to standing again, then sat when they sat. The girls waited a few seconds, then looked at each other again and shot to standing. Juan stood and smiled at them.

By now, Pilar had gone to the counter to put the pot back on the stove, but kept watch over her shoulder. She warmed at the sight of their game and smiled. After another couple of rounds of, 'Let's see if Officer Rodriguez will stand,' their mother said, "Alright, that's enough. You've tortured him plenty. Here. Eat." She set their plates in front of the four and sat next to Juan with her own.

They ate in silence for way too long, until Rose said, "Someone say something. Please. This is weird."

"Rose!" Pilar chastised.

"What? We're not dumb. We know you like each other." The other two girls nodded and laughed, shooting the adults a precocious grin.

Pilar turned every shade of red on the spectrum. Juan guffawed. "It's okay Pilar." He reached over and took her hand. The girls all looked at each other, picked up their plates, and headed for Rose's room.

Pilar looked away, embarrassed, following her daughters' retreat from the room.

"There's nothing to be upset about here. They're not wrong." He put his hand on hers and Pilar heated all the way through to her bones.

"But why should they know, or even be okay with...this? Aren't they too young?"

"I think we're both being naïve here. Kids today know way more than we did at their age." Juan went back to eating. "This is the best palomilla steak I've ever had."

"Thank you," said Pilar turning her gaze toward him. "I'm glad you like it." They looked at each other for what felt like forever. Pilar nodded, and without looking up, she said, "And I'm really glad you're here."

Carmen and Phoenix went back inside after taking care of all the personal stuff. She found Carlos on the couch flipping through channels.

"Can I ask about your family?" Carmen wriggled in next to Carlos, sliding her back over his chest.

"Of course. What would you like to know?"

"I don't know. How much do they know about me?" She

tapped the sofa and Phoenix wiggled in behind her bent knees, curling like a tabby cat.

"Just that I met someone I'm head over heels for. That one day without her is impossible." Carlos swooned, batting his long lashes.

"What if they don't like me?"

"They will love you. You'll see."

"I'm going to invite my kids next."

Carlos looked at her. She'd been resistant about inviting people into their space. "Why now?"

"It's time."

"Have they asked about me?"

"No, not really. But I'm sure my mother filled them in. Gloria has her way of telling things."

Carlos laughed, "I'm sure. Let's go to bed. We've got an early day tomorrow. Gabby will need all of us."

The morning of the big day had arrived and cars loaded with ferry passengers wheeled in and out of the hotel driveway. Deliveries for both the restaurant and the hotel rolled up every thirty minutes. From the outside, it appeared to be the busiest place on the island; a flurry of activity everywhere.

Gabby had one employee assigned to accept deliveries, while another organized where to place the crates in the storage room of the restaurant.

While Angela delt with guests, Diego organized the hotel's

own deliveries. Every time they passed each other, they exchanged a quip or a high five, and sometimes a knowing half smile or wink. Contact of any kind seemed to bring them closer together, and they both knew it, but would never admit to it.

Angela found herself walking a few extra steps or going the long way, so she'd 'accidentally' run into him, unaware that Diego had the same plan. More and more, they'd stop to chat for a minute here and there. Their bodies shifting side to side, arms crossed or folded, with nervous laughter. Angela would adjust her hair, or Diego would straighten the end of his beard at his chin, sharpening to a point.

Sometimes, Angela felt herself sweating, heated by his musk as he passed her by. She'd fan herself with whatever paper was closest. And if Carmen were close by to witness the utter discomposure, she'd laugh and shake her head.

"We've arrived!" announced Nina, waving an arm in the air as if she was the opening act at La Scala in Milan. Mary laughed at Nina's wiggly saunter toward the check-in desk. Her hips swinging wild, making the fringe on her skirt flip this way and that.

Angela hadn't had the full Nina experience yet, and she smiled at the woman's exuberance. Mary glanced at her from behind and winked, making Angela giggle and Diego swing his head toward the laughter, then he moved to stand in Angela's very personal space. Both Mary and Nina noticed the attraction right away and couldn't wait to dish with Carmen. The pair magnetized to each other in an obvious way, and it was something everyone witnessed.

It had been a whole three months since their last adventure, and Carmen had been excited to see her friends. Gabby insisted they come for opening day, and the two had dieted to prepare for what they knew would be a gastronomic showcase. They designated the extra ten pounds they'd carry back with them 'extra baggage.'

"You're here!" yelled Carmen. "Good flight?" It was almost a silly question, since the flight is only about forty minutes, gate to gate. The plane is barely level when it has to begin its descent, and you barely had time to get comfy. She hugged each of her friends and held out a room key.

"Perfect!" said Mary. "I'm ready to relax by the pool with a Piña colada."

"Me too! Let's go change," said Nina, snatching the key.

Carmen led her friends to the room they'd share for the weekend. There were no free rooms because of the restaurant opening. The hotel filled up the minute Pilar posted the advertisements.

Nina and Mary were relieved that Carmen's decision to stay in New Cuba had worked out. It took them a while to get used to not having her nearby every day, but they also enjoyed running away to the island every chance they got.

Within minutes, the friends were by the pool in their bathing suits, sunglasses, and hats. To prepare for this visit, they bought new long sleeve, full length cover-ups that made them look glamorous. The trim on the bell sleeves had gold or silver lace. They paired the ensemble with cute one-inch heel slide sandals and a straw handbag.

Nina had an enormous ivory bangle on her left wrist that matched her huge white sunglasses. Mary wore no bangle, just giant gold hoop earrings that glinted in the sun. They were so big, they scraped the top of her shoulder.

The two looked like they'd stepped out of a 1960s magazine advertising a tropical vacation. "Look at that sign," Mary laughed, pointing to a dragonfly and mariposa decorated metal placard unable to hold in the chuckle. Her face turned a crimson shade as she covered her mouth.

Nina read aloud,

"The common areas are for

the enjoyment of all guests.

Please refrain from inappropriate

conduct in all public spaces."

Mary snickered. "I want to hear all about *that* when we see Carmen later."

"Sounds like something scandalous happened," agreed Nina.

They'd just settled in when a server came over with their drinks. Nina lowered her extra-large, white sunglass to get a good look at the guy in the white linen trousers and guayabera. She saw a nametag, but was too captivated by his physique to take note.

This guy was tan. Not sun-tanned, but what seemed to be his natural color. "If you need anything else, just press this button here and it will ring my phone." He set a black box on the table between Nina and Mary. It had a red button in the center, and a gold plate identified the owner. Nina picked it up, "Alvaro." Then she eyed Mary and turned to watch Alvaro walk back toward the house with his tray in hand.

"No."

"What? I didn't say anything."

"Nina, we're here for Gabby's grand opening. That's it."

"I wasn't thinking anything."

"Sure you weren't. I know that look."

They both laughed. The three friends knew each other well and had no qualms about keeping each other in check and from making poor choices.

For now, they sat by the pool, sipping their cocktails and watching the bustle that went on around the pool. Families with children, couples enjoying umbrella clad drinks, and hotel workers racing around with towels and food and drink orders. "I'm so proud of Carmen. She truly turned things around," said Mary. Nina agreed with a hearty nod.

"I don't know what would have happened if she'd forgone this and stayed in Miami. She'd have been stuck in some office somewhere with no windows. Look at this place."

"Yes. It's magical." Mary exhaled pure contentment. The subtle hints of jasmine from the mariposa perfumed the air with its relaxing scent. "I might retire here."

"No. You wouldn't leave me, would you?" Nina was rightfully concerned. The last couple of years had been difficult for Mary. Her mother had passed, and her children moved away. After the Covid virus wreaked havoc on the school system, things just weren't the same. Mary's once preppy attitude diminished. In its place, a deep resignation. "I might."

Chapter 9

Opening Night and an Oniony Smell

As the sun idled its way past the horizon, Nina and Mary made their way to their room to rest and change for dinner. They'd planned to head to the bar at some point and share a few drinks.

"Maybe Alvaro will be there," said Nina.

"Just reminding you, we're here to support Gabby. Nothing else."

"Yes, yes. Okay." Nina rolled her eyes just as they saw Carmen speed walk in their direction.

Busy helping Gabby with the restaurant, she didn't have time to stop and chat, but spat out, "Sorry, I'll catch up with you later," as she flew past them hording menus like they were a secret two thousand year old Egyptian papyrus map that leads to unforetold riches.

Turning toward one another, eyebrows on the rise, they recognized their friend was in her glory. The pair walked up the stairs, chatting about how excited everyone was about the restaurant opening and the progress they'd seen on the island since their last visit.

"What would you do if you moved to New Cuba?"

"I don't know. It was just an idea." Mary didn't look at Nina, and her answer floated on a long sigh and hung in the air above them.

Nina worried it wasn't 'just an idea,' and soon she'd be down one more bestie. "Well, for now, let's get dazzling for the opening."

She hooked her arm around Mary's. "I can't wait to see the menu. Did you see how Carmen shielded them as she hurried past us?"

"Yeah, I guess it's a big secret."

Afternoon in the Caribbean is a boiler. Carlos designed the landscaping at the restaurant's front with the idea that people might wait outside in the sun for their reservations.

Royal palms, like the ones that line the hotel's driveway, continued on to the restaurant. Smaller ceiba trees were left in their original spots since they provided extra shade.

Carlos had spent days watching the sun set so he could arrange extra trees, bushes, and plants to keep the area as shaded and cool as possible. He managed to keep the setting sun from hitting the outside seating areas, which lowered the temperature about twenty degrees. Carmen enjoyed watching him strategize and giggled at his excitement.

For the grand opening, Gabby had slotted out tables for friends and family that would attend, and reservations for the first ten people to join the newsletter email list. The rest was first come first serve, and no reservations.

Back in the kitchen, she gave an impassioned speech to the staff and sent them to their stations. Jose stood by, beaming with pride as he watched his girl in her all her wonder.

He'd never seen her like this. She'd left the hustle of the restaurant world before he met her, but she filled him in when they started dating. And he was excited for her, though he feared her return to it, might bring on more anxiety for her than she'd want.

At five, she lined up the waitstaff, cued the hostess, and had Jose open the front doors.

The line of hungry, or hangry, people stretched beyond Jose's line of sight. One by one, guests gave their name, and their server seated them, leaving each with a menu, and then returning to the end of the line to get their next set of guests. Everything ran smooth.

Once they accomplished the first seating, the servers made their way to their tables to get drink orders, and bartenders swiftly dispatched cocktails.

Gabby arranged a table for Carmen, Carlos, Nina, and Mary, and they were seated before the doors opened. Carmen had already put the girls on notice to be on their best behavior. She knew that after they'd had a few drinks, all bets were off.

From their table in a far corner, they eyed each person who entered. Gabby tasked Carmen and Carlos with taking notes of anything they saw amiss, or needed improvement. She'd trained her employees well, making their task a breeze.

Carmen watched in awe as they moved about. Everyone was on point. Gabby had pulled off a great start. Nothing had gone wonky, and it was a relief to not have to give Gabby bad news.

Meanwhile, Nina and Mary enjoyed people watching. Some came in typical tropical evening attire, and others in clothing too fancy for the unconventional restaurant. Nina knew she'd go back with stories to shock even the craziest of her co-workers. Her favorite pastime. And it took no time for a good story to unfold right before her.

"Gomez!" yelled a woman at the hostess stand.

Carlos looked over. "Oh, no."

"What is it?"

"Maria."

"What? Why?"

"I don't know. Should I do something?" He moved to stand, but Carmen's well placed hand on his arm prevented him from interfering.

"No. Just wait."

Every person at every table stopped talking and turned to stare at the scene unfolding before them. "Can I help you?" asked Jose, dressed in a suit and tie.

"I have a reservation. This bitch won't seat me." Maria heard about the reservation lottery scheme and immediately enlisted.

"Name calling isn't necessary." Jose looked through the reservations, "I don't see your name," he said while trying to keep calm and not make a scene on opening night.

"It's Gomez. G.O.M.E.Z.." Maria blasted out each letter with an icy stare.

"Oh. Here it is, under your first name. I'll seat you over here." Jose walked her to a small table in a corner of the restaurant. With every step, her very tiny skirt snailed up, revealing the very bottom of, well, her bottom.

The spaghetti straps of Maria's dress strained to hold up her ample bosom. A lot of her spilled out the sides of the top. Patrons behind her hoped there was something under that skirt to cover her other parts.

"Why are you sticking me in the corner? Am I not good enough to sit in the middle?"

"The middle has tables for larger parties." Jose took a deep breath, but Maria continued to push. "This is the only table for one I have left. If it's not to your liking, we have outside seating."

"Outside seating? Who do you think I am?"

"I don't think anything. I'm trying to accommodate you. If you're not happy with your table, there are other restaurants in the area that will be happy to seat you."

Jose placed the menu on the table and walked away. His calm demeanor infuriated Maria. She sat hard, slammed her purse on the table, and slapped the menu open. Her vigorous breathing caught the attention of nearby guests. "What are you looking at?" she snarled.

Maria placed her order, which came faster than she thought possible, then looked out through her brow at everyone staring when her plate arrived at the table. It appeared so fast; she wondered if they were trying to get rid of her.

From another single table, far on the opposite side, Margot Sanchez watched. Waited. Noting every person who sat at a table.

Every person who worked in the restaurant, and then, turned her attention to the distasteful woman causing a scene. She lifted her blood-red glass of wine and took a sip, careful not to drip any on her white suit. Margot set the glass down and continued watching the room.

Maria leaned back and grabbed the fork. She turned it over in her hand while looking around the place. In the back, she sees Carlos at a table with Carmen and two other women. They were laughing and pointing at each other. *'That better not be about me,'* she thought.

Maria blew out a hot breath, then tossed the fork on the table, hitting the plate with a clank that reverberated around her. People craned to find the source, then went back to their own gatherings.

After straightening herself, she took a moment to glance around the restaurant again. Everyone continued to go about their business. She looked down at the dish and closed her eyes. Waving down the hostess, she paid her bill and left. Her cocktail drained. The plate untouched. No one even noticed her leave, except Margot, of course.

Opening night was a tremendous success. Gabby met with the staff at the end of the night, thanking them for a great start. Her days of training them paid off with their providing a smooth first evening and excellent service. She promised to keep her anxiety in check.

Carmen and Carlos had done as instructed, but the items on the list had to do with first night stumbles and nothing had gone wrong.

When everyone left, Gabby turned to Jose. Tears surged as

she rocked, hugging herself tight, then she blew out all the frustrations and angst the opening bestowed, stretching her arms overhead. "You did a fantastic job tonight. Every plate looked beautiful and every single person loved what they ordered. You should be proud." Jose walked over, put his arms at her waist, and pulled her close. Gabby searched his eyes. There, in the restaurant he built for her, she allowed herself to believe.

"I am. I forgot how this feels." Gabby was fanning herself. She removed her white coat and set it on a chair back.

As she turned white, Jose leaned in. "Are you alright? You look a little... pale."

"Yes, just nervous, I guess."

Throughout the night, she'd remove her cooking coat and put on the coat and toque her mother gave her to check on guests. Wearing it gave her all the confidence in the world as she made the rounds. Now, she hung it on a hanger in her office like an award she'd won.

"Let's go," said Jose. "Tomorrow is another day."

The next morning, Gabby had trouble getting out of bed. Every time she'd lift her head, a wave of nausea rose in her throat.

"Here's some saltines. What did you eat?"

"I don't know. It's just nerves."

"You should stay home and rest. Should I make some tea?"

"No..." Gabby leapt from the bed and rushed to the bathroom, sliding in on her knees. She'd just made it to the toilet.

Convulsing and dry heaving, bile burned its way up her throat and into the toilet water.

After vomiting yellow slime, Gabby's legs went slack. The cold bathroom tile a relief, her body shivering with cold sweats. Ready to stand, she struggled to lift herself. Jose swooped her up in his arms and laid her to bed. A quick call to Luis and he was at their door.

"You don't have a temperature. You sure you didn't eat something that might have disagreed?"

"No. I'm telling you, it's just nerves."

"Keep hydrated. If it doesn't pass, you'll have to go to the E.R. Getting dehydrated is dangerous in this heat. Believe me, I know."

A little while later, Jose insisted she stay home in bed until she felt better. He had to run out to meet an inspector, but intended to come right back. Gabby's mind raced around, thinking about all the things she had to do at the restaurant. She didn't have time to be sick.

By early afternoon, the nausea subsided, and she could keep some toast down. She showered and dressed and headed in to work.

The whole place buzzed with activity, practically running itself. She made it all the way to the bar before a fresh wave of nausea rolled up, and she leaned her head onto the cold, raw wood edge of the top, then leaned on a stool and covered her mouth.

"Are you alright? You don't look so good," said Jessy, the bartender. "Food poisoning?"

"I think it's the onion smell in here."

"What onion smell?"

"You don't smell that?" Gabby was sure there were raw onions in the room.

"Maybe in the kitchen?"

Gabby held a hand to her mouth and slugged her way to the kitchen, using the wall for support. "Hey. Where's the onions?"

"Onions? We took care of them last night. They're ready to go for this evening," said her sous chef. "Do you need me to fetch them from the cooler?"

"No." Just then, Gabby turned for the nearest trash can and hurled air. The assistant chef ran over to help. "I'm okay. I think I better go back home, I might have a stomach bug. Can you all take care of the restaurant today?"

"Of course. Go home and rest. Should we call Jose?"

"No. I'll see him back at the house. Are you sure you can handle all this?"

"We got it, boss. Feel better." The chef walked her to her car where she climbed into her seat, then leaned on the steering wheel, a life raft. "Should I be driving you home?"

"I can drive, thank you." Gabby made it home safely. After all, it was only a few miles away. Hollow-cheeked, she shuffled back into the house, barely making it to the sofa where she lay her head down on a throw pillow, falling asleep before she even realized how exhausted she was.

Jose found Gabby asleep on the sofa and covered her with a throw. He was certain the pressure of the opening had gotten to her and she couldn't keep her head up.

Later that day, Gabby awoke to Jose puttering around the kitchen. "Hey. What are you up to?" she asked.

"Well hello. How are *you* feeling? You were out when I got home."

"Yea, I'm okay. I think it was all the pressure of the opening finally making its way to the surface. I tried going to the restaurant, but the smell of onions got to me and I had to come right back."

"I asked you to stay here and rest. You trained them well. They can handle it."

Gabby nodded and sat at the table for some tea and toast. Jose turned the conversation to their wedding. They needed to set a date.

"I think we should wait until I'm more confident that the restaurant can run itself."

"Your restaurant is already running itself. Besides, not that much will change. I want to make it official."

Gabby smiled, but her insides were roiling at the thought of planning a wedding, never mind getting married. Her anxiety began twisting its way up into her chest and she let out an exhaustive sigh.

"What's the matter?"

"I'm feeling...pressure. Too much pressure." She rubbed at her chest.

"Too much pressure?"

"Between the restaurant and the engagement, and now you want to set a date. Pressure." She looked up at him, her eyes pleading.

"But isn't that why people get engaged? Don't you want to marry me?"

"Of course I do. Can't we enjoy being engaged for a little longer?"

"Yes, but setting a date doesn't mean we have to get married on the spot. We have to plan. We've been together for over ten years. It's time."

"Hmm."

"Don't you want to get married, start a family?" Jose's petition wasn't landing the way he thought it would, and her hesitant answer gave him cause for alarm.

"I do. I really do."

"Then, let's set a date so we have plenty of time to plan."

"Alright." Gabby agreed. Knowing how much she loves Jose, and that they'd been together a long time, she saw no other choice. Not to mention, her clock was ticking louder and louder, and so was his (she could almost hear it). In her head, there was a lot of ticking. She worried it would go off like a bomb if she wasn't careful. "Tomorrow."

The next morning, Gabby jerked awake, sitting upright. The nausea was back, though not as bad. She thought for sure it had passed, whatever it was. Leaping from the bed once again, she hurled her empty stomach fluids into the toilet with Jose right behind her, rubbing her back. "Are you okay?"

"I don't know." Gabby stood, rubbing her forehead, and left him kneeling on the floor. She flushed the toilet, then washed her hands and rinsed out her mouth. The acid from her stomach burning in her throat. "Wait." She turned to find him sitting on the covered seat, leaning over his folded hands. "What's today?" she covered her mouth.

"The eighth. Why?"

Carmen woke the next day to the sound of laughter coming from outside her window. She drew back a corner of her blackout shades to peek at the scene. Having Nina and Mary in town, she wanted to spend as much time as she could with them, and after staying up late the night before, she thought it safer to sleep off all the wine in her room at the hotel.

Outside, Carlos was busy in the garden with his weekly horticulture presentation for guests who'd signed up for the adventure. The tour stopped at the rose garden he'd planted outside her window. Through an infinitesimal movement of the shade, he caught her leaning on the window frame peeking at him, and he smiled a secret smile.

She envied the way Carlos schmoozed with people. He knew when to joke and not offend. It seemed he could say just about anything and get away with it. Carmen knew she took herself too seriously and sometimes people picked up on her unease.

Carmen loved watching him talk. The way his arms called everyone's attention to whatever he was talking about. The way he walked. Strong, sure steps, and the pure magnetism that drew her close when he was nearby. Any whiff of his attar and Carmen heated from the inside out.

From the window, she saw the guests laugh at his jokes, endearing him even more. His speech commanded respect and drew people closer to hear him talk. He shot her a knowing half smile that sent shivers to her very core, and she rolled her eyes at him before stepping away from the shade.

When the lesson ended, the guests clapped and exchanged nods as the group dispersed. He loved being the entertainment. Most of all, he loved talking about plants. He knew the Latin name for every plant he came across. His memory impressed Carmen; she couldn't remember the everyday name for the most common plants.

Saying goodbye, he headed to the kitchen for some coffee and Carmen. "What time are the girls getting up?" he asked as he poured his cup, then pulled out the chair next to her, kissing her as he sat.

"I'm not sure. We were up really late, talking." She sipped from her mug, eyeing him over her the brim of her glasses.

"Gossiping... *I'm* sure."

Feigning offense, she giggled and slapped his arm. "Noooo." Carmen dragged out the o's. "Okay, maybe a little."

"Let's review, shall we?" Carlos counted off on his fingers. "Diabetic comas, sex in public places, school explosions, engagements…"

"Okay," she stopped him and he laughed. "We gossiped. It was very dishy and fun. Oh, and let's not forget Maria's outburst at the restaurant," she added a count with her middle finger.

Carlos laughed. "Oh, let's forget."

Just then, Mary and Nina appeared in the kitchen. The latter heading straight for the pot of black coffee. Nina had on her 'Do not disturb' sunglasses and didn't turn to wish them a good morning. Her head felt like a wrecking ball was trying to get in. Mary seemed alright. She walked behind Nina and paused at the table to say hello. Carmen put a finger to her lips, motioning for Carlos to stay quiet.

He couldn't help himself. "How was your night?" he asked. His voice was at least two to three decibels too loud. In an instant, Nina covered her ears.

"Nina was up late. Drinking." Mary told them as she pulled out her chair and sat.

"They don't need to hear the rest. Shhh," ordered Nina from over her shoulder. She made her way to the table, handed Mary her coffee, and slid a chair out for herself as quietly as she could before covering her face with both hands.

"With. Alvaro." Mary gave a long pause between the words, for dramatic effect.

"The pool boy?" asked Carmen in a snicker of disbelief, or rather, belief. "Really, Nina?"

Carlos smirked. He'd heard about Nina's…nature, so it came as no surprise that she'd found someone as quickly as she had.

"Believe me, he was all pool *man*," Nina dragged out.

"She changed just before coming down here. Go ahead, tell them about your walk of shame." Mary could barely hold in the laughter.

"I will not. I think they've heard enough."

After a lot of coffee and even more aspirin, Nina spent the rest of the day with Carmen and Mary. She and Mary were leaving on the last ferry, so they had a limited window of time to spend with Carmen. They asked about what prompted the 'appropriate behavior' sign, and the story had them roaring with laughter.

Mary ratted on Nina's earlier visual devourment of the "cutie patootie," as Nina started calling Alvaro, and it didn't surprise Carmen. Then, in a tit-for-tat moment, Nina told Carmen that Mary was unhappy and thinking of retiring to New Cuba.

"Really? That would be fantastic! You'll love it here." Carmen's eyes went wild with excitement.

"Maybe. I said maybe," Mary cautioned.

Later that day, Nina and Mary hopped into their Uber and headed for the port. They talked about everything they'd seen. Carmen's success and how happy she was. The restaurant's fantastic opening and Gabby's engagement. Mary turned quiet, contemplating all the life-changing events going on in New Cuba, and thought about how she was standing still.

Pilar leaned on the granite at the front desk while checking her online marketing campaigns. Reservations were up, and they had a waiting list. The restaurant was now open and started taking reservations as well. Everything was falling into place exactly as she'd planned and expected. Except for Juan.

She hadn't planned on Juan, or anyone else for that matter, but here she was. Worse, her daughters knew before she did. Humiliating. Everyone seemed to be alright with it, except her. Embarrassing. She stopped to rub her face. Her eyes stung, and she'd grown tired of worrying, tired of crying and thinking about it, all of it. Her phone chimed with a new message.

Thank you for dinner the other night. It was delicious. I had a wonderful time with you and the girls. Maybe I can cook for you all soon?

Pilar stared down at the message and took inventory. The girls already knew, even before she did, and they just met him but have asked repeatedly when they can see him again. They obviously like him. She likes him, and can't stop thinking about him. Pilar knew there were more plusses than minuses in her chart, yet she still stared down at the phone without answering.

Unaware of Angela's presence, "You know you like him. Whatever he's asking, just say yes."

150

Pilar looked up. She sighed so long that Angela thought for a moment that Pilar would fire her, and she took a step back. "You think so too?"

"Everyone thinks so besides you," Angela stated without blinking, looking straight into Pilar's eyes.

Without answering her, Pilar picked up the phone and typed out a response.

Just say when.

Pilar closed her phone and went back to work without looking up. Angela grabbed her radio and strutted away, chin high in the air, quite satisfied that she hadn't been fired, and despite her young age, had given advice, and that advice was taken.

Angela reached the back patio, all smiles and practically skipping. "What's this?" asked Diego as he set down a folding aluminum ladder he was carrying.

"Nothing. It's just a great day." She sauntered away in her snug tropical print pencil skirt. The light breeze blew the tank top's fabric, creating waves of ivory silk. She could feel his stare sliding down her back, to her tightly wrapped bottom, to her flexed calves and her high sandals, and she warmed deliciously at the idea that he was ogling.

"Hmmm," grunted Diego, shaking his head before picking up the ladder and going back to work.

"What about the date?" asked Jose. Gabby ran for her phone with Jose right behind her. "What is it?"

She swiped up and pulled up her calendar. "Oh." Gabby collapsed on her side of the bed, staring up at him. "I'm late."

Chapter 10
Shock and Geriatrics

"Late for what?" asked Jose. His brows knit in confusion. Gabby tilted her head, fluttered her eyelashes, smiled, then waited.

"Oh! Really?"

"Might be."

Jose pulled her up and swung her around before giving her that dip and dive deep kiss she loves so much. "That's great news!" he said, way too excited for someone not having all the facts.

"I said, might be. I need to take a test." Gabby was relieved he was excited. She had friends that had gotten pregnant on purpose and their partners weren't excited nor supportive. The thought had crossed her mind many times. *'Would he be happy to be a dad?' 'Will he stick around if I get pregnant?'* His reaction relieved some of her worry. "I'll make an appointment and get tested."

"Okay. Soon."

"Yes. As fast as they'll take me. But, if I am, let's keep this to ourselves until after the first trimester. I don't want to jinx anything."

Gabby and Jose sat in the exam room at the hospital in Pinar the following week. The doctor had ordered a blood test and performed an ultrasound. The couple clung to three small black and white printouts. Like a receipt. Proof of life.

Gabby stared at the doctor. "I'm pregnant? But how?"

The doctor tilted her head and stared up at her.

"I never miss my pill."

"It's only 99% effective. When a child wants in, they want in. Looks like this one is no different." Gabby's doctor was tall and thin. She wore a white coat with a stethoscope hanging from around her neck. The typical garb of any doctor. Gabby wasn't sure how she felt about her demeanor until the doctor said, "We will need to keep a close eye on you. This is a geriatric pregnancy."

"Excuse me?" Gabby's offended tone sealed how she felt about *this* doctor.

"There are guidelines about how we treat a mother at different life stages. At your age, it's considered a geriatric…"

"Stop. Please stop saying that. Do you mean to say I'm too old to have children?"

"No. But, at your age, there can be complications and we need to prepare for them, just in case."

"I'm… I'm shocked. Can't they come up with another name for it?"

The doctor laughed. "Don't I wish. I was in your shoes a few years ago, so I get it. I'm going to put together a pamphlet and give you a prescription for the right prenatal vitamins. If you have any questions, please call. Anything at all." And with that, she'd redeemed herself.

Gabby and Jose left the doctor's office elated that they would be parents. They held hands, swinging their arms as they walked to the car. "Well. How do you feel, daddy?"

"Daddy?" Jose turned to face her. "I love you, I love our

baby, and I love the sound of that."

"Good."

Gabby cut down on her workload between the sandwich shop, the hotel, and the restaurant. They kept their secret as long as they could until someone noticed.

"Hey Gabby." Pilar's eyes went wide.

"What is it?" Gabby touched her face, looking for whatever made Pilar's eyes bulge.

Pilar whispered, "How far along are you?"

"What? How did you know? I'm *just* pregnant," she whispered.

"I've had three, and I know what it looks like."

"Almost two months. Does anyone else know?"

"I don't know. Don't worry, I'll keep your secret, but don't wait too long. I don't know when my cork will pop." Pilar laughed at Gabby's shocked reaction. "It's your first child. I think with the first one we all look preggo immediately."

"We want to wait until after the first trimester."

"If you think you can hold out, by all means. So when's the wedding?"

"What, you too?"

"You're engaged. Now you're…you know…why wouldn't that be the next natural question to ask?"

"No. Sorry. You're right. I'll talk to Jose."

Carmen showed up for her shift at the front desk just as Gabby walked away in silence, swinging her arms and shaking out her hands. "Everything okay?" she asked Pilar, looking back at Gabby.

What? Oh. Yeah. Okay. Everything."

"Boy. You really can't keep a secret, can you? Spill."

"I don't know what you mean. I have to pick up the girls." Pilar gathered her files, her phone, and her purse, shuffling everything into a messy pile, and headed out, but Carmen knew something was up.

She squinted, following Pilar as she walked out the front doors, with papers hanging on for dear life as she ushered herself away. Pilar could feel Carmen's stare burning the back of her head, but she didn't turn around.

"Angela, can you please hold down the fort here? I'll be back."

"Of course. Everything alright?"

"That's what I'm going to find out."

Carmen walked the gravelly path to the side of the restaurant, entering through the corresponding door to the center petal of the outside seating area. "Gabs? Hey Jessy. Where's Gabby?"

"In her office, I think." Jessy was polishing glasses behind the bar until they were spotless, then replacing them in an exact space apart.

She found Gabby at her desk in the office with her hands on her forehead. Carmen closed the door behind her. "So. What's going on?" Carmen sung, dragging out the 'n' as she rocked forward and back with her hands behind her waist, then sat in the chair across from her.

"What did Pilar tell you?"

"Nothing. But she is not one to keep a secret, so spill."

Gabby leaned forward. "You can't tell anyone."

Just then, the door opened and in walked Jose. "What's going on?"

"Pilar figured it out. Carmen is asking."

"We're pregnant!" said Jose.

"What happened to waiting until after the first trimester?"

"Can't help it, sorry."

"What? Oh wow! How exciting!" Carmen leapt from her chair and gave each a hug. "Congratulations. That's fantastic news."

"I'll let you two chat and I'll see you at home later." He kissed the mother to be and closed the door on his way out.

Carmen tilted her head. Gabby's hands had gone back to her forehead. "What is it? Aren't you happy?" Carmen rubbed her shoulder and upper back before getting back in the chair across the desk.

"I'm thrilled. Really. But mostly terrified, and feeling rushed. Rushed to get married, rushed to have a baby, rush, rush, rush."

"One day at a time. One item at a time. You and Jose need to sit down and decide the next step."

"It's a lot of pressure."

"I know. And you're still under pressure from the restaurant opening. But you don't need to take on everything at one time. Just one thing. Go home. Talk to your man. I'm here to fill in wherever you need me."

Gabby got up from her desk and gave Carmen a tight squeeze. "Thank you." She gathered her things and left the restaurant.

Luis and Cristina were out in the yard collecting produce for the farmer's market. The scorching sun blazed over the field, drying the ground from the previous night's rain, leaving the air thick and humid.

A light breeze blew through the avocado tree, rustling the leaves and cooling down the old couple. Extending a long pole with a red fruit picker basket on the end, Luis grabbed a branch. Using the wire prongs on the end, he tugged avocadoes free into the safety of the waiting basket.

Once he got the fruit down, Cristina would collect and place them in a waiting crate, careful not to bruise. They swayed in a harmonious rhythm as they listened to Celia Cruz playing on a radio in the kitchen. Cristina would sing along, Luis chiming in every other chorus and smiling at each other.

To watch them, you'd never know they'd been mortal enemies. To know them when they were mortal enemies, you'd have never guessed they were once, long ago, each other's first love. Back and forth they went, smiling at private jokes or singing.

Dragonflies zipped through the trees, and birds chirped above them. In the back, chickens buck-buck-buck to get their own space in the coop, no doubt laying eggs. The ones in the yard cackled away, while the rooster crowed, a symphony of farm life.

"Here's a chair. Sit down Cristina. You don't have to stand the whole time."

"Leave me alone. I'm fine. I can't live like this carajo!"

"Don't curse at me when I'm trying to take care of you. Damn it right back!"

Cristina sat in the folding chair fanning herself with an old lace fan that had seen better days. Some of the lace hung in ragged pieces, while stains from coffee spills dotted the floral pattern. Sweat beaded on her forehead, though she fanned furiously.

"Let's go inside, my love." Luis took her by the elbow and led her inside through the back doors. "Why don't you lie down for a little while? I'll put the crates in the car." He watched her walk down the hallway, slumped to the side and using the walls for support.

"Okay." Cristina was out of breath, and labored to get to their room. Luis's heart shattered at the sight of her.

Outside, he struggled to move the produce crates into the truck. His thoughts and heart heavy with worry, when Carlos spotted him and ran over to help. "Here. Let me do this."

Luis took hold of Carlos's forearm, stopping him in his tracks. "Listen to me. Don't wait. I know how you feel about her. Don't wait."

Carlos felt the massive weight with which Luis was expressing himself. Every word came out strangled with fear. He turned and looked at the front door of the house, then back at Luis. "Is she alright?"

"I don't think so."

Carmen left Gabby's office making the rounds in the restaurant to ensure everyone had what they needed. Leaning on the bar, she put one foot on the brass footrest and thrummed while taking it all in. "Good Times Bad Times?" asked Jessy.

"Yeah. You a Led Zeppelin fan? Feels like the theme today."

"Always been a fan. You don't have to worry about the restaurant. We've got this." She leaned on the bar and pulled up two glasses, pouring each a shot of Havana Club Maximo Añejo rum. Carmen knew how expensive the bottle was because Gabby had reviewed the invoices with her just before opening night. The new restaurant owner insisted on having some extra special bottles on hand for any high rollers that might show.

"I know I don't *have* to worry, but sometimes I feel like it's my middle name. Do you believe in signs?" Carmen asked Jessy. "Sometimes. Depends I guess. It would have to be something blaring in my face."

"Well. I do. A lot. I seem to get this feeling of foreboding, then I wait around for the other shoe to drop."

"Hmm… Have you considered that maybe all the shoes have already dropped?"

"In my experience, there are always more shoes." Carmen's cynicism spoke volumes.

"That's life. What you *can* do is find a place to put them. Every time a shoe drops, shove it there...until further notice."

The two women called, "Salud," swigging the shot.

Carmen looked her over. Jessy was still too young to understand. "I'll leave you to it. If there's anything you need, call me. Let's let Gabby rest. She hasn't been feeling well."

"You got it."

Carmen walked out humming. The memory of her Corvette's rumble called her name. She shot a quick text to Gabby, letting her know everything was running smooth. Another to Angela, letting her know she was going for a ride, and a third to Carlos with the same message. She revved the engine and turned up the volume. Within seconds, her iPhone connected Jimmy Page at the precise moment he slid his cello bow across the strings. "Let's go, sexy butterflies," Carmen hummed.

Weaving her way through the town and up the hills to Soroa, she thought about her family. And now, getting to know Carlos's family brought that sinking feeling back to the pit of her stomach where it grew and throbbed.

The week seemed to stretch on forever, and finally, they were due to arrive on the morning ferry. She had prepared the house, stocked food and drink, and still she couldn't strip the feeling that something was amiss. *'Maybe it's just nerves over meeting his kids,'* she thought.

Carmen zipped up through the Viñales Valley, passing Las Terrazas, pulling in to the Orchidarium. Since moving to New Cuba, Carmen visited the historic site whenever she needed to feel grounded.

Back home, her escape was often the cemetery where her father lay resting, or the street in front of the house where she grew up, and her mother Gloria still lives. And when the mood struck, she'd take her vintage Mustang down US 1 to Haulover Inlet.

The unmistakable grumble of the Corvette, not to mention the loud music, alerted Carmen's new friend Pancho to peek out at her from the upstairs pavilion.

She'd visited so often, she made friends with the caretaker, often hearing stories about famous visitors, or a new variety of orchid he grafted.

Sometimes, he'd find her sitting in the same place he'd met her. Carmen would sit and take in the sights and scents of the exotic flowers, or watch vacationers listen to tour operators explain the history of the place with unmatched artistic performances. The cool coquina bench beneath her, a grounding surface.

"Hola, Carmen. So nice to see you. How's the hotel coming?"

"Muy bueno, gracias, Pancho. How are the orchids?"

"They're good. And the ghost orchid I gave you?"

"Growing slow. So slow. Don't forget, you promised to come down and check it out."

"Yes, yes. I will."

Pancho went back to his task. Carmen sat on her bench; it was the only place she could sit and just be.

She watched Pancho's routine; pruning this one, repotting that one, watering and fertilizing. After a time, she got up and left. No one knew her secret run away place.

Here, there were no cemeteries she'd visit, or a street that left her longing for simpler times, or the crashing of waves at a beach she enjoyed as a teenager. She found serenity in this botanical garden, strolling through the labyrinth of roses or descending the stone stairs that made up the outcroppings of garden tiers.

Carmen stood and made her way over to the white railed stone bridge. Standing in the center, she looked down into the pond below. The fish swam in circles. Not a care in the world. "Bet you guys don't worry that your boyfriend's family won't like you." She waited, but of course, fish don't know we're up here. Why would they answer?

Back in her car, she flipped the ignition and glanced up at the large stone building. Pancho's head popped up, looking through the window of the stone wall. He could always hear her coming and going. Today was no different, and he waved. Carmen waved back; their own secret language.

Pancho looked forward to her visits. Turning away, he went back to his practice with a smile, pushing his extra thick coke-bottle glasses up the ridge of his nose. His slicked back hair harkened bygone days of thin mustaches and pursed lips. Traditions only the older generations remembered, or kept a light on for.

Gabby reached the home she shared with Jose. Upon hearing the VW's gurgling engine approach, he moseyed to the driveway. "Are you okay?"

"Yes. Tired. I need to rest."

"You lie down. I'll take care of everything."

"We need to pick a wedding date, so grab your calendar and we can get going on that."

Jose flinched at the fast turnaround, but he wasn't about to argue with a pregnant woman. He grabbed his calendar and quickly sat at her side.

"I would like to get married soon, since I'll be showing and won't fit into a dress."

"Okay. You sound like you're in a 'get this over with' hurry." Her haste disheartening, but he went along anyway.

"That's not it. I'm just tired and I don't want to think about this anymore."

Jose bit his lip and nodded. "How about September fifteenth? It's only a month away, but I know we always said it would be a small wedding. I think we can pull it off."

"Perfect."

"Let me talk to Pilar and we can sort it all out."

Gabby gave Jose a much needed hug and a deep enough kiss to reassure him then went to bed. Jose pulled out his phone and went to work planning their wedding.

Chapter 11
Visiting Relatives and Bad News

"Quick, they'll be here any minute." It was Saturday morning and Carmen's anxiety kept her up the entire night. "How do I look?" She'd worn a wide leg teal jumpsuit. The tiny white polka dots on the flowy fabric danced when she walked. She wore low-heeled shoes that were tight, but she planned to remove them the minute his family left for the house where they'd be staying.

"Babe, relax. They will love you. You'll see."

Carmen exhaled and shook out her hands. She went into the kitchen, popped the sheet in the oven, and set the timer. Ten minutes later, the house smelled like chocolate chip cookies. As soon as it chimed, she pulled out the pan, set each one on a cooling rack, and went back to the porch to wait. Phoenix had to know something was happening; she paced and made circles, staring at Carmen and waiting.

Minutes later, a van pulled up and a crowd of people poured out. It resembled a clown car at a circus. Carlos's sons looked like an amalgamation of what she imagined Carlos looked at their age. He held tight to her hand and walked over to the van.

"Hi everyone! This is Carmen. Carmen, these are my sons Rafael, his wife Adela, and my grandkids, Kenny and Emma. This is Frank, his wife Alba, and my granddaughter Olivia." The kids took to Phoenix immediately, running around the front yard with her.

"I'm so happy to meet all of you." Carmen smiled but shook from the inside out. She went over and hugged each one and welcomed them to their home. "I have cookies in the kitchen. Let's go inside." Upon opening the door, the warm and welcoming aroma of chocolate, sugar, and molasses emanated from the kitchen. The children's eyes lit up.

Carlos's family was friendly, and they were happy to meet Carmen. Since their father had gone on and on about her, they felt as if they already knew her.

After a few minutes of warming up to her, and the cookies, her fears were eased. Carmen attempted to observe the interactions and get a sense of where she fit in. The wives' closeness was obvious and the comradery between the four adult children warmed her, reminding her of her own.

"Well, we've set you up in the house down the street. There are snacks, drinks, fresh food in the fridge and clean linens on the beds. We've planned for lunch by the hotel pool whenever you're ready."

"Thank you Carmen. That sounds perfect. Three children under ten need to be kept entertained," smiled Rafael, the oldest. Carlos's family didn't even sit since they were looking forward to relaxing poolside, so the kids grabbed extra cookies before being herded back outside. Phoenix bobbed along behind the children, who'd been sneaking cookie pieces to her the entire time.

The women gathered their little ones and got back in the van, followed by their respective mates. Carmen stood on the porch with her arms folded, rubbing her shoulders. Carlos came up behind her, wrapping his arms around her, and smiled at his family over her shoulder. She leaned her head on his cheek, then both waved as the van drove away.

"That went well," she said.

Carlos turned her to face him. "I told you."

"Frank seems quiet."

"Yes. He takes a while to warm up. Don't worry."

Carmen saw that as a sign; there's something he doesn't like about her. "They waited a long time to have children, didn't they?"

"Yes. They were in grad school when their mother passed away. Then they threw themselves into their careers, trying to focus on something else. They put family life out of frame until they were ready."

"Well. My grandkids are in college. Guess there won't be any playdates in *their* future," she laughed.

Carmen and Carlos went to the hotel to check on the activities they'd laid out by the pool. It was important for Carlos's family to feel wanted and welcome when they visit. Carmen remembered how Mary felt at her mother's funeral.

Mary's brother had just gotten divorced, then his mother died, and he blamed everyone around him for the collapse of his family, Mary included. It had been a few years now, and she still didn't feel welcome or comfortable around him. Carmen didn't want that for her and Carlos. She'd make it work no matter what.

Before long, the two couples and their rambunctious kids were poolside. Luckily, they all knew how to swim. Carmen had hired a lifeguard, and he was on duty as long as the pool was open. Phoenix pretended to be backup lifeguard, lying at the end of the pool eyeing the kids as they ran alongside the pool and jumped in whenever the mood was right.

"Hey kids! Carmen ordered a bounce house for you. It will be here soon. Gabby's is preparing lunch and we'll eat right here," said Carlos.

Carmen and Carlos had worn their bathing suits, intending to enjoy family time by the pool. His grandkids were so excited they called him to jump in. He took off his shirt and flip-flops, and made a cannonball splash so big, the waves popped the three kids up out of the water. Their laughing and giggling had Carmen smiling a mile wide, and Carlos's family ogling her reactions.

"Hey! What's that?" yelled Frank, pointing at his father.

"What's what?" asked Carmen, turning toward where Frank jerked a finger.

"My dad. His stomach." His voice tight, halting.

"Frank, wait." Rafael shot to standing and tried to hold his brother back, but failed.

"Dad. What happened to your stomach?" Frank waved his arms in a frenzy.

"It's nothing. Relax. Everything is fine." Carlos's stomach revealed a story he hadn't shared with his family. He swam to the edge of the pool and hoisted himself out.

Carmen hurried to intercept. "Frank, let me explain." Rafael stood between them with his hands separating them.

"No. Not. You." he pointed at Carmen. "Dad?" Frank spoke in short, severely punctuated words.

Alba and Adela sprang from their lounges and called the children from the pool, leading them away toward the conservatory. "Come on kids, let's go exploring and see what's in there," said Adela. Carmen watched the women take the kids away faster than anything she'd ever seen before. Like they saw a storm coming and ran for shelter.

"What happened? Did she have something to do with that?" Frank's words came out searing as he pointed at Carmen.

"Frank. Stop." Carlos got out of the pool, threw on his shirt, and took his son by the arm, leading him away. 'Talk about timing,' thought Carlos.

The wind blew the scent of mariposa through Carmen's hair, and she slid the wayward locks behind her ear. She watched the men walk away and that sinking feeling took hold again, her insides cartwheeling on a balance beam. She took a deep inhale and exhale, then looked over at Rafael, who stared after his father and brother. "Did I do something?"

Turning toward Carmen, he placed a hand on her shoulder. "No. That's Frank. He's quiet, then if anything bothers him, he explodes. He has no gray areas." Rafael rolled his eyes and exhaled.

Carmen gave a slight nod, then looked down at her feet before throwing on her coverup. "I'm sorry. I wanted your first visit with us to be memorable."

Rafael looked away. "It'll be memorable alright. It's not your fault. I promise. Frank just…" Shifting his stance, he looked down at his feet and tilted his head while squinting one eye at Carmen. "He's still not over our mother's death, so he's kind of touchy. What happened to my dad's stomach?"

"I think you should ask *him*. I promised not to say anything."

Rafael nodded, "Excuse me," then jogged to catch up to his father and Frank as they walked to the other side of the sugar cane. He made it just in time to hear his brother's tirade. Carmen watched them walk away thinking, *'Secrets of the sugar cane.'*

"Frank, stop." Carlos went into 'dad mode' and his happy-go-lucky personality got tucked away. For the next ten minutes, Carlos explained what had transpired the day he took a bullet. The way Carmen's attorney, Machado, was trying to swindle her out of her inheritance.

"I knew it was her fault!" yelled Frank.

Rafael grabbed his arm and stared him down. "Stop. This isn't about Carmen. You know that."

"Son, your mother has been gone a long time. No one is replacing her. But I deserve happiness too. Don't you want me to be happy? Have companionship? Or would you prefer I die alone?"

"No dad. I want you to be happy. Just. Why her?" Frank shifted from side to side, looking away and wiping his eyes.

"Who would you rather it be?" asked Rafael.

Frank paused too long. "I'd rather it be mom. But I know that's not possible."

"So, what you mean is that dad should be alone. Mom is

gone. What would you have him do? Be alone?" Rafael stared his brother down. They all knew what Frank's problem was. Carmen was just a scapegoat.

"Get to know her. You'll see why, *her*," said Carlos. Rafael clasped his father's shoulder.

"It's okay, dad. Give him a little more time. He just met her."

"How are you okay with her already?" asked Frank. "Have you been down here to meet her?"

"No. This is my first time, too. Don't you think dad deserves happiness? He loves her. Have you noticed how he looks at her? How she looks at him? Make your peace with it and stop creating tension where there isn't any. Stop imagining she's done something she hasn't done. Come on, dad."

Rafael and Carlos walked away, giving Frank some much needed space. By now, the women had brought the children back to the pool. Carmen sat at the steps talking with Adela and Alba, all three smiling while the kids play.

"Hey beautiful," said Carlos. At the sound of his voice, Carmen's sexy butterflies woke up, threatening to escape.

Adela and Alba looked at each other as Carmen seemed to lift right out of her body. She straightened her back and looked up behind her. Carlos squatted down and planted a deep kiss right on her lips. The women gaped at their father-in-law's demonstrative conduct. They'd never seen him behave that way in public before, and it was clear why. Adela pointed at Carmen's toes, curling up right in front of them, and the two women smiled coquettishly.

"Hey yourself. Everything alright?" she looked behind him at Frank.

"Yes," said Frank from right behind Carlos. "I'm sorry, still working on my…"

"I'm sorry too. It was a very scary day. I thought he'd told you all what happened." She looked at Adela and Alba, who gave an empathetic smile.

The silence stretched on until one of the restaurant servers appeared with a large, covered, mobile serving station. He wheeled it right up the side of the pool.

"Ms. Carmen. Lunch is served."

He moved behind the table. "We have pan con bistec with shoestring potatoes. We use only the best cut of thin sliced beef steak. Over here we have pressed Cuban sandwiches, tamales, and macaroni and cheese for the kiddoes. For dessert, I brought guava and cheese pastries, and Cristina sent coconut cookies. After the kids eat, if it's okay, Gabby sent a snow cone machine. There're seven flavors for the kids and a few spiked ones for the adults."

"This is fantastic," said Rafael. "So kind of you, Carmen."

"You're very welcome. I know you're only staying until Sunday morning, but I wanted to make everything as special as I could. We have dinner reservations at Gabby's for tomorrow, and I arranged for our concierge, Angela, to babysit."

All enjoyed the rest of the day, except Frank, who didn't smile, leaving Carmen's anxiety screwed up.

The wives thanked Carmen for the attention garnered to

their families. The children had a wonderful time, leaving with purple or green lips from their snow cones.

That night, Carmen and Carlos sat on their back patio. She still had that look. The one she always got when she stared at the sky, looking for a flying shoe.

"Everything is fine. Please stop worrying."

"Not fine. Frank is still upset, and he didn't have any lunch. He didn't speak, and blames me because you got shot."

"He doesn't blame you. After my wife passed away, I left and came here. He wanted me to stay, but I needed to go. We all do whatever we need to do, and I think it's just part of being human. Maybe he felt like he'd lost both his parents."

"I'm so sorry. There's nothing anyone can say to him to make it better. Believe me, I know."

"It's my fault. Looking back, I realized I rushed to get away from the house we lived in and the lifestyle we had. And though they already had their own lives, it had to be hard to feel like they lost us both. Ofelia needed me soon after my wife's funeral, so I sold everything and came here. The timing was a sign."

"Oh, so now you believe in signs, do you?"

"That, to me, was a clear sign."

Pilar, Rose, Daisy, and Lily pull up to Juan's house. He didn't live too far away, but also not near their street. She dressed the girls in coordinating outfits. Not the same outfit, but each one had something special about it. A ribbon that matched a sash on one, or a bow that matched a ruffle on the other. Just enough that they looked cute and not so much they looked like triplets.

Her days of convincing a teenage Rose to dress like her younger sisters were coming to a close. She'd already started rolling her eyes and stomping her feet. It wouldn't be long before there was a boyfriend she had to contend with, and with her Quincéañera around the corner, it was inevitable.

Juan heard the car pull into the driveway and he sprinted to the door, throwing it wide open and calling out an 'hola ladies' before they'd even gotten out of the car. He was sure the neighbors heard. As the four approached the door, "Wow! You all look so beautiful."

"Thank you, Juan," said Pilar.

"My mom made me wear this," complained Rose. Pilar rolled her eyes toward the sky and Juan giggled.

"Come in, come in. Lily, I left some art supplies on the table. Rose and Daisy, I thought you'd like these bracelet making supplies."

"Oh my. You didn't have to go through so much trouble."

"No trouble. I want them to have something that's theirs when they come here."

"That smells wonderful. What did you make?" asked Pilar.

"Broiled snapper. My cousin, Carlito is a commercial fisherman, and he brought me his catch of the day. May I offer you some Pinot Grigio?"

"Yes, thank you." Pilar walked around, admiring the photos on the walls.

"Here you go. Girls, I have juice boxes. Is that okay?"

"Yes, thank you," they each replied.

"Is this your family?" asked Pilar as she eyed a large photo of a group of people.

Juan pointed to each person in the photo, starting in the back row. They were his grandparents, then aunts and uncles, parents, "And this is my cousin Carlito, and me in diapers."

"You were a cute baby," she smiled.

"Thanks. There's very little of us Rodriguez's left. Everyone has either moved away or passed. My cousin Carlito, the angler, and myself are the only ones left here."

"It's sad, ya know. How we lose family, by any means. Death is just one way." Her melancholy over her own parents crept in.

"What is it?"

"Another time." Pilar glanced over at the girls, then looked back at him, and he nodded.

The couple headed over to the sofa and sat next to each other while the girls continued their crafting fun.

"Rose. I understand your mother is planning your Quincéañera. That's exciting."

"I know just the dress I want and the cake. I want all my friends there. Mom says I can't have a court, even though it's tradition." A quick change came over her as she talked about her coming of age celebration.

176

"Well, I'm just trying to keep it reasonable."

"I thought the point of building up New Cuba was to 'keep the traditions' alive," Rose mocked and air quoted, her comment dripping with sarcasm. "You and Papi talked about it my entire life."

"We'll discuss it later."

"Pilar, if there's any way I can help with Rose's Quincé, just let me know. I'm here for you…and them."

"Thank you, but I'm still planning. Carmen and Gabby have jumped in with the details."

"It's only a couple of months away. When are we going dress shopping?" asked Rose.

"I'm sure your mom has a plan." Juan smiled, but could tell Rose's attitude was wearing thin on her mother.

Pilar was tiring of Rose's petulant attitude. Next time, she thought she'd hire a sitter and avoid the embarrassment. Then it occurred to her. She needed her daughters as chaperones. She couldn't imagine being alone with the man. And then that exact thought heated her all over and she felt herself blush.

Juan left the living room to check on dinner. "Alright everyone, dinner is served." He had a special plate for each of the girls. They sat down and he began serving.

"Ew… is this fish?" asked Rose.

"Rose!" admonished Pilar.

"It's okay, Pilar. Rose, I have macaroni and cheese I made, just in case. Would you like that instead?"

"Anything but fish."

Pilar looked like someone had spilled a bowl of borscht on her face, and the red soupy mess flowed down her face and neck, heating her skin as it washed over her. She planned on having a word with Rose when they got home.

Daisy and Lily looked at each other, hiding a sheepish grin and gobbling up the fish with a side of mac n cheese. After dinner, the two went back to coloring while Rose sat on a club chair with her arms folded tight at her chest as Dory looked for Nemo on the television.

Pilar and Juan began clearing the table. "Here, I have an apron. I don't want you to mess up your pretty dress." Facing her, he reached over her head, and with great care, draped the apron around her neck while staring into her eyes.

In one slow, smooth move, he took hold of an apron string and traced her waist with his index finger until he reached the other side, where he took his time tying the two ends in place. Pilar could feel his hot breath on her neck, then his palm slid across the small of her back as he moved past her and walked to the sink.

Pilar looked down at the front of the apron, pulling it straight. She chortled and waited. An impulse took over, and she walked over to Juan, who was placing the dishes on the counter. When he turned toward the table, she pulled down on his shirt collar and kissed him tenderly on the lips. The move both demanding and soft. Juan could feel his blood rush down below his waist, and attempted to make out his fantasy baseball league in his head, though it wasn't working very well.

178

When she pulled away, he gazed into her eyes, then tugged her back and kissed her long and hard, running his hands through her hair, twisting it around his fingers.

She could feel the kiss down to her toes, who were curling inside her shoes, and she pictured them screaming; no little piggie went to market, no little piggie stayed home, but every little piggie screamed wee, wee, wee, take HIM HOME! Pilar wrapped her arms around him and pulled him close. Feeling his erection, she gasped, but didn't move herself away.

"Uh, I didn't expect that," said Juan.

"Neither did I. I was just following directions." Pilar pointed at fancy white stitched embroidery on the front of the black apron he'd covered her dress with that read, 'Kiss the Cook.'

"Lucky there's a wall here between the kitchen and the family room…" he said, "…and your kids are here

"Tell me about it."

The pair were cleaning up; a comfortable and familiar dance, though it was a first. Then his phone rang. "Rodriguez." Pilar watched him listen to the person on the other end of the line, though he couldn't take his eyes off her. "I understand." He looked at her as though he wasn't hearing whatever was being said.

Pilar removed the apron and hung in on the hook next to the refrigerator. She headed into the living room, where she sat across from Rose. "We'll be talking at home." To which the child let out a snort and another eye roll.

Juan came out of the kitchen and waved at her to come back. "They found the custodian." Pilar put her hand to her lips. "They're charging him with domestic terrorism and hundreds of counts of attempted murder. I'm sure there'll be other charges." Juan threw the dishtowel over his shoulder and looked into Pilar's worried eyes, tugging her close. She laid her head on his chest and inhaled.

Chapter 12
Abandonment and Moments of Joy

Twenty-eight-year-old Maria leaned on the old wood table in her empty kitchen, scratching at the surface with her fingernail. Its fragmented edges snagged her clothing every time she walked by.

While rubbing the same spot, she looked up at the empty walls of her tiny house; the dirty sofa in the living room, the open shelves of kitchen cabinets revealing mismatched, chipped, and cracked dishes. There were no photos on the walls, no books on any shelves, and no knick-knacks collected, evidence of a life well lived. Maria didn't consider it home. It's where she grew up too soon. Where her parents abandoned her when she was ten.

In this kitchen, her parents let out all their anger. All their contempt for each other. In one of their last fights, her father had come home sloppy, and smelling of liquor and perfume. Her mother threw plates, pots, and pans around without regard to the impressionable child in the room. Maria watched her mother go from a woman scorned to something carnal; her fingers curled up into fists and her arms went rigid with rage. When she opened them, from across the room, Maria could see small slits of fresh blood where her mother's nails punctured the flesh.

That day, he didn't just smell like alcohol; he was drunk. He wasn't just sloppy. There were lipstick stains on his neck, his shirt, and even the front of his pants. Her mother vowed not to clean that mess up again. She turned to him and cried, accusing him of the obvious transgression. She threatened to take Maria away and never allow him to see her.

In his rage, he picked up a sledgehammer and started swinging at the upper cabinets. Shards of wood fled to the counter, the sink, and the floor as her mother leaned on the wall at the end of the row, covering her mouth, and stifling a scream.

Maria saw her mother's face tighten and contort. She watched her tug and rip at the top of her yellow dress, screaming at him to stop. Maria cried, wailing for her mother.

Her father moved closer to the end of the row of cabinets, dragging the sledge with him. Maria ran and stood between her mother and father. The front of her little pink dress stained with salty tears. "Papi, stop!" she yelled through her sobs. Her father cocked his hand back, ready to backhand Maria. She turned her face, giving him her cheek, but she didn't leave her mother's side. Maria cried again, "Please stop, Papi!"

Her father stopped, only to toss the sledge one last time on the wood table. The same table she occupied so many years later. The semi-circular dent from the iron was the same one she's picked at every day since they left her. Its edges were no longer as sharp as they were on the first day. Her fingers had worked the relic for so long, she'd smoothed out the fringes.

After he threw the sledge, he cursed Maria's mother, then stormed away. Her mother didn't speak to her again for days. The last time Maria saw her mother, she stood at the door with a suitcase. Turning to Maria with her dead black eyes, she said, "He left because of you. I'm leaving. Because of you. Do not come looking for me." Her words stabbed through Maria's tiny heart, and she blamed herself, though she wasn't sure why.

Ten-year-old Maria sat at the wood table in the kitchen, rubbing her fingers on the dent. The dent her father made a few days ago, before he left her and her mother, and a couple of days after her mother left her. Day after day she sat at the table, sure that one or both would return. No one ever did.

Maria got up from the table, got herself dressed, and brushed the knots out of her hair the best she could before walking to school every day. Averting her gaze, she didn't want to look at anyone, but through a small part in her red hair, she could make out where she was going. She didn't tell anyone what happened, and tried to look normal.

Maria didn't appear as clean as the other girls at school. Though her mother had taught her how to use the washer and dryer, she'd run out of detergent, so she'd put her clothing to wash in plain water. As she walked, she dragged the smell with her while the other girls taunted her.

Feeding herself was becoming more and more difficult. Her dark circles and sunken complexion showed, and when her bones began peeking through her clothing, the cafeteria staff at school would sneak her an extra helping.

By the time she was fifteen, she'd left school behind, and worked at any minor job she could, lying about her age. She watched as the other girls had their Quincéañeras. Not her. If she passed the dress shop and saw one of them picking out a dress, she'd scowl, pinch her nose, and make sure they saw her.

Maria had grown up too fast and without the proper guidance of a loving parent. No one knew she was alone. No one noticed or cared.

Her loneliness drove her from man to man. She'd suffered painful rejections that left deep boot prints on her heart and a continuous ache. Maria no longer cried for the parents that didn't want her. She cried for the future she never got a chance to have, and now, time was up. Maria knew what she had to do.

Carmen spent the following day catering for Carlos's family. She made sure there would be plenty of food and snacks for the kids, and enough supervision to support some leisure time for the adults. And every day, she'd check on the hotel. Everything ran as smooth as melted marshmallow on a warm cake.

Carlos stayed poolside with them throughout the day, enjoying much needed time with his grandkids. Carmen watched through the window. Her heart throbbed every time he smiled while throwing the children back into the water with a loud splash. The kids loved it. They'd climb back out and run to push him in, and he'd fake the conquest.

On the other side of the pool, several other hotel guests ordered drinks and food, while other groups walked through the garden and the conservatory.

184

Carmen remembered the first time she walked outside and felt the garden's embrace; a welcoming like no other. Glancing at the gazebo, brought to mind the day she found Carlos's grandmother Ofelia, dead on the floor, and her smile slipped away.

Despite everything that had happened since she first came to New Cuba, Carmen was thankful she stayed. Everywhere she looked, her spirit was renewed, and she placed her palm on her chest, patting, perhaps to calm the flutter she felt. Looking back to Carlos, her smile returned and brought her sexy butterflies with it until footsteps behind her broke her reminiscing.

Pilar arrived in time to relieve Carmen from the hotel duties and found her staring out the back window. "Stalking is illegal, you know."

"I know. But I don't care. Look how happy he is with his family."

"He looks happy. Aren't you afraid he'll want to go back with them?"

"Not in the least. We've made a life, here. I'm not leaving, he's not leaving. This is it. It was all about timing." Carmen turned, her eyes fluttered at Pilar.

"I'm going to pretend there's no hidden message behind those lashes. I have some news. They found the custodian."

"When? Where was he? Did they find out why he disappeared?"

"It seems he locked and chained the doors from the inside before setting the pilot light in the boiler room to blow. They're not sure how he got out."

"Why? Why would anyone want to hurt children?"

"Carmen. He had the scorpion tattoo on his neck. No one ever saw it because he always wore a turtleneck under his uniform."

Carmen listened to what Juan had told Pilar. She pressed her lips together, then wiped her forehead. "Wait. When did he tell you?"

"Oh. Last night. At his house." She'd blurted the words out as if it was a normal occurrence that she'd be at his house, before she realized Carmen didn't know they were becoming an item.

"Realllly." she turned on her heels to face Pilar, crossing her arms. Her sarcasm dragged out the l's and her eyes glittered at the news.

"Alright, alright. We'll talk about it when we get with Gabby." Pilar turned beet red and covered her face when the giggles took over. "I can't help it," she laughed again.

"I can see that. Whatever it is, I'm so happy you're open to possibilities."

At six-thirty that evening, Rafael and Frank showed up with their families. Angela had enlisted Diego to help with babysitting duties. He was looking forward to spending time with Angela any way he could. He tried not being too obvious or overly invested, but her invitation to help couldn't have had better timing.

Angela told Carmen that Diego would help with babysitting. It wasn't so much that she was providing information, more that she worried it would cause an issue. But all Carmen could think about was how these two were coming together on their own. "Okay then," she told her. The smile on the outside couldn't match the one on the inside.

"Hi kids. I'm so glad you're here." Carmen enjoyed being a grandmother, and with her grandkids grown, she missed them being little. "This is Angela and Diego. They have all kinds of fun plans for this evening." She made introductions, and the children followed Angela and Diego as they headed for the bounce house that Carmen ordered.

"Wow! It's a pirate ship," the three kids hollered as they ran for the opening and climbed in.

Diego grabbed two chairs and set them in front of the giant inflatable ship. The outside had painted wood planks and sails that inflated above the bouncing area. They were pivoting in the gusts that blew across the field.

The chaperones watched the kids jump around for over two hours. Their plan had been to tire them out before dinner and the movie. Everyone heard laughing from all over the grounds as the children walked the plank, exiting the castle out of breath.

"Looks like you guys had a blast," said Diego.

"How about some dinner?" asked Angela.

The brood walked with Angela and Diego toward the

kitchen. There, on the table, large pepperoni pizzas had their stomachs growling.

"We've set up a projector in the room upstairs that Carmen set aside for you. She decided on, 'My Neighbor Totoro,'" explained Diego, "It was *her* kids' favorite."

"We've never heard of it," said Kenny.

"It's awesome. You'll love it," Angela told them. The rest of their night went off without a hitch. The kids were entertained and well fed. By the end of the movie, they'd fallen asleep, and Angela and Diego sat in the conversation circle just outside the room, whispering stories about themselves.

Carmen and Carlos took his family to Gabby's for dinner. They were given the large round table in the center of the restaurant. Within minutes, Gabby was table side to say hello to her friends' relatives and describe the tasting menu she'd planned for their visit.

"I'm so glad you're all here, and I hope you're hungry. Tonight, you'll have a taste of some dishes I plan to incorporate. So yes, you're now my guinea pigs. First, an appetizer of sriracha glazed seared scallops on a bed of arugula. Then, a medium rare steak au poivre made with cognac and a dijon that just arrived from Burgundy."

"Is that Burgundy, France?" asked Alba.

"Yes. Specifically, the Edmund Fallot brand. They produce wonderful varieties. I visited the mustardary years ago. It's been there since the 1800s. Anyway, I'm serving it with parmesan crusted, split fingerling potatoes and green bean almandine. I have individual cast iron paella Valenciana with Spanish chorizo and lemons I imported from Sorrento. A creamy chicken piccata with angel hair pasta that I guarantee you'll want to come back for a full serving."

"Gabby, that sounds fantastic. Doesn't it, Frank?" Rafael struggled to get his brother out of the funk he's been in since their mother passed. He couldn't help but wonder how Alba puts up with him.

"Sounds great Gabby. Thank you," said Frank.

"I'll send someone over to get drink orders."

When Gabby walked away, she couldn't help but think something was up with Frank. He was always quiet, but today, he seemed to stew over something, and was in rare form. Alba has always been quiet, keeping her opinions to herself, and never intervening when he was being a dick.

After the drinks were served, the group started talking about the children and how much they've grown in the last couple of years. Rafael talked about business, and Frank about his job. Their wives sat quietly, taking it all in, waiting for an opportunity to speak.

Carlos and Carmen held hands under the table and listened intently when the others spoke. All the while, she'd rub her thumb over his knuckles, and Carlos would give a squeeze, or he'd slide his hand between her thighs, warming all parts north.

"So dad. What are your plans with Carmen?" asked Adela. Her smile so wide, he read volumes into her question.

"That was quick. Have you been sitting on that question all

day?" Carlos asked. She wiggled in her seat, waiting for an answer.

"I've been sitting on that question since you first spoke of Carmen. We haven't seen you this happy in a very long time," continued Adela.

"Yes. The two of us have been talking about how lucky we are that you found someone," said Alba.

Frank slammed his hand on the table, startling Alba. "I can't believe you two have been talking about our dad behind our backs this whole time. Alba, I don't want you talking about this anymore."

"Excuse me. What's the problem here, Frank?" Carlos furrowed his brow at his son's outburst. "I know it's not my business, but don't speak to Alba like that again. Do you hear me?"

"What's your plan, dad? Are you going to marry her?" he spat. He threw Carmen a look that made her so uncomfortable, she pulled her hand away from Carlos.

Just then, a cart rolled up to the table. A cast iron pan, hot as the surface of the sun, sat in the middle. Everyone at the table went dead silent.

One by one, the server added the scallops, searing on each side, then flambeing. Using twelve inch kitchen tweezers, the server pinched each one from the fire and set them on a bed of arugula on individual appetizer plates, serving his masterpiece. The awkward silence making him avoid eye contact. As fast as he could, he placed a dish in front of each and then scurried with his cart back toward the kitchen.

"How's it going at that table?" asked Gabby.

"Don't go over there," answered her sous chef, his voice shaky. "I don't know which is hotter; my pan or that situation."

Carlos paused and looked down at his plate.

"Well?" Frank's tension gripped the table. No one dared look up or interject.

"Frank. You're being rude. I've tried to be patient, but you've crossed the line. Hear me now. I'm in love with Carmen. Nothing anyone says is going to change that. You can either accept it or not. That's on you. But you *will* refrain from talking to your wife or anyone else in that manner."

"You didn't answer my question."

"If you don't like who I'm with, that's your choice. You will not disrespect Carmen." At this, Carlos turned to Carmen. "I'm sorry. My son is being so rude."

Carmen put her hand to her chest. "It's alright. I understand." Prickling tears threatened. Adela grabbed Alba's hand as a befuddled Frank looked around the table. Unblinking, Rafael glared, his nostrils flaring. Alba was still a little shaken from his outburst.

Over at the bar, Jose and Gabby watched. Waiting. The pair intertwined and squeezed their hands, worried about the scene unfolding.

Rafael grabbed his brother by the arm and dragged him off his chair. The wood seat slammed to the floor as he led him out the front doors of the building.

Jose rushed over and picked up the chair. "Everything okay?"

"My son thinks he has a say in what I do with my life. Don't worry. He'll get over it," Carlos said, but looked for Carmen's reaction as he said it.

Carlos's family boarded their ferry home the next day. Frank barely spoke again before he left.

"I'll talk to him, dad, don't worry. He has stuff he has to sort out for himself. Be happy." Rafael hugged his father tight. He had always been the most sensitive of his sons, often tearing up over sentimentalities. Whereas, Frank had a very short fuse and seldom listened. Instead, his response would involve some kind of grunt or explosive behavior. Afterwards, he went over to Carmen. "I'm sorry. My brother loses himself in things he can't control. Thank you again for everything. We had a great time and can't wait to come back.

The next afternoon, Luis and Cristina stood at the bus stop waiting for Rose, Daisy, and Lily. They enjoyed shade from their umbrellas as the scorching sun roasted the asphalt at their feet. The rain from the previous night had already evaporated as steam rose from nearby puddles.

"We should stop by McDonald's and get them some ice cream," said Luis.

"Maybe they're hungry. Food first."

The school bus arrived, dragging road dust, water, and debris in its wake. As the driver set it in park, the familiar hissing of the brake, and the stop sign squeal as it flipped out, had the waiting parents stand or exit their waiting cars to collect their children. Kids laughing and screaming jogged down the stairs and out the folding doors, while the bus driver called to them to 'slow down.'

"Hola Mima! Hi Pipo!" they called at the same time.

"How was school?" asked Cristina.

"Boring," said Rose with an eye-roll. The bus pulled away and gravel ground through, shooting in different directions.

"You always think everything is boring," said Lily.

The old couple took the girls to McDonald's. Each ordered their favorite: a Happy Meal of chicken nuggets and fries with a soft serve ice cream cone. The girls ended up eating the ice cream first as the blazing heat turned it into a river of vanilla and chocolate that oozed down their arms.

"You girls clean up and start your homework. Your mother will be here to pick you up soon." Cristina said. She loved playing grandma, and Luis relished his grandpa role.

More and more, Luis noticed his wife was out of breath and needed to sit. Her refusal to get checked out had been a point of contention, so he let it lie, but decided he couldn't leave her alone anymore.

Later that afternoon, the loud scrape of their metal gate called the girls to the door. Pilar approached with a basket of baked goods from the store. "I brought you these to sample. Let me know what you think." She placed the basket on the kitchen table.

"What's this for?" asked Cristina. As Luis reached into the basket to grab a cookie, Cristina swatted his hand away. "You can't eat this right now. I'm making dinner." Luis made a funny face and shrugged at the girls. Their laughter was worth the smack on the hand.

"I wanted you to see what cookies for diabetics are available in town. I know you can do so much better. Making cookies is easier than working in the garden or the field, and not as hot. Plus, you're the better baker. Not to mention, it would be a great addition to the farmer's market. Just an idea."

Cristina gave her a sideways smirk. "Okay. I'll try them. I'm not promising anything."

Pilar took her children and went home. She hoped Cristina would consider doing something else. Farming is difficult, add to that the Caribbean heat, it's a recipe for disaster. She'd rather see her create edible recipes that would keep her safe. Besides, there seemed to be a high incidence of diabetes in town, and Pilar thought they could come up with something to help.

After she'd fed the girls and put them to bed, she sat at the table looking over her marketing strategy for the hotel and restaurant. Her vantage gave her a look across the street at Cristina's house. The couple sat at their table eating dinner, and in the center sat a large platter of all the baked goods Pilar had brought them.

She watched as they talked and laughed. Cristina would slap Luis's hand away from the cookies in the basket. A warmth washed over her as she gave a half-suppressed laugh, thinking it resembled an old thyme silent movie. All at once, everything stopped. Silence veiled the room, and the hairs on the back of her neck stood on end. Then her phone rang.

Chapter 13

Thorns and Scorpions

While still dark out Tuesday morning, Carlos decided it was time to trim back the magenta bougainvillea that had grown haphazard against the gazebo. The branches wove through the iron posts until there was no space.

It had grown so large; it obscured the entire eastern side of the conservatory. Abundant, gorgeous blooms cascaded down from the edge of the roofline in mammoth bunches, fulfilling the superstition that it welcomes visitors and ignites passion. He knew it was a shame to remove it, but it had been creating a mess on the floor and he'd grown tired of raking away.

Carlos avoided the task for years. Removing the branches with extra thick, long thorns was a job too treacherous for a novice. The last time he'd trimmed it back, his arms, neck, and legs looked like a cheese grater had attacked them. The spikes became larger the bigger the plant grew, and more vicious.

Late July was too hot to work outside, so doing it before the sun came up was paramount. "Don't go. Come back to bed," groaned Carmen. Phoenix lay her head on Carmen's ankle and watched Carlos get dressed, her eyes darting from side to side.

"I don't want work in the sun all day, but that bramble has to go. I'll see you later." He kissed her, but she was so sleepy, she didn't even realize she'd *been* kissed. "Let's go Phoenix."

The dog loved traipsing around with Carlos. A living link between him and Carmen. She popped off the bed as if she'd known adventure was afoot. When he opened his truck door, Phoenix jumped right in, making herself at home in her copilot seat.

This was their routine while Carmen was away, and any time Carmen was busy, Phoenix would tag along behind Carlos. Carmen would joke, calling Phoenix 'the other woman.' She loved the way the dog gravitated toward him. "Just another one of your bitches," Carmen joked. Carlos could never tell which made her jealous; him, or Phoenix?

Carlos set the car in park next to the vine and opened the door. The dog leapt over him before he could get out and went to make her rounds. He watched her prancing toward the restaurant like she owned the place. He smiled from ear to ear because he knew the dog's routine; pull up for a treat at the kitchen door, sit like a pretty girl for the bartender's nuzzle, then pronk to the hotel front desk where she'd collapse for a belly rub from Angela.

In fact, Phoenix spent most of her days going from one person to another, garnering as much attention as she could get. From people she knew as well as strangers. A welcome change from the standoffish behavior she exhibited when Carmen rescued her.

Carlos laughed and reached into the truck bed, grabbing his rawhide gloves. He'd found them online, hoping they'd help with the daunting task. The thick, tanned leather went up past his elbow. Specific for working with thorny vegetation, he prayed they'd do the trick, and he'd leave the job unscathed.

Besides the gloves, he'd prepared various tools to make the

job easier. He honed his clippers and whetted his hedge shears until they could slice through just about anything with little or no effort. After pulling on the gloves, he began trimming the thicket.

"Crap. This is going to take all day," Carlos hissed. It appeared the gloves were working, and though he wore work pants and the thick leather apron, now and then a thorn would impale him or carve a deep ravine where a streaming crimson river coursed through, staining his clothing. Every now and again, he'd let out a 'shit' or 'crap' that no one else heard except him.

"Hey. How's this coming?" Carmen asked, giggling as she walked up next to him, overhearing the vitriol.

"Good morning. You were out of it. It's coming. Slow and steady." He leaned over and gave her a quick peck.

"I can see the thorns are drawing new designs on you. We'll have to buy a truckload of Neosporin to take care of those wounds." She touched his cheek, wiping away a trickle of blood that seeped through the line carved by a thorn.

"It's alright. They'll heal. Phoenix is making her rounds. This is going to take me all day. I've been out here over two hours and I haven't made a dent."

"I wish I could help, but there isn't any other protection equipment." Carmen was genuine in her sentiment, but deep down, she was thankful there wasn't anything she could do to help. She'd had her fill of removing bougainvillea to last her the rest of her life.

Back in Miami, after her divorce, she'd purchased herself a

cottage. In her rage, she'd bought clippers to remove the nasty vine that the previous owner allowed to overgrow. Neighbors heard her yelling at it, cursing the 'day it was born.' "Alright. I'll bring you some cold water. Lunch later?"

"Okay. But I don't want to stop until I'm finished."

A short while later, Carmen delivered him cold water, then continued on to the restaurant. On her way there, Phoenix pranced up next to her, just as she had day after day. Gabby's morning sickness had taken hold, and until it normalized later in the day, she'd stay in bed. Carmen made sure everything ran smooth in her absence, and it always did.

Next, she made her way to the front desk, where she found Angela trembling and talking to the police, Diego standing close behind her. "Hey, Angela. Is everything alright? Where's Pilar?" she looked from one to the other.

"Hi Carmen. The officers are investigating a police shooting."

"Police shooting? I don't understand."

"Someone shot Sergeant Rodriguez. He's in the ICU at the hospital. It doesn't look good," said the young rookie. His partner studied both women as they reacted to the news.

"Oh no. Pilar." Carmen's face tightened as she looked back at Angela, then yanked her keys from her pocket, and turned to Phoenix. "You stay here with Angela, sweet girl." The dog froze in her spot while the police watched Carmen leave on a full run, the older officer following.

Turning back to Angela, the rookie continued questioning. "It appears Sergeant Rodriguez was investigating the custodian. Do you know anything about that?"

"No. I wish there was some way I could help you," replied Angela. "But I don't know him very well. Pilar has been spending time with him. I think they're dating?"

"We know. He listed her as an emergency contact. We've already spoken to her and she's at the hospital."

Angela and Diego looked at each other and raised their eyebrows at the news. "That's new," said Angela.

Outside, the senior officer called, "Ms. Coronado, may I have a word?" jogging down the steps.

Carmen had her car door open and stopped, turned to face him. "I need to get to my friend at the hospital."

"What do you know about the custodian that tried to blow up a school full of children?"

"I know nothing. Just that he had the scorpion tattoos and that he was in custody."

"I understand you've had run-ins with this organization before."

"Yes. But what does that have to do with this case?"

"We're investigating all angles. Thought you might have something more to offer."

Carmen closed her car door and ambled toward him, blowing out her tension. "A couple of years ago, I inherited this property from my father," she pointed at the building. "There were people who wanted the property that were involved with that group. You know, the scorpion tattooed idiots. They were in my home trying to coerce the property from me. My attorney shot my…boyfriend…in the exchange, and they were all arrested. After that, we testified to what we knew, and that was all."

"That was all?"

"Yes. Wait. Are you implying I was involved?"

"No. We're just exploring all possibilities, and if you had anything else to offer, it might help us with our investigation."

"Well, if I think of anything, I will get in touch." The officer thanked her, then waited for her to get in her car before heading back inside when the rookie headed his way.

"There's nothing here," he conveyed. Carmen eyed them, straining to hear what they were saying from her open car window. She gave up and left, careful not to speed out in front of them.

Luis and Cristina were home with Pilar's girls. They'd received the call and were attempting to distract the girls from the violence that seemed to crop up around them. Cristina had convinced them to join her in making cookies. "Your mother thinks I can start a new business. At my age, no less. What do you think, Rose?"

As she took bite after bite of Cristina's coconut cookies, she smiled. "Totally."

"Does that mean you think I can do it?"

"Si, mi amor. That's what she means. These teenagers are

speaking less and less full sentences." Luis laughed as he handed Lily and Daisy another cookie.

"I'm not dumb, you know," said Rose. Cristina looked over at Luis and both waited to hear more. "Mom likes Sergeant Rodriguez, and I can tell he likes her, too."

"We don't think you're dumb. You're very observant. What's with the attitude?" asked Cristina.

"I know something happened, and that's why mom isn't here. Just tell me."

After quite a few soulful looks between the couple, Luis took the two younger sisters to another room.

"Gunfire hit, Sergeant...Juan. Your mom is at the hospital."

"Is he going to be alright?" Rose turned to Cristina, the knot in her throat tightening as she fought to contain her anguish. "We like him too. We want mom to be happy. He makes her happy." Rose started to cry, a deep, strained sob.

Cristina understood how Rose was feeling. She'd lost her father, and now this glimmer of hope for happiness for her mother might be taken away. "I'm sure they're doing everything they can and he'll be alright. Now, help me mix these guava chunks into the next batch of coconut cookies."

The rest of the day, they experimented with cookie dough flavors; coconut, guava, and chocolate. Flour had floated through the air, landing on the floor, the sink, and the table. Particles had attached themselves to their hands, leaving fingerprints on every appliance and cabinet handle in the kitchen; it even snowed on Rose and Cristina.

There was no more conversation about Juan or Pilar. Cristina and Luis kept the girls busy with baking and drawing or watching a movie while they waited, hoping good news would arrive soon.

By early afternoon, Carlos had emptied the truck bed of cuttings several times. The pile was a safe distance away where he could burn them without fear of fire spreading.

After clearing away the bulk of the vine, he stepped back to look at his progress, and noticed the outline of what appeared to be a narrow door frame. Though there were still a lot of branches to cut away, he was certain it was a door.

Carlos dropped his cordless chainsaw and stood with his hands on his waist. He had never noticed a door in this area before, and he still couldn't get to it, since the thorns in this area were thicker and longer than any other spot he'd already cut away.

He took off the gloves and pulled his hair back into a man-bun. Walking to the conservatory, he stomped his boots before lugging open the right-hand door. Inside, everything was normal.

Heavenly scents emanated from exquisite orchids, colorful rare black rainbow hibiscus bloomed in the corner from their enormous pots, and pink and white fuchsia dangled from macrame hanging baskets. He scanned the walls looking for an opening, drifting over to the Forever Susan lily's orange and purple petals burst of color.

He saw no door outline in this main room. Sliding the barn doors to the bedroom and bathroom, he looked at every wall. No door. He thought the previous owner might have constructed the rainforest style bathroom to conceal the opening. Carlos tried walking around to the back of the indoor waterfall but found no doorway there. He scratched his head, then went back outside to the straggling remnants of the bougainvillea.

After pulling his gloves back on, he was more determined than ever to rid himself of the irritating plant. The closer he got to revealing the door, the more aggressive he became. Once he removed the last of the bush, he grasped his shovel and unearthed the plant's roots to prevent it from returning. When he finished, he stood back. The outline revealed a doorway, complete with a lock.

Carmen reached the hospital, parking in the nearest spot, and strode to the check-in desk where she got a visitor's pass and the room number from the attendant. In the elevator, she pondered why, if she was in a hurry, the elevator needed to stop at every floor. She worried it was a sign.

She exited the elevator doors, looked left, then right. Carmen spotted the familiar crowd of uniformed officers milling outside the ICU. Anytime one of them was in the hospital, especially when caught in the line of fire, they all showed up. The odor of disinfectant and rubbing alcohol assaulted her nose, and she rubbed at the sting. As she approached the door, several officers halted her, questioning who she was. From behind them, Pilar called her name, "Carmen?"

"Pilar," she shoved them aside, navigating the sea of constables to get to her friend. Pilar's face sunken, her eyes puffy and swollen. The friends hugged, and Pilar began crying again. "What happened?" Pilar pulled Carmen into the room and closed the door.

"We don't know. They think he was close to figuring out where the Scorpions were coming from. That's what they're calling the gang, and one of them must have shot him." Pilar cried again. "I can't believe I'm here again."

Carmen took hold of Pilar. "Look at me. He's going to be fine. You are not in the same place again. This is entirely different."

Soon, Pilar got hold of herself and stopped crying. Her body was stoic. She remained expressionless, focused on the beeping and blinking machines that seem to keep Juan alive. Her thoughts spun round and round about the future. A future she had accepted was certain to include Juan. She stepped away from Carmen and went back to where she sat next to the helpless man on the bed, wove her fingers through his, bent over, and placed her cheek on the back of his hand. He was cold and pale.

Carmen looked down at the floor and blew out the gargantuan lump in her throat. *'Don't cry, don't cry, don't cry,'* she repeated in her head. "What can I do?" The overwhelming helplessness was back. She couldn't help her friend by healing him. She couldn't find the people responsible. And she couldn't take away the pain Pilar was sure to carry forever if she lost Juan. She was too young to be going through this.

Through her runny nose and tear soaked face, "Nothing," answered Pilar.

The phone in Carmen's pocket vibrated, jarring her from her thoughts. "Hello," she whispered, then listened to the voice on the other end. "Okay." She stood to leave and told Pilar to call if she needed anything.

"Luis and Cristina may need a break from the girls soon. They've been with them since last night when I got the call."

"Of course. I have to stop by the hotel, but then I'll get right over and relieve them. Can I bring you anything?" She waited, but Pilar didn't answer. She opened the door and slipped out. As she passed the window, Pilar remained unmoved, her forehead on Juan's hand.

Carmen's heart cracked wide open. She waded through the sea of police officers before reaching the elevator bank and pressing the down button again and again as if it would come to her, without delay.

Chapter 14
It's About Time and Unopened Doors

On the drive back to the hotel, Carmen went over and over it in her head. There were no other details she could share with the officers. Over the last two years, she'd been able to put the entire ordeal behind her. She'd been able to learn to trust people again. It seemed to be a cycle in her life: she's betrayed, has to relearn how to trust only to find herself betrayed again, then start the cycle all over again.

Her mind wandered back to the days before she came to New Cuba for the first time. How her family warned her it wasn't safe enough yet. She shook her head, and much like shaking an Etch-a Sketch, she wiped the slate clean of that memory. Carmen worried what would happen if the violence that plagued the darker spaces of the state showed up at her door once again.

Phoenix's head popped up as she felt the thrum of the Corvette before it even reached the driveway. She bolted through the front door and sprinted across the deck, dodging guests that milled around on the front porch, her rear end drifting at the turn. Phoenix's claws and paws trying to gain purchase, she scampered out the other side, chasing the candy apple red car.

Carmen drove closer to where Carlos was waiting for her, setting the gear in park and shutting off the engine. The dog slid next to Carlos with a huge dust up. The second the door opened, Phoenix leaped in like she hadn't seen Carmen in a year. After some quick pets and slobbery kisses, "You called? I came as fast as I could. What happened?" she got out of the car with the dog and closed the door.

"First, what happened with Pilar?" asked Carlos.

"It's Juan. Someone shot him last night. They think it was a group they're now calling the Scorpions. They have no leads, but they questioned Angela and Diego earlier."

"Is he alright? Just when he and Pilar were getting to know each other. Talk about bad timing." Carlos shook his head.

"You should have seen her. It was Eduardo all over again." Carmen looked away, fighting back the sting in her eyes. She crossed her arms and covered her mouth while she looked for solace in Carlos's eyes, then looked down and shuffled the gravel under her sneakers.

Carlos threw off his gloves and wrapped her close to his heart. "Should I head over? And why question Angela and Diego?" Carmen backed away. "They're questioning everyone. They asked me out front if I had anything to offer before I left. Anyway, what did you find?"

"This isn't the right time," said Carlos.

"It's always about time, isn't it? Show me."

Carlos walked Carmen over to the outline of the doorway. The lock was old and rusty, but had the familiar outline of keys she'd seen before. "Is that…?" Carmen scrunched her nose and narrowed her eyes. She looked over the rim of her glasses, then walked over and ran her fingers over the antique doorknob and tried to open the door. Locked. She moved her hand away, peering down at the remnants of iron oxide that streaked her hand, and brushed her hands together to rid herself of the orange metal residue.

"I think so. I didn't want to open it without you." Carlos jangled the keys, then put them back in his pocket. "Let's take care of Pilar now. We'll deal with this later."

Lucrecia approached the small house with the blue Nissan out front. The two men at her sides stood too close. The stink of hot breath flowed down the back of her neck. A rotting stench that forced itself past the malodor of their cologne.

She turned to look at them over her shoulder. A cemented stare locked eyes with them, her nostrils flaring. Without a word, the two men backed up, clasping their hands in front of them, staring her down.

Lucrecia opened the heavy iron security door, fisting an intense knock on the wood, making Maria hitch at the sound. From her seat on the couch, she remained quiet, craning to see who was there. "Maria. I know you're home. Your crappy old car is in the driveway. Open the door. It's Lucrecia."

Maria stood and straightened her clothing, pulling down the skirt of her short dress, and pulling the top higher. She'd stayed out of the public eye for days following her last attempt at getting Carlos's attention.

Her disheveled red hair matted to the back of her head, her glittery nail polish chipped, and her clothes had splotches of various colored stains. She wasn't wearing any shoes, and the bottom of her feet were charcoal. She looked down at herself, loathing the very skin that swathed her.

"Come on Maria. I'm waiting." Lucrecia's grating voice cut through the air, leaving a thick venom quality in its wake.

Resigned, Maria walked barefoot to the door, tugging her dress down as it crept up when she walked. After looking through the window, she spots two menacing thugs flanking the creepy woman. "What do you want?"

"Open. The. Door. You don't want my friends to open it themselves, do you? It's hot out here. You don't want them to get angry." Lucrecia's savage stare through the small glass window of the front door scared Maria to her core, and she shuddered.

It was then that Maria realized they could break the door down; she hadn't locked the iron security door. Over her shoulder, she searched the kitchen behind her. If she brandished a knife, she might survive.

Panic started building in her gut, a serpentine coil that tightened with every passing second. She had no choice. "Okay. Coming." She tiptoed to the kitchen and grabbed the biggest knife she could and held it tight to her side as she headed for the door.

She stalled as she unlocked the four deadbolts, slowly, one at a time. Upon reaching the brass chain at the top, she hesitated. "Who are those men with you?"

"None of your business. The chain, Maria."

Maria's fingers went numb and her hand shook, but there was nothing she could do. Her legs wobbled and trembled, making her knees knock. She thought any minute they wouldn't be able to hold her up. Lucrecia and her men were getting in. Her eyes flicked around the room. It occurred to her she should never have talked to Lucrecia. She knew the woman ran with that gang. What was she thinking? *'She's no different from Guerrero.'*

Now, a reckoning has shown up to her house. Maria leaned her forehead on the door, taking a deep breath, and without hurrying, slid the chain across until it was out of the track. She took the doorknob in her hand, turning it by degrees before opening at a snail's pace, the hinges displeased, the wood crackling.

Without warning, the two men burst through the door, grabbing her by the throat and pressing her into the opposite wall. The knife she held clanked to the floor, bouncing and rattling, a discarded trinket. Maria tried to slip her hand between the attacker and her throat. One man held a filthy hand to her mouth while the other held her to the wall, as she gasped for air.

Lucrecia sauntered into the house, turned, and closed the door, locking it with a blast. Her hideous chartreuse skirt flipped as she turned back to look at the terrified woman. Her garish sandals clacked against the floor.

Maria eyeballed Lucrecia from top to bottom. She'd drawn in her eyebrows and she looked like a clown. Her hair was sparse and patchy, and her teeth were yellowed or gray. Her heels were so cracked there was no question she didn't take care of herself.

Maria shook free of the dirty hand, "What are you do…" and the man clasped his hand over her mouth again, this time tighter.

Maria could smell the alcohol on his breath. The men pulled her from the wall. One stood at her back, holding her hands behind her. The other was in front, warning her not to scream when he removed his hand. He reached for the top of her dress and ripped it off.

"Move aside." Said Lucrecia. She pulled over a kitchen chair and sat in front of her. "Maria. Recently, you threatened to expose me. Look who's exposed now. You threatened to tell the authorities that I know who the Scorpions are and how they operate, how they're getting to this side of the wall. My friends here don't like threats."

The man released Maria's mouth. "I just wanted your help. That's all." Maria's voice, tight with fear, choked out every syllable as tears flooded from her eyes. "Please. Lucrecia. You know what it's like when…"

"Quiet." Lucrecia stood, picked up the knife, and made her way over to Maria, her pace prolonging the inevitable.

By early afternoon, Gabby was eager to get back to work. She didn't care if the restaurant could run itself. Right now, she just wanted to cook. To get her hands into the vegetables and specialty meats she'd ordered. To chop the herbs she'd asked Carlos to pick from the herb garden.

The marvelous knives her friends had given her were begging to be used. To work on the dishes she'd planned for so many months, and serve the food from the menus she'd painstakingly designed. She was sick of being *sick* and wanted to get back to her life.

"Just don't overdo it, please." Jose knew how headstrong Gabby could be, but still tried to impress upon her how important it was to take care of herself, especially now, with *this* pregnancy.

He'd reserved the use of the word 'geriatric' as a last resort to stop his fiancé from going a little too far with her insistence to do everything herself. After seeing her reaction to hearing the obstetrician use the word, he was in no hurry to get on that shit list.

Before she arrived at the restaurant, Jose called and gave them the heads up she was on a mission. By the time she got to the kitchen, the sous chefs had laid out all the items Gabby blustered about that she wanted to work with.

"What's all this?" she asked.

"Today's menu items. Don't worry, we're on it," said the head chef, and went back to what he was doing. Jose asked him not to be obvious or tell her he'd called.

Gabby eyed the short cook and squinted. She noticed the containers of food and everything she'd need set on the counter for cooking. The only thing her staff *knew*, without exception, was to *never* touch her knives, so her knife roll was nowhere to be seen.

She sidled around the corner of the counter, dragging her hand along the edge of the cold metallic worktable, slow and steady, and set eyes on the dessert chef. "Did Jose call you?" Gabby spun her head down, around, and up in one motion to catch the pâtissier's expression.

The poor girl kept to her task and said no. She wasn't lying.

Jose had spoken to the other chef, and she wasn't about to throw him under the bus. Gabby walked over to the pots that were simmering and peeked in, grabbing some spoons and tasting each one as she walked past. She looked at her head chef and raised an eyebrow. There was nothing to say. They'd followed every recipe to a T. He smiled at her and went back to work.

Gabby sighed and walked over to where they'd set up the containers and got to work. She pulled out her tools, and unwound the leather knife roll, spreading out her cutlery. She caressed the handles, picking up the seven and a half inch santoku and gripped it tight with her palm. The metal of the blade caught her reflection, and she smiled.

The vegetables were all washed and ready. Taking a carrot from the bin, she began to julienne into transparent strips. Only with a knife this sharp could she accomplish such a task. Soon, Gabby was humming to herself while she prepped the rest of the vegetables.

After taking the herbs Carlos left for her, she prepared a chimichurri marinade for her coffee-rubbed steak and set it all in the walk in until service time. When she exited the cooler, a sharp, stabbing pain sliced through her abdomen and she dropped to her knees, doubling over and gasping.

Carmen and Carlos had picked up Pilar's girls and brought them back to the hotel, where they could go swimming and have a bite to eat. It was getting late, and they hadn't heard from Pilar. "Can you keep an eye on them? I'd like to bring Pilar some food and clothes?"

"Of course. I'll be right here. Give her my best."

Carmen grabbed some food from the buffet and headed over to Pilar's house to collect some items that would make her friend more comfortable. She knew what it was like to watch the person you love fading away. Carmen didn't want to go through that again, and she was even more positive that Pilar didn't want to go through it again, either.

Once Carmen took the girls, Luis and Cristina dragged themselves off the sofa, walked to their house, and headed straight for bed and a long nap.

"I hope Juan survives this. Pilar can't take another loss," said Cristina.

"Whatever happens, we'll be here, just like last time." Luis shook his head, a sadness enveloping the space he occupied. He watched Cristina hold on to the walls as she made her way down the hall to their bedroom in the back of the house and it rattled his composure.

The officers milling outside Juan's room could smell the aroma coming from the elevator before the doors even opened.

As Carmen exited the lift, the hungry assembly of officers was already at attention, staring at the tote she carried. Without a word, the detectives parted like the Red Sea, allowing her passage. Carmen smiled and nodded as she passed.

"I brought you some stretchy clothes. Thought you'd be more comfortable. But first, I need you to eat while it's still warm. There's a roast pork pressed sandwich, rice and red beans. And I snagged some ham croquetas on my way out the door. I'm sure they're not *ice* cold." The breaded and fried ham croquettes gratified the soul of anyone who took a bite, whisking your memory back to home and family, and your abuela frying them up in the kitchen.

She set the food out on the table and looked at Pilar, who hadn't moved from the spot where she'd left her. "Come on hon. You need to eat something." Carmen helped her up and sat her at the small table in the corner of the room.

"Thank you. But I don't think I can swallow."

"Now you listen to me. You have three daughters who need their mother. Eat. Now." The severity of Carmen's tone was so firm Pilar didn't dare defy her. "I'm calling in an order for the guys outside. They looked like they were about to devour me as I walked past."

Pilar took a bite from the succulent sandwich. Garlic, onions, and lime mojo filled her mouth with tangy juices. "This is good. Thank you," she exhaled while chewing., and the bite went down like it came straight from heaven. And though she wasn't hungry, the offering filled her with warmth and hope.

The crunch of the pressed Cuban bread followed by the tangy mojo danced on her tongue as a small drop of gravy escaped from the corner of her lips. She grabbed for a napkin and wiped it away while looking at Carmen, and smiled.

"See. You need your strength. I brought you a change of clothes, a towel, your toothbrush, and soap."

As the women talked, they didn't notice that behind them the machines were bleeping louder and faster. "Ohhhh…" groaned Juan.

Pilar threw her sandwich and ran to his bedside. Carmen opened the door and screamed for the doctor. The officers in the hallway all stared at her, then hiked themselves higher to look inside the small room like a bunch of gophers popping out of their holes.

"I'm here," said Pilar.

"What happened?" he asked.

Before she could answer, the doctor fought his way through the crowd of law enforcement and burst into the room. "How long has he been awake?"

Carmen blanched. "Miguel?" asked Carmen.

"Who's Miguel?" asked Pilar.

"Carmen?" the doctor questioned back, then turned toward his patient.

"What…?" Pilar looked at Carmen. Her lips squeezed tight and her face strained like someone was pulling at it from both sides. She breathed what Pilar could only imagine was hellfire. "Carmen!"

At Pilar's urgence, Carmen snapped out of her fiery stare, looking back at her friend who's eyes had bugged-out at her. The doctor turned to Juan, taking vitals as a nurse turned off the loud machines that squawked around them.

"Doctor?" asked Pilar.

"Juan's vitals are looking pretty good, considering we weren't sure he'd wake up." The doctor looked over at a stunned Carmen, then back to Pilar and Juan. "He's not out of the woods yet. We had to remove his spleen, but should recover fine. Let's give him a few days and see how he's doing." He clicked his pen into his pocket.

"Can I see you outside?" asked Carmen.

Without a word, the doctor held the door open and Carmen walked out. Pilar looked at the nurse who was changing Juan's dressing, and the two women unblinking stared at each other, raised their brows while turning their heads, and watched the pair through the window of the small room, pivoting to watch them as they disappeared down the hall.

Chapter 15
Blindsided and A Visit to the E. R.

Cristina woke to the sound of Luis arguing outside in the front of their home. She tottered down the hallway, straining to hear the conversation. Peeking through the window, she sees him on the phone, yelling. His arm waving wildly. She heads over to the stove, setting her Cuban coffeepot on the burner, and leaned hard on the edges of the counter with both hands, straining to make out what he was saying.

After a long exhale, she turned the ancient knob, listening for the hissing of the gas as it flowed into the burner tube, then the ignitor's click-click-click and spark, burning the strong gas smell that was filling the air. Cristina turned the knob and set the flame on high, then took out a couple of bowls. She cut up strawberries and mango in bite-sized pieces, then placed them on the table.

Minutes later, Luis, catching the whiff of strong coffee, hangs up his cell and heads inside. "Buenos dias, mi amor." With a calm demeanor, he kisses Cristina as she spoons raw cane sugar into the carafe, then splashed a few drops of brewed espresso, and ground it against the side to make foam.

Without looking up at him, "Who were you talking to?"

"What do you mean? Nobody."

Cristina dropped the spoon on the counter with a loud clank. "I heard you yelling from way back in the bedroom. What's happening?"

"It's nothing. I promise."

Cristina squinted at him. "Don't lie to me, old man."

"Settle down. I was talking to Carmen. She called to ask me for help with a situation."

"What situation?"

"I'm sure she'll talk to you when she's ready."

Cristina couldn't stand not knowing what was happening. She had no choice but to let it go; Carmen had called Luis, not her. For now, she'd let him handle whatever problem was plaguing their friend.

"What the hell are you doing here?" Carmen whirled on Miguel. The doctor was six-foot-three and towered over Carmen's five-foot-four frame. He stood tight-lipped, with one side of his mouth in a derisive curl. "Well?"

"Relax. You look...tense." Miguel quirked up the right side of his mouth again. His eyes fast-squinted. "I didn't have a choice. The hospital wanted all doctors to have a rotation in New Cuba. I never thought we'd run into each other." He looked down at her with his chin held high and his cold dark eyes provoking her to scream.

"How long do you have to be here?" Carmen asked, and he stared down at her, rocking on his heels and avoiding an answer; like he knew what he'd done, and it gladdened him, seeming to secrete some kind of nasty ooze only she could see. He flipped up his iPad and began tapping away, ignoring her presence.

Carmen fumed like an oil rig after it struck oil. She willed herself not to assault him, especially while so close to the officers that watched the scene unfold from down the hall. So she raised an eyebrow and waited, clenching and releasing her right fist at her side.

"It's a six-week rotation. I'll be back on the mainland before Noche Buena. You should see someone about that…anger you're carrying around." Miguel rolled his eyes and looked back down at his iPad. "I have patients to see. If you'll excuse me." He walked past her without another word. His strong cologne overtaking the bleach smell that had taken up residence in her nostrils. Carmen preferred the alcohol-bleach smell to the lingering stench of his odor.

Carmen didn't turn. Instead, she went back into the room and collected her things, picking up each item as though it had offended her. Pilar was still at Juan's bedside, and the nurse had gone. The two were talking.

"Hey Carmen. Do you know the doctor? Seems like you know the doctor." Pilar said in a joking tone, accompanied by a smirk, but Carmen missed it.

"Yes." Carmen answered curtly, then looked over at Juan and told him how grateful she was that he would be alright, and hoped he'd get out of the hospital soon. "I have to go."

"Wait. You didn't answer me." Carmen's seriousness alarmed Pilar, and she kept her eyes on her through the hospital room window as she boarded the elevator. Once inside, Carmen turned and glowered. Pilar thought she saw steam coming out of Carmen's ears.

As soon as she reached the car, Carmen called her oldest

son. "Antonio. Did you know your father is in Pinar?"

Tony knew that if she was using his full name, that she was not happy, and it put him on the defensive. "No. Why would I know or care where he is?"

"Does Andres and Hope know?"

"Ma, none of us are in touch with him. You know that. None of us know or care where he is or what he's doing as long as he stays away from us, and you."

"Okay. Okay. It just…caught me by surprise, I guess."

"It's alright. Calm down. What's he doing there, anyway?"

"A rotation at the hospital. He said it would only be six weeks."

"Wow. You *actually* talked to him?"

"I didn't have a choice."

"So, what happened?"

"Well Tony, he was his usual glib self, like there was no room for anyone else. I swear, I think he sees a spotlight wherever he goes. And if he doesn't see one on him, he fabricates a scenario where it will shine on him. He pretended I'm the one with the issue. Like I was intruding in his life or something."

"Typical narcissist. They all act as though their presence is doing us a favor. And God forbid you're on to their manipulations. That's why Miguel spread rumors about you. He even tried making up lies about you, to *us*. Can you imagine? You're our mother. Asshole thought we'd believe him and take his side. That's why he told us we were a 'mistake he *deeply* regretted.'"

222

Hearing what Miguel had said to their children infuriated Carmen even more. She'd told her son how much she loved him and hoped his father's idiocy didn't cause too much pain. She'd shared nothing that happened between her and their father; sparing them any pain they might feel if they knew the whole truth. Carmen and Tony finished their conversation on a high note, then hung up, promising to talk again soon.

After sitting in traffic for far too long, and thinking too hard about this unexpected turn, she called Luis for help. Since he was the only one she'd shared details with about her ex, she knew she could count on him. He reminded her of her father; thin Cuban mustache, skinny frame with broad shoulders, and always wore a Perro camiseta under his button-down shirts; exactly like her father. The undershirt peeked out from the top, exposing the three buttons. One call later, she told him that Miguel was there as part of an assigned rotation.

"Yes, that happens sometimes. I got sent all over the place, and it was difficult, but I'm glad I had the experiences or I wouldn't be the dashing doctor I am today."

"Cute. Could he have *chosen* the assignment?"

"Yes."

"Well, I don't want him here!" she yelled into the phone.

"Don't yell at me, muchacha!" Luis yelled back, waving his hand. "Stay away from him the best you can, and tell Carlos."

"Why? It has nothing to do with him."

"You called me for help. I'm telling you to tell Carlos, so

there's no misunderstanding. You know Carmen, you can be so stubborn!" Luis shouted into the receiver, then the aroma of coffee beckoned and he hung up without even saying goodbye.

Carmen tossed her phone on the passenger seat and pressed her palms to her eyes. Her hospital encounter had taken her by surprise. She didn't know where to turn, but Luis got his point across. She needed to tell Carlos right away, and she found him parked by the gazebo where he'd removed the bougainvillea.

"Hey gorgeous," Carlos said, smiling, as she strode toward him. "I'm finishing the cleanup, then we can look. See what's in there."

"Oh. Okay." Carmen looked down at her feet.

"What is it? Is Juan alright?"

"Yes. We need to talk."

Luis and Cristina sat at their table eating breakfast, sipping coffee, and going over their plans for the week. There would be a lot of babysitting now that Juan was going home.

Over the clangor of silverware, they talked about how they were relieved that Juan survived the shooting and that Pilar had found someone. Though, in his line of work, they worried it could happen again, but it was important the girls have a positive male influence in their lives and Juan was as worthy as they come.

"I want her to be happy, and not alone. When I'm gone, what will she do?" asked Cristina.

"Don't say that. You're not going anywhere."

"My father used to say, 'Me quedan dos afeitadas.'"

"I've heard that expression. 'I have two shaves left,'" and he laughed at the memory of old timers using that saying when they reached a certain age. Luis realized there were so many forgotten expressions and shook his drooping head. It worried him it was an aftereffect of becoming a state. All the little cultural things that make Cuba special would be gone one day.

"That happens in every culture. My mother had expressions I'd never heard because they were before *my* time. Stop blaming statehood for any little thing you see." Cristina knew she was right, but Luis had his beliefs and there were times no one could convince him otherwise.

"I know you're right. Sometimes I get too invested in how I think things *should* be. I'm trying."

"Alright." Carlos took her hand and led her to a shaded concrete bench in one of the more secluded areas of the garden; the one in an alcove near the ceiba tree. Something deep down had coiled tight and up into his chest.

"What is it?" He grasped her hand and wove his fingers through hers, covering her hand with his.

Before Carmen could say anything, someone ran out the back door screaming her name, Phoenix trotting behind them.

"Diego? What is it?"

"They've taken Gabby to the hospital. Something's wrong. She doubled over at the restaurant."

"What?" Carmen bolted up from the bench.

"Let's go. I'll drive," said Carlos, who threw his gloves in the truck bed while yanking his truck keys from his pocket.

"Take Phoenix inside," said Carmen. "What is happening? If it's not this one, then it's that one, or the other one."

"Timing, I guess." Carlos drove as fast as he could toward the hospital.

Miguel pulled up to the house where he was staying near the hospital. His friends, who own the mansion, offered him a place to stay while they were abroad. They were a prestigious Cuban family that escaped the incoming regime with the clothes on their backs during the 1956 revolution, and the enormous house became a piece of nationalized property.

Over the years, the house suffered decay from lack of upkeep; crumbling walls, rusty pipes, and a myriad of other deficits that made the place most undesirable, and unlivable.

Following annexation to the Union, the family reclaimed their stolen property, and hired engineers to step in and restore the home, sparing no expense to bring the house current with the rest of the world.

As Miguel's car approached, wrought-iron gates opened to a lush royal palm driveway, and at the pinnacle, white marble steps led to a solid Cuban mahogany double-door entry inlaid with Murano glass.

Sculpted hedges framed every walkway, and like any other respectable property on the island, the heavenly scent of mariposa filled the air.

His very young fiancé, dressed in a skintight mini dress that ended too high on her thighs, leaned on the doorframe, smiling a wide, buck-toothed smile. She twirled a white mariposa bloom in her left hand, looking out at him as she sniffed its perfume.

Miguel insisted she wear heels whenever he was around, and she complied, no matter how uncomfortable they were. He also required her to keep her long blonde hair in a braided ponytail when they were at home. Out in public, he instructed her to wear it down. The strands landed squarely on the top of her bottom. She needed little makeup; her porcelain skin always had a pinkish glow, and revealed her age.

Once he made it to the door, she threw her arms around his neck, pulling him in for a kiss that was all tongue, teeth, and saliva. Sloppy, just the way he liked it. He fisted her pony tail and roughly yanked her head back to look at her, biting her neck as she gasped. After righting her, she shrugged off his aggression and followed him into the house, touching her fingers to her sore lips, then placing a palm on her neck.

"Where have you been? I made dinner, and it's gotten cold," she half laughed, half whined pursing her lips.

He walked into the room, removing his sport coat, and tossing it on the floor. "I had a stop to make." Miguel loosened his tie, ripped it off, and threw that on the floor. He kicked off his shoes, leaving a trail of articles from the hallway to the living room. Bianca scrambled behind him, picking up the pieces of discarded clothing. "Leave it on the floor."

"Why? It looks messy. I want our home to be neat and clean." The woman carried a bewildered expression, as though she waited for something. Something she might want him to say, that deep down, she knew he never would.

What Bianca wasn't aware of was that he would always be the same narcissistic person he always was. She was so naïve, that it never dawned on her that she could never change him, and now it was too late.

Ignoring his order to leave the mess right where it was, she quickly and quietly picked up the pieces and set them down on the nearest chair. "Can I get you a drink or anything? I can reheat dinner." The woman stood still, with her hands folded in front of her, waiting for instructions. Her feet were cramping in her shoes.

By now, Miguel had thrown himself in the corner of the couch, turned on the television, and unzipped his pants. He stared blankly into the screen, and without looking at her, commanded her to kneel.

Carmen and Carlos reached the hospital within minutes and leaped from the truck, running for the emergency room doors where they found Jose hoofing in front of the waiting room chairs. "What happened?" asked Carmen.

"I'm not sure. They called an ambulance because she

couldn't stand."

"Has anyone said anything?" asked Carlos.

"No. I got here about ten minutes ago. She's in surgery."

"Jose. Do you think it's the baby?" Carmen asked, fearing she already knew the answer. Her hands trembled. "Come on, sit."

"I don't know. I hope not."

The three took turns sitting and pacing until a short while later, a surgeon came out.

Jose froze in his seat while Carmen and Carlos stood. "What happened?" asked Carmen.

"Jose. Gabriela is going to be alright. She got here just in time."

Jose stood, but couldn't speak. His body quaked, releasing the dread he'd been holding. With a loud discharge of air, he bent over, placing his hands on his knees, then stood straight again. A flood of tears spilled down his cheeks.

The doctor explained that Gabby's appendix burst just as they'd reached it on the operating table.

"What about the baby?" asked Jose.

Once they'd left the hospital, Carmen quivered at the end of the truck's bench seat. Carlos could feel the vibration of the bench under him and looked over at her as she stared out the window picturing herself in the first car of a rollercoaster; everything is alright until it reaches the top, then drops you and you feel like your insides were left behind. Once you think you're alright again, another loop.

Carmen pondered all the positive changes that drew her to move to New Cuba. She reflected on how much everything has changed since her arrival. How much *she* changed. And now this. She was certain this would ruin everything. Somehow, Miguel would find a way to make her suffer like he had so many times before.

Carlos remained silent, waiting for her to be ready to speak. Carmen shifted from one leg to the other, blowing out enough air to fill quite a few balloons. She bent forward, searing her forehead on the hot dashboard, causing her to twitch back up.

"Okay. I can see something's eating at you and I'm trying to wait, but I can't stand to see you this way."

"Pull over."

"We're almost home."

"I don't want to bring this into our home."

That statement jabbed right through him like some jagged, wayward lightening leaving a rip he hoped wasn't permanent. It's points stabbing every nerve on the way through. Whatever it was, was bad enough that she didn't want to taint their happy home. "Alright." Carlos found a shady spot and shifted into park.

"I realize I have discussed very little of my past with you." Carlos didn't speak. He listened as she began with the admission. "My husband...ex-husband, is in town." Carlos decided long ago that he would never ask about her husband. It just wasn't worth rehashing something that didn't matter. Not to him.

"I don't understand. Why is this..."

"Miguel's a doctor. He got assigned to the hospital in Pinar. When I went to see Juan and Pilar, he walked into the room to check on him. Juan was his patient."

"I guess I still don't understand. Why is this an issue? Did he try something?"

"Miguel likes to…create problems everywhere he goes. He's never satisfied until he's ruined everyone's life, and turned everyone against everyone else. I never noticed it until much later, but he'd befriend people, then bad mouth them behind their backs until he'd get everyone around him to hate them as well."

"Quite a narcissist."

"That's what my son Tony said."

"Well. The only thing you told *me* was that he left you because he said you were too old. Am I remembering that correctly?"

"Yes. But there was *so* much more." Carmen closed her eyes tight, then opened them again, staring out the front windshield before turning toward him, her eyes hooded and red.

Carlos pulled her close to him in the truck. Carmen leaned in, nestling her cheek against his chest. "It'll all be okay. You'll see."

"I stayed as long as I did for the kids. I wanted them to have their father around. When he decided I wasn't good enough anymore, it was a relief. He left, so technically, I wasn't the bad guy."

"Your kids would have understood."

"No. There were aspects of our life I can never share…with anyone. Especially my children."

"You don't have to." Carlos waited for her to say something, anything.

"I don't know. This whole thing just…blindsided me."

"I hope you don't have to see him again. He'll do his time at the hospital and leave."

"Because of everything he did, our kids don't even talk to him unless they have to. After he left me for this much-much younger woman, he took their college funds away, and got one of his lawyer friends to transfer their trust funds to *her*, or so I hear."

"What a scum-bag! I don't even know…" Carlos's voice jacked-up along with his breathing. She could see anger blossoming in his face. Carlos wiped his mouth and chin as he let out a hot breath.

"There's so many things he did to us trying to prove that he's better than everyone else. Our friends no longer wanted anything to do with us. Towards the end, his dysfunctional family made us uncomfortable to be around them with their smirks and nasty looks. I don't know how I got through it."

"You're aware that he's not. You know, he's not a good person. What kind of father steals his children's education and future out from under them?"

"This one. This father. He spent a lot of time berating them. You know. That's the worst thing anyone can do. Be malicious to your own children, or any children, for that matter. He hurt them. I could have killed him for messing with my kids. He's a despicable person."

"I can see that."

"That's not all. When I started my business, he tried to sue me for part of it, claiming it was all his idea. Meanwhile, the whole thing started a couple of years *after* our divorce. And by then, we weren't speaking at all. It was over. That's what led to my next mistake."

"What mistake?"

"I had to draw money from the business to hire an attorney to dispute his claim. By the time we settled, I had only pennies left, and my business was in trouble." Carmen paused, then held up her hand. "He got nothing, by the way. But then I needed help to get it off the ground again, and that's when I met that asshole that stole the whole thing out from under me. I'm such an idiot. Too trusting."

"It's not you. There's just bad people in the world. You hope that at some point, they'll get what's coming to them."

Carmen let out an exhaustive sigh and looked up at Carlos. "I'm so lucky to have you."

"I think I won *that* lottery. Be honest with me if he approaches you. Please don't hide this. How long will he be in town?"

"He said it was a six-week rotation and would be gone before Noche Buena."

"Yeah, but Noche Buena is over three months away. I think the best we can do is pretend he's not even here. Can you forget he's on the island?"

Carmen nodded and reached her hand behind Carlos's neck, pulling him down for a soft kiss.

Chapter 16
Babyville and A Date for Saturday Night

Carmen and Carlos arrived at the hospital just in time to hear the news. "The baby is fine. We've had obstetrics run a full check, and all is well. If you have any questions, call my office." The doctor handed Jose his card, and he jutted forward, hugging the doctor, who patted him back. "Everything will be fine," he told him as he pulled him away.

Carmen and Carlos smiled and hugged Jose. "She'll be alright. If you need anything..." said Carlos.

Jose exhaled long and hard and nodded, choking back a sob. "Thanks."

"I'm going to wait to see her. I'll see you at home," Carmen said to Carlos. She gave him a peck on the cheek and a hug. She knew he had things to do and didn't want to hold him up. He said his goodbyes and headed for the ER doors. Carmen plopped down next to Jose and waited until they could see Gabby.

"Diego," said Angela. "Carmen called and Gabby and the baby are fine." She'd waited hours until he appeared at the check-in desk. Many times she'd wondered where he disappeared to throughout the day, but she didn't ask. Didn't want to seem needy or jealous.

"That's great news." Diego stared at Angela.

"What's the matter?" she asked.

Diego tapped the counter, then began rubbing at the surface as though there were a deep stain he couldn't remove. "I...I've been wanting to ask you something, but it feels like there's never a good time," he pushed away, sliding his hands into his back pockets.

Angela looked around. There were no guests in the lobby, and a calmness blanketed their space at the moment. "What's up?" She wobbled as she stacked and shuffled papers, straightened her hair, adjusted her skirt, and folded her hands over the pile she'd just accumulated and adjusted for the twelfth time since he'd stopped by.

"Can you, I mean," he took a deep breath. "Would you like to go to dinner…Saturday?" he looked up at her fast, like she might run away.

Angela halted. She'd dreamed of the moment so many times that now she wasn't sure if he'd asked her out or she'd imagined it. They'd been playing catch-me-if-you-can for months now, and she'd just about given up. "Oh."

Diego waited for her to say something, but she stood, transfixed by his strong features. Her eyes gliding over his face, his chin and neck. She loved how his muscled chin rippled when he clenched his jaw. Her once-over continued down to his chest, and she thought about what it might look like under his pressed uniform, and what it would feel like to be *that* close to him, under him. "Angela?"

"Yes. Yes. We have a room."

"What? That's not what I asked you. Will you go out to dinner with me on Saturday?" The question came out in an exasperated tone.

236

Angela shook herself from her motionless gape and robotic answer regarding a room. She tried to move, but her knees were weak, paralyzed. She felt herself leaning on the counter, and the room seemed to slide around behind Diego.

"Angela." Diego said louder than before. He scrunched his brows and angled his head so she could look into his eyes.

Angela's eyes jumped back up to his in answer. "Oh. Yes. Yes. I'd love to go out...with you...on Saturday," She could feel herself sweating under her clothes. Inside, she prayed, *'Please don't let me look nervous...'* over and over again.

Diego waited, but she was still stunned. "Are you alright?"

"Yes. It's just. Okay. What time?"

"Great." Diego beamed as he drummed on the counter. "I'll meet you here at the desk, say six-thirty, on Saturday?"

"That's good. Great. Perfect." Diego began walking away, and when his back was turned, "Um...where are we going...so I know how to dress." Angela stuttered like a fish that was just hauled up, flipping and flopping uncontrollably on a river bank. She pictured her face on a fish's body, gasping for air.

Diego turned back and she could tell he was holding in a wide smile by the way he bit his lips. "Whatever you wear will be perfect." He ogled her like a favorite dish he hadn't had in a long time. "See ya." As luck would have it, he saw no scales on the fish he'd caught.

Angela watched him walk away. His pockets did that enchanting dance she loved to watch. One of his nubuck construction boots came untied, and she called out to let him know. Then she realized it might have been a bad idea, and she looked down at the papers that were now all over the counter, and scattered on the floor.

"Thanks," he called back. As he bent to tie the laces, he wondered if she was checking him out the way he checks her out. He hoped anyway.

Carlos drove toward home, and as he passed the familiar houses, Luis saw him coming and flagged him down.

Reaching the truck window, Luis leaned in. "Hola Mijo. How's Gabby?"

"She's going to be alright. The baby too. How's Cristina feeling? I haven't seen her."

"She's okay. I'm keeping her out of the heat." He rolled his eyes, which solicited a chuckle from Carlos.

"Good luck with that," he rolled his eyes back and laughed. Luis took hold of the door handle and opened the door, then climbed up and sat inside. "Drive."

Carlos pressed his lips and then the gas. "What's up?"

"I know this is none of my business, but I know about Miguel."

"Annnd?"

"Carmen is…annoyed. Be patient with her. That guy put her and their kids through the ringer."

"I know. She told me."

"Good. That's not what I wanted to say. Don't wait."

"For what?"

"To ask Carmen to be your wife. I should have insisted Cristina's parents allow us to be together. I should have pushed harder." Luis made a fist. "It's the biggest regret of my life; letting her get away. I wasted so many years. So much time." Carlos listened as Luis's voice cracked. "Now we're old, and neither of us is worth a damn. Don't be foolish, like I was. Nothing should stand in your way. Not even Carmen."

"Okay. I hear you pop, and I understand." Carlos worried his friend had some hidden news about himself or his wife. This insistence on him proposing to Carmen happened one too many times. "Let me get you home."

By now, Cristina was outside. Luis leaned back in the truck window. "Remember what I said," and he waved a stern finger. Once they went inside, "What did you say to him?"

"Nothing. Stop trying to control everything."

"Look who's talking! What did you say?"

"Just that I love you with all my heart." Luis swung around and stared into her eyes. "That I've always loved you. Every day. Even when we were apart."

Cristina looked into Luis's eyes and beamed. "I love you, mi amor." The two hugged and kissed as though they'd just started out; young and uninhibited. "No meddling. I mean it, viejo." Cristina laughed, knowing full well what Luis had done. Calling him 'old man' in both English and Spanish was now his pet-name.

A few hours later, Jose and Carmen could see Gabby. She was still a little groggy when she saw the two of them standing over her on either side of the hospital bed. "Huh, the baby!" she yelled, rising and grasping at her abdomen, then winced at the sting of her stapled stomach.

"The baby's fine. It was your appendix," said Jose as he helped her back down onto the pillow.

"I'm so relieved you're alright. Can I get you anything?" asked Carmen.

"No. I'm okay. Just tired. I want to go home," her eyes pleaded with Jose to get her out of there. It wasn't the first time she'd been in the hospital in recent years and she always felt like she was being punished; to be kept away from people she loved.

"The doctor said you're staying the night and you can go home in the morning. No arguing." Jose was firm. He had to be, since she ignored anything that was for her own good.

"But, the restaurant..."

"The restaurant is running like a well-oiled machine. Everything in its place, and everyone doing their thing. There's no reason for you to be there," Carmen tried easing her worries. "Besides, I keep checking in and they are so well trained, I just get in their way."

"I'll be here until the three of us can all go home," said Jose. Carmen stayed for a little while longer, then took an Uber back to the hotel. She smiled as she looked out the window, relieved that her friend was recuperating and that her baby had survived. Her mind wandered to Babyville, where she starting thinking about the baby shower and the baby's room. Then, to all the things a baby would need.

Boy or girl? Breast or bottle feed? Would they be the 'it takes a village' type of parents, or the dreaded newfangled parents that joined parenting support groups online and only followed the advice of the 'online community,' family be damned?

She couldn't help but think of when *she* wanted *her* kids. Carmen was thrilled to have her parents and in-laws involved. It made her kids' lives all the better, the bonds of family strengthening them. Then her mind drifted to other, darker places.

Getting pregnant was an ordeal for Carmen. Her sister got pregnant when the wind blew, but she wasn't as lucky. She remembered the excruciating tests. Most technicians described the tests as, 'you'll feel some pressure.' Carmen believed they were confusing their adjectives.

The endometrial biopsy involved the scraping of uterine tissue. This test would check to see if the uterine lining was thick enough for a fertilized egg. Not 'some,' but lots of pressure. The hysteroscopy wasn't as bad, but still uncomfortable, to say the least, with lots and lots of pressure.

But the worst was the hysterosalpingogram. The doctor called it HSG for short, and used the phrase, 'you'll feel a little pressure.' It was the most erroneous description she'd ever heard since there was tremendous pressure. Carmen called it the 'medieval-torture-device-constructed-by-hell for women who couldn't produce an heir.'

The design of this test had the technician insert tubes into the cervix, uterus, and fallopian tubes -all at the same time- along with a camera that would help the doctor find any obstruction that might impede the progress of an egg once it left the ovary. On the end of each tube, a dye filled balloon would be 'blown,' covering everything in enough dye to light up the place.

In those days, they called it, 'getting your tubes blown.' After the test, they handed Carmen a maxi pad (that she felt was more appropriate for horses) and told her she 'might have some spotting.' By the end of the day, she couldn't even stand and had to lie down. She mused how their use of the word 'spotting' was quite inaccurate.

Carmen shook off the images of all those painful days, replacing them with memories of her children. It was all worth it. Every scrape of her uterus, every tube inserted with 'some pressure,' was all irrelevant. Her kids were worth every bit of pain she felt and every trickle of blood she shed.

Just then, the cab pulled up to the hotel. As she exited her car door, Phoenix had already sprinted down the steps, meeting her halfway. "Hi my sweet girl," she bent for a hug, "What's happening?" Phoenix's answer, of course, involved prancing alongside Carmen, nuzzling up to her hand, and capering her way into the hotel lobby like she owned the place, then plopping back in her spot next to the check-in desk by Angela.

On the front porch, Carmen chatted up some of her guests,

242

creating familiarity with them she was certain would bring repeat business and word-of-mouth accolades. As she listened, her thoughts rolled around how everything was once again right in the world, and she sighed.

Inside the hotel lobby, she spotted Angela, whose smile and complexion attempted to give away all her secrets. "Hey. So, what's with that smile?" she pointed. Angela turned crimson before she could even speak. Her hands went up, covering her hot cheeks. "Wow, I don't think I've seen that shade of red."

Not able to hold it in any longer, "Diego asked me out. We're going out Saturday night." Angela was giddy with excitement, bouncing up and down and fast-clapping her hands.

Carmen smiled from ear to ear. "Reaallly?" her face turned sideways, shooting her a provocative smirk.

Angela froze and said in a whisper, "Yes. Oh. No. Is it alright?" her brows knit as she looked at Carmen, not daring to blink.

"Is what alright?"

"Employees dating," she whispered. "You know, all that 'workplace' stuff," she looked around.

"Oh. Yes. It's alright. Here. If it doesn't work out, you'll have to flip a coin for your job. I don't want any animosity on premises. Understand?"

"Yes. Yes. I'll let Diego know."

"Try not to be so serious," Carmen said then walked away.

"Oh, Carmen. I forgot. You have a message from a Ms. Sanchez. She called several days ago, but with everything that was happening, I didn't get a chance to give it to you. She was asking if you gave any thought to what she said, but wouldn't elaborate."

Carmen took the slip of paper where Angela had written the information. "Ugh. That's the realtor I pulled my listing from a couple of years ago. I don't know what her deal is. From now on, if she calls, tell her you'll give me the message, but don't bother writing anything down."

Angela looked up at her boss. Carmen's mouth turned down in the corners and she pressed her lips tight. Not a side she'd seen of her before; not even the day she had to remove the people who were having sex in the pool. Her boss walked around happily talking with patrons, or with Carlos, or just...there. This new Carmen was someone not to be trifled with. "Alright." Angela answered her in a semi-silent tone and didn't ask questions. If she wanted her to know why it bothered her, she would have said something. Carmen tore the message and flung it on the marble tabletop before walking away.

Carmen floated toward the kitchen, already forgetting the message from the realtor. She'd seen Angela and Diego's romance budding every day since the day she hired Angela, and Angela took one gander at Diego. She saw it the day Maria intruded on Gabby and Jose's engagement party, and every time she put them together on a project. Carmen laughed, thinking her matchmaking skills were perfectly honed.

Outside, the sun was beginning its gradual decline, settling behind some ominous dark clouds. Once in a while, a few rays peeked through, blinding anyone looking up. Carmen turned back and sat on one of the porch sofas. She looked out over the grounds as she had so many times before, grateful for the little things that now make up the life she'd chosen. Her heart swelled, and she placed a gentle hand to her chest, looking up, thinking about her father's gift.

The sound of children frolicking in the cool waters of the pool got her attention, and she glanced to her left. She could make out parents begging their kids to come out and get ready for dinner. Like *her* mother had done with *her*, and *she* had once done with her own kids.

Echoes of bygone days bounced around her mind. It was time her kids came for a visit. They hadn't been able to be there at the same time since she'd moved to New Cuba. The couple of times they visited were quick weekends, and they were off on their next adventure. She desperately craved having her family together, all in one place, all at the same time. She'd set aside a date and insist they all gather.

The sun glinted off one of the domed panels on the conservatory roof, blinding her. The once so imposing structure, now a stately edifice, was an invaluable accent for the hotel. She looked up at the center. Over the top, she could make out the exhaust from the restaurant kitchen, a strange aroma filling the air.

She looked right toward the ceiba tree and a soft breeze blew through her hair that smelled like summer rain. Hot and green, like fresh, cut grass. The dark cloud undulated closer.

In the distance, she could hear sirens closing in. She stood at a gradual pace, placed one hand on her waist and the other across her forehead, shielding her eyes from the setting sun. Her gaze tracked a rush of fire engines up the restaurant driveway, and an explosion shook the ground, tossing furniture and pulsating up her legs.

Chapter 17
Sirens and A Basket of Baby Stuff

Carmen ran to the edge of the deck, near the tree, dodging the furniture that had fallen over. She peered around the corner of the conservatory toward the restaurant and covered her mouth.

Black smoke billowed from the rear of the building. The wind blew ash toward where Carmen stood on the patio, and she covered her nose and mouth. Carlos came up right behind her, startling her when he wrapped his arms around her waist, and she screamed. Turning to look at him, "Oh my God! Why is this happening?" she cried.

"I don't know. We need to stay back here in case there's another explosion. Don't forget, there's propane back there," said Carlos.

"Gabby," Carmen broke down. Carlos turned her, cocooning her in his arms until nothing could sneak through and hurt her. "Why does this keep happening?" she buried herself in his chest, her body shaking. "What has anyone to gain by blowing things up?"

"I don't know, but someone needs to do something."

It was a stroke of luck that it was a Monday afternoon. The one night a week the restaurant is closed. If the restaurant had been open, Gabby's employees and customers might have been injured or killed. Carmen could have been inside on one of her check-ins, and Jose might have been making the rounds just the same.

As soon as they arrived, the fire department turned off the underground propane. The men scrambled to connect the fire hoses to the onsite water line, delivering over two hundred gallons of water per minute, extinguishing the flames that shot through the roof.

By the time the fire was put out, the kitchen had been destroyed, as well as all the restaurant's equipment and food supply. Carmen was thankful she'd insisted Gabby purchase enough insurance to cover something like this. She and Carlos stood just outside the perimeter of the disaster, waiting for someone to give them information.

The fire chief walked the periphery of the building, ensuring there were no hot spots remaining once they quelled the blaze. He spotted Carmen and Carlos walking toward the front of the restaurant and met them halfway.

"Hello. I'm Carmen. This is my property."

"Carlos."

"Hi. Lieutenant Smith, I'm the Fire Marshall." He shook both their hands. "We got it under control. Any idea what might have happened?"

"No. The restaurant is closed on Mondays," said Carmen.

The lieutenant turned and looked at the building. "I think the fire started in the kitchen. Was someone working?"

"No. Gabby wanted one day a week that no one was to come in for work."

"Well. It's definitely a propane fire. Here's my card." The lieutenant's quick assessment and apparent dismissal left them both a little dumbfounded. He was a short, rotund sort of man with a receding hairline. With a name like 'Smith,' and his complexion, they knew he wasn't Cuban. He seemed a little put out that he had to come out to extinguish the fire. Both Carmen and Carlos looked quizzically at each other and shook their heads at his shortness.

"What's that about?" questioned Carlos.

Jose put everyone on notice; Gabby was not to hear a word about the explosion. Fortunately, Gabby was none the wiser about what had happened since the obstetrician put her on bedrest and only her friends visited.

Her fiancé continued to reassure her that the restaurant was in expert hands and business was going well. All the while, Jose hurried his team to put it all back together before she demanded to see the place. They could start as soon as the fire marshal cleared the investigation.

Meanwhile, Carmen kept her busy in Babyville. She'd brought over magazines and books to help pass the time. She'd gone shopping and filled a basket with neutral baby items to help keep Gabby's mind off the restaurant. There were white onesies, a package of soft colored binkies, a few bottles, a sound machine, and assorted board books and rattles. The hodgepodge all lay on top of the softest baby blanket Gabby had ever felt.

Gabby picked up each item, holding them up and giggling at whatever caught her fancy; the tiny size of a newborn onesie, the black, white and red fabric rattle, and the sound machine. "Isn't it too soon for a sound machine?"

"I thought you could use it to relax in the meantime," laughed Carmen.

Best of all was the basket. Carmen had the overlapping part of the yellow gingham fabric liner embroidered, 'Little One Martinez' in a brown color. "Aw, that is so sweet," cooed Gabby. "Jose will love it."

The rest of the day they talked about Carmen's experiences with getting pregnant and childbirth, and all the little things in between, and the many little things since. Carmen avoided any of the big things.

"By the way, my kids are coming in a couple of weeks," Carmen told Gabby, her voice squeaky high with a little too much excitement. "They're all coming at the same time."

"Wow. The last time they came, it was just one at a time. That's exciting." Gabby grabbed her notebook.

"What are you doing?" asked Carmen.

"Planning a menu for when they're here."

"You're not about to get up from this bed. Do you understand that at your age…"

"Stop. Don't say it."

"I just don't want you to have to go through losing this baby because you think it's important to cook. Let it go. Focus on growing this Little One." Carmen patted Gabby's belly. Gabby tossed the pen and notebook on the nightstand, landing with a whack. Ever since that day, Gabby called the baby 'Little One.'

"Good. You'll see. It's only a few months. You'll be back to yourself in no time at all."

The next day was Pilar's turn. She showed up with several boxes of leftover baby items from when Lily was a baby.

"What's all this?" asked Gabby.

"Cleaning supplies. Time to clean up this place."

"What? Why?"

"No. Baby stuff, ya goof. Do you think I'd bring you cleaning supplies?"

Gabby rolled her eyes and giggled. "No, I guess."

After three trips to her car, the two spent the afternoon going through boxes and organizing the booty Pilar had brought over into neutral colors and girl colors. "This is all so…great. Thank you so much. If it's not a girl, I'll return the rest."

"No. Hold on to it. The next one might be."

"Let's not talk about 'next one.' So, how are you doing, Pilar?" asked Gabby.

"What do you mean?" Pilar looked away.

"Well. It took you a long while to gather all this stuff. I'm thinking you've got to have some feelings going on in there."

Pilar expelled a very loud breath. "I've talked myself through most of it. Eduardo is gone. He wouldn't want me mourning forever or wallowing in self-pity. Not so sure he'd want to see me with someone else, either. My girls are growing up without their father."

Pilar sniffed, then put down the pink dress she'd been holding. She ran her fingers over the lace ruffle at the bottom, then looked over at Gabby. "But they are growing up so fast. Rose is driving me crazy about her Quincé." Then she held up the pretty pink dress once again. "Before I know it, they'll be off to college."

"But first, Rose will want a car." Gabby smiled.

"I am not ready for that." Pilar shook her head. Gabby chuckled.

"It's alright. You need to have something for yourself."

"I know. I'm okay. Don't worry."

Gabby heard Pilar's words, but who knew the truth?

A few days later, Sergeant Rodriguez called Jose. "I have the report from the fire marshal. It would appear the explosion was an accident. There was no clamp on the intake and water got in the line."

"I clamped those myself. Could someone have removed them?" said Jose.

"It's possible. Do you think someone was out to sabotage the restaurant?"

"I think anything is possible these days. Don't you?"

The sergeant set a time to meet with Jose and the fire marshal to examine the point of origin for himself. The following morning, they all met in the back of the burned out building. Jose went over to the gas lines. "These were clamped. I tied them off myself," he repeated for the benefit of the Fire Marshall Smith.

The men moved debris from around the pipes that lead from the ground connection. "Here," said Smith. He squatted down and picked up several clamps. "They've been cut. See here, the clean edge? I'll have to change my report to arson." The man left without warning, leaving Jose and Juan to work things out for themselves.

Jose paced, rubbing his forehead and pulling back his curly brown hair. "Who would have done this?"

"Can you think of anyone who might want to hurt Gabby or yourself?"

"No." Jose turned and walked in the opposite direction, before whipping around. "Yes. That woman. Maria. She was here on opening night. Created a scene, then left without eating the meal she'd ordered and paid for. Crazy."

"I've seen her. But why? What motive would she have to destroy this place?"

"I don't know. I know she's always had an irrational thing for Carlos, but this has nothing to do with him. He only designed the landscaping, and eaten here a handful of times." Jose continued to scratch his head. "That *can't* be it."

"I'll look into it. Hang tight," he started walking away, then turned. "Oh, how's Gabby feeling? I heard she had a scare."

"Yes. She's fine. It was her appendix. Baby's good. As luck would have it, she's on bed rest or this would kill her." Jose had his hands on his waist.

Juan took his notes and left. There wasn't anything else to investigate, so he was clear to rebuild the burned out areas. Jose's only focus was to fix it before Gabby found out.

Just then, Carlos showed up. "Hey. I saw the sergeant leaving. What happened?"

"Someone cut the clamps on the gas line. Water got in."

"Wow. Why would anyone do that?"

"I don't know." Jose looked hard at Carlos.

"What?"

"That woman. Maria. Do you think she would have done something like that?"

"Maria? Not a chance. She's just a lost and lonely person. No one wants anything to do with her. I can't imagine her grabbing a pair of wire cutters, breaking in, and clipping the clamps. I don't even think she's smart enough."

"Maybe you're right. Juan is going to check that lead, just in case."

"I'm sure he won't find anything incriminating her in all this." Just then, Carlos noticed Gabby's knife set, picked it up, and rolled it around in his hands.

"Well, that's lucky," said Jose as Carlos handed him the knife set they'd given her as a restaurant warming gift.

"I'll say," said Carlos. "I'm happy to help with this whenever you're ready," he pointed.

"We can't let her find out about this. It will crush her."

"Of course. I know Carmen is keeping her occupied. We'll make sure it's back to normal before she can make her way over here."

254

Juan arrived at Maria's house within minutes, planning to question her about her whereabouts on Monday. He figured she must have just gotten home because she'd parked her blue Nissan out front with the windows down. Juan knocked on the door and waited. He tried calling her name, but she didn't answer. He walked to the side window and peeked in.

"Maria Gomez. It's Sergeant Rodriguez. I need to speak to you. Maria?"

Juan walked the perimeter of the house through overgrown weeds and brush, over discarded plastic containers and furniture, and scouring through every mildewy window. The back door and the transom were both locked, and he couldn't see inside. It wasn't until he reached the tiny bathroom window that a pungent smell almost knocked him to the floor.

The small window was open a smidge, but high on the wall where he wasn't able to look inside. He knew that odor. Too many times he came upon it by accident. Too many times that same smell was called in to the precinct, sending him to follow up on the call.

Juan raced around to the front of the house while calling for backup, and pulled open the metal door gate. With the weight of his body, he threw himself on the wood door. A few slams later, the jam splintered, and the door gave way. The stench causing Juan to gag. He covered his nose and mouth with his shirt, and his eyes watered, impairing his vision to where he had to blink away the sting. Still, he trudged on.

As soon as he got his bearings, he spotted the smear of blood that dripped from the kitchen wall, and drew his weapon. The red stain swiped down to the floor, where it streaked through the hallway. He followed the clumps of blood and mangled hair that left an easy to follow trail. Three sets of footprints stamped on the terrazzo floor. The closer he got to the bathroom, the stronger the odor. Juan tugged at his collar to cover his nose as he held his breath.

Behind him, he could hear the sirens as squad cars screeched to a stop, spitting gravel and dust into the air, and officers drawing guns, moving toward the open front doorway, calling out his name.

The bathroom door was ajar. Slowly, he used his foot to swing it open and peek inside while holding his weapon. Several walls had splatters where it appeared a body was heaved against it. There, in the tub, was Maria's mangled body. She couldn't have survived. "All clear," yelled Juan, his mouth and nose still covered while he swung his head.

Maria's fingers were all broken, bent in unnatural directions. The bones in her arms protruded through her skin, and her knees were bent backward like ostrich ankles. One leg was missing a foot, and when another officer entered the bathroom, Juan closed his eyes and said, "No one deserves this."

As the others approached, he could hear running steps out the front door and one of them retching on the porch. The splash of lunch slapping the ground. At the door, he holstered his gun, as did the other officers. "Call the coroner."

Pilar had stayed home that following Friday. She hadn't seen Juan in a few days, and wanted to make him a special dinner. After the shooting, she'd taken care of him until he was up and around. Then he went back to work, and things went back to normal, though cooled off.

Tonight, she was making a simple arroz con pollo with beer. In her opinion, it was the only way to make the dish. Juan was bringing fresh Cuban bread and the whiff coming from her kitchen even caught Cristina and Luis's attention.

"Hola Pilar. Are you making arroz con pollo?" she could feel his smile through the receiver.

"Yes, Luis. I made some for the two of you as well. Juan is coming for dinner. Would you like to join us?"

"We'd love that. Cristina, Pilar invited us to dinner with Juan," Luis called over his shoulder.

"No, old man. We're not intruding on their night. Give me that phone." Cristina grabbed the receiver out of his hand. "Thank you Pilar. We wouldn't dream of encroaching on your night." She shot her husband a look that seared.

"It's no intrusion. We'd love for you to join us. See you then." Pilar laughed as she hung up. She fantasized that she and Juan would one day be the old couple across the street and the whole idea surprised her, making her stop to ponder what that meant.

Soon, Cristina and Luis were at the door. Cristina had her coconut cookies, and Luis brought over a bottle of Cardenal Mendoza. The brandy came in a tall, narrow cork box, and though he knew she didn't drink brandy, he brought it with him, anyway.

"This isn't for you, Pilar. I want to have a drink with Juan."

"It's all yours Luis."

Cristina and Luis stood together, then went to the back to see the girls. "Hola. What are you three up to?" asked Cristina.

"Hola Mima and Pipo. We're reading this story about a girl who no one wants, so she has to live alone, far away from everyone," explained Lily.

"That sounds like a very sad story," said Luis.

"It was. In the beginning. Now she's found a whole new bunch of people, and they seem friendly, so far," said Rose. "She's a warrior."

The old couple stayed in the room listening to Rose read aloud to her sisters. Sometime later, they heard the front door open, then close, and looked at each other and smiled. It was quiet in the other room, and their smiles grew as they straightened, then looked at each other with a knowing glance, until they heard Pilar scream.

Chapter 18
New Regulation and Strange Stairwells

During the early boon in New Cuba, people quickly purchased and developed land, causing real estate prices to soar. The promise of a better place and a fresh start attracted many people to make the move. Start over. It was this promise that kept everyone in Cuba on their toes. The welcoming of people from different walks of life did not squash or diminish the essence of the Cuban people. In fact, it was the soul and aura of them that attracted people from all over the world the most.

One example was Fire Marshal Smith. His wife had left him for a woman she'd met online. They had no children, and he didn't even fight to change her mind. He just stepped aside so she could leave.

Soon, he'd grown bitter at seeing her happy with her new wife, and moved as far away as possible. The humiliation hit his male ego right where it hurt.

One day, there was a posting for fire marshal for the city of Pinar del Rio in New Cuba on the job board. Without hesitation, he applied for the assignment. Little did he realize what he was signing up for.

Decaying wiring, decrepit plumbing, and an infrastructure needing revamping was just the beginning. He recognized when time caused a breakdown and when it was something more sinister.

The deliberate damage of random buildings across the state didn't go ignored. In no time, the U.S. government sent in the

National Guard to keep order, and new legislation ruled to deport anyone guilty of treason and subversiveness to live on La Isla de la Juventud.

This island remained Cuban territory, and not annexed as part of *New* Cuba. The land there held no value for the U.S., and therefore it was an unnecessary burden. The old Presidio Modelo prison sat empty on the island, and this would be the revolutionists' new home.

Soon, most of the die-hard communists living on the other side of the wall at Guantanamo gave in and moved to the island as well. Not all were violent criminals, but wanted to keep living the same wretched existence they believed was the best way to live. Bartering for necessities of food and clean water was their way of life, and they saw no better way to live.

The streets in Guantanamo echoed an emptiness that beat in the agonal rhythm of a dying heart. The only sound anyone could hear was the periodic arguing of malcontents.

Small groups of subversives gathered in various locations plotting an end to the U.S. occupation in what they believed was *their* Cuba. Lucrecia, a long supporter of the socialist agenda, rallied behind their new flag. An amalgamate of the Cuban flag with a black scorpion setting it ablaze appeared on fliers and tagged on buildings everywhere.

Anytime the image cropped up, crews painted over them, removing all graffiti. Whomever found fliers with the same symbol would throw them into the trash where they belonged. There was no conversation to fuel its ongoing aim, and the Guard was swift in collecting those responsible, yet Lucrecia seemed to get away every time.

Pilar felt sick after hearing the news about Maria, though Juan spared her the sickening details of how they found her, she only imagined how bad it was from the look on Juan's face. "Let's not tell Carmen and Carlos just yet. They're busy with Jose to fix the restaurant and Gabby's pregnancy, it might just be too much to hear."

"Alright. If you think that's a good idea, I'll keep it to myself."

"Lucrecia's fingerprints were found in the house. Do you know if she knew Maria?"

"No. Maria was not someone…"

"I understand. Apparently, no one has seen Lucrecia in months. We need to question her about Maria and the other fingerprints we found at the house."

"I'm sure you know what kind of person she was. Those prints could be anyone's."

"Good morning," said Carlos as he nuzzled in behind Carmen.

"Good morning to you."

"We still didn't open that door we found." Carlos grabbed the keys from the nightstand and jingled them.

Carmen turned toward him with a wicked smile. "Okay. Let's grab a bite and get over there."

As they approached the rusty door in the rear of the glasshouse, Phoenix jotted over, sniffing the ground and the casing around the sealed opening.

Carlos stopped and pulled Carmen's hand, and she turned toward him. He wrapped his left arm around her waist and hitched her forward. He slid his right hand up her spine to her neck, and with a meager slip, he dipped her head back, kissing her so profound, that her legs went slack. "I love you, Carmen. Phoenix, pre-sent."

Phoenix trotted over to where Carlos called and "presented" a small box at Carmen's feet, then sat, and looked up at her, wagging her tail as she waited for Carmen to pick up the offering.

"What's this?" she bent and picked up the wooden box. Wiping the slobber from the lid, she examined the intricate dragonfly carving on the outside. "Is this another box you found?"

Carlos tipped his head, dropped to one knee, looked up at her, and said, "I love you, Carmen. From the moment I saw you in your kitchen. That day you stood on the chair screaming at rats, then at me. The andiron, the small moments that made up every day until this moment and so many other moments, are woven through every fiber of my being. I can't live a minute without you close to me, and I don't want to. I'd like to spend the rest of my life making you happy. Will you marry me?"

Carmen's mouth dropped so far she'd need special equipment to hoist it back up. "Uhmm..." she stared down at Carlos's imploring expression, while he held his breath. "Yes! Yes!"

He grabbed her legs, hugging them tight and pulled her down to the ground, then wrapped her hair around his fingers and kissed her until they were both breathless.

"Here," Carlos took the oversized wood box, opening it to reveal a large, heart-shaped diamond. On both sides of the heart lay amber colored diamonds of varying shapes set in a dragonfly pattern. He removed it from its mounting and slid it on her finger.

"Carlos. This is…" Carmen's eyes stung and when she looked up at him, a waterfall of tears came down her cheeks. They'd forgotten all about the door they were opening.

"Are you going to call your kids?" asked Carlos.

"They're coming in a few days. We'll surprise them. What about you?"

"They were just here. We'll FaceTime later."

"Oh, let's bring dinner over to Gabby's and give them all the news there. We'll invite Pilar and Juan, and Luis and Cristina," said Carmen.

"That's a great idea. Now. Let's open up this bad boy. See what's behind door number two."

Jose and his crew stopped every job they were working to devote all their resources to rebuilding the restaurant. He'd given his current clientele complimentary meals at the restaurant, and they knew how important it was to maintain a civilized state, and continue to grow New Cuba, so they waited for their jobs to continue. Besides, Jose had vowed to complete their jobs on time and they trusted him.

"Jose, I'm bored. I want to see my restaurant."

"Gabby. The doctor hasn't cleared you. Please give it a couple more weeks. It's important. I brought you all the newest issues of every culinary magazine I could find. Why don't you see if you can work out some new recipes?"

Gabby was tired of sitting around and even more exhausted from thinking about recipes. She wanted action. She wanted to be in the nitty-gritty of it. To get her hands on her knives and slice and dice and julienne. She wanted to season and sear and sous-vide. Carmen's family was due to arrive the next morning, and she wanted to be the one to prepare the menu and the food. It's all she could think of since she'd gotten the news.

As soon as Jose left for the day, she got up from bed and got herself together. Nothing fancy, she was already showing and was excited to be seen. She promised herself that she wouldn't stand too long or lift anything too heavy. She climbed into her van and puttered off.

Zipping down the hotel driveway, crunching over gravel, she saw how busy the place was and slowed down to observe. There were people milling around on the front patio, and some walking around the perimeter to the back. "This is what Carmen dreamed of the day we talked about making this a hotel, Little One." Gabby smiled and she filled with contentment. She drove toward the back at a moderate speed since she didn't want to get caught.

Peering around the corner, she spots Jose's pickup and screeched to a stop. He was talking to one of his captains and he didn't look too happy.

Piles of burned wood littered one end, and piles of blackened kitchen equipment the other. Groups of construction workers carried fresh wood and supplies into the building. Her heart raced, and she placed a hand on her belly. "We're okay, Little One." Gabby couldn't help herself. She drove on, parking in a shady spot under one of the ceiba trees. Exiting the car, her breath caught as she bit back the gargantuan lump in her throat. The smell of burned everything hung thick in the air; wood, metal, and gas, mixed with food. She spotted Jose, who hadn't seen her coming. She struggled with the urge to drop to the floor and curl up in a ball when he turned to see her trudging up.

"Babe, what are you doing here? You should be in bed." He hurried over, taking her forearm, then giving her a hug.

"What happened here, Jose?" Her eyes stung as she fought the tears that were sure to spring when she heard the news. She'd been hormonal for days and cried at the smallest bits of news and even tearful supermarket commercials.

"Come on. Sit down." They sat under the large outdoor pavilion. He radioed Jessy at the bar and sent for some ice water to cool Gabby down and keep her hydrated.

"Jose. Please. What happened?" she pleaded.

He spent the next twenty minutes giving her every detail of the last week. "I've ordered replacement kitchen equipment, we've already eradicated the damage, and I've clamped the lines again. I even put them under a lock box. It won't happen again."

Gabby attended to every word Jose said and nodded. Her mind raced with visions of her employees getting blasted apart, along with anyone else in the vicinity. This was too close to home. It *was* home. She glanced up at the neon sign at the front of the building. "People are going to be afraid to come here, aren't they?"

"No. Don't be silly. People have been calling to make reservations for when we reopen. Now. We've talked about this. You need to rest. Let me get you home."

"I can drive home." Gabby stood and began walking back to her van.

Her downtrodden expression devastated Jose. "Hey. We have a wedding to plan. This is the perfect time."

Gabby turned around and walked back to him. She put her arms around him and kissed him long and soft. Resigned. "Okay. I'll call Carmen and Pilar."

"Rose. Rose?" Pilar called to Rose, who'd locked herself in a dressing room, trying on dress after dress at Quincé Couture for her Quinceañera. The place had wall to wall racks of dresses in every color of the rainbow, and in every style a young lady could want. The location smelled of roses and fresh rain. "I want to see what they look like. You need to come out." Pilar held a lavender dress with lace outlined teardrops that hung in swags from around the waist.

"Ugh! Let me try them on first!" she shouted. Rose had grown into a beautiful young lady. Her long dark hair and black eyelashes emphasized her fair skin, provoking the dots of black in her hazel eyes to dance about. Pilar saw Eduardo in her daughter's eyes. His same eyes.

Rose had turned into a full-blown teenager. Every morning, she needed to be shaken awake, then hurried to get ready for school. She'd sit in front of the mirror applying layer after layer of makeup- in twelve stages- then brushing her hair, one hundred strokes on each side before leaving the house. And she wouldn't leave the house without completing this morning ritual.

Rose played less and less with her younger sisters, often snubbing them with an eye roll and a door slam. When it was convenient for her, she'd watch a movie with them or apply makeup for practice. Pilar was tiring of her attitude and threatened to cancel her Quincé if she didn't 'change her attitude.'

Every time Pilar caught herself betwixt and between one of Rose's poor dispositions, she'd catch herself echoing her own mother. Something she swore she'd never do. And here it was, creeping in again.

That thought would lead to another reminding her that her mother would never know her children, and her children would never know their grandparents, and other, more unpleasant thoughts that kept her awake night after night.

After so many years of estrangement, she didn't know if they were even alive. Being an only child herself, she couldn't understand why it was so easy for them to delete her from their lives. Nothing *her* girls could *ever* do would make her remove them. Thrown away like so much trash.

Those were the most painful. The ones that ripped at her, shredding everything. Her childhood, her education, and all the things she'd accomplished in her life. Her children.

They'd missed out on so much. It had always been a subject she side-stepped whenever Rose would ask. Daisy and Lily were far too young to ponder the bigger questions of life. One day, they'd be front and center with questions Pilar would have difficulty answering.

For now, Pilar would enjoy her children the best way she could, whenever she could. The highs and the lows and all the little things in between. A friend once told her, "You have to take the good with the bad." The good was Eduardo. The bad was her parents disowning her. She regretted nothing.

New thoughts went to what she believed she would say if they knew of Eduardo's murder. In New Cuba. What they would say if they'd witness the last two years of private hysteria, or about her new relationship, with a police officer.

An officer of the law, she could lose at any time in the line of duty. *That* was certain send them into another dimension. Pilar exhaled hard. All the anger she felt over her dismissal blew out along with all the pain she'd felt over the years. She wasn't about to allow their hate to leech into her new life.

Rose came out of the dressing room wearing a dusty pink dress with subtle lace trim bordering the bottom. Delicate lacework covered the flouncy skirting, while the oversized crinoline gave it the right amount of volume.

There were dusty pink pearls sewn throughout in no particular pattern. A classic Quincéañera dress. Pilar thought she'd choose something non-traditional, and she took one look at her and a deluge of tears flooded down her face and on her clothing. "Mami. This is the one."

At that moment, Pilar understood. Rose wanted to be the one to pick her dress with no outside influence. It was something *Pilar* wanted for her own Quincé, but her mother had chosen her dress, her theme, and every guest. She had no say, and no friends at *her* party. It was all adults. All her parent's friends.

"It's perfect, Rose," she said, and love just poured out as she marveled at her daughter. Pilar would do this differently from her mother. Rose's celebration would be all about Rose; she'd pick the guests, the food, and the music played.

Carmen spent the next while gawking at her ring. Large iron keys dangled from Carlos's hand, clanking her back to the moment.

"Ready?"

"Yes."

Taking the largest key, he slid it into the slot and turned until he heard the click. He turned the knob, and pushed the tarnished door, and it grated along the cement floor, scraping and boring along a pre-dug trough.

The other side of the door revealed the same corroded metal as the front. As they stepped through the doorway, flecks of oxidized rust tumbled off the edges and into their hair and shoulders.

While stepping over the threshold, Carlos peered through the doorway. About five feet in front of him, he saw a railing and a dark opening in the dusty ground. Carmen held his hand tight as they stepped forward and squinted into the abyss.

The two stood upright again, and Carlos shined his flashlight to the left, then to the right. The light disappeared into a long tunnel that stretched in both directions.

Carlos held on to the rust-covered iron rail and together, they looked over the edge and into the hole in front of them. The space below was swallowed in darkness; not even sunlight could reach it from the open doorway. The flashlight lit up the other side of the rail, and they could make out a set of stairs, and even more railing when they looked down.

Carmen crossed her arms and held her stomach as she peeked over the edge. There were no sounds, save the whistling of the wind that came from the tunnel.

"Okay. Let's walk down a few steps and see what's down there." Carlos shined his gear light onto the stairs. He'd bought it the day after the fire at Gabby's for its impressive ratings for night vision and battery. Today, he could use it for excavating.

Carlos took the first three steps down and shined his flashlight toward the opening of the cavern. He took Carmen's hand and walked down the next three steps, careful to see where he was walking in the dark.

A sinking feeling of dread crept into his chest, like something was pulling down on him. He looked over at Carmen. There was a small, almost imperceptible shake of her head. She felt it as well. Besides the heat in the space, there was an odd odor wafting from deep in the hole. One they didn't recognize. Like something old. Something long forgotten.

Chapter 19

Tunnels and Internet Cat Videos

Upon reaching the bottom of the stairs, Carmen and Carlos discovered a lower chamber. The floor was cement, and the walls were a rough grade of stucco. Electrical lines hung from the walls, held in place by bolts that were set into the plasterwork. The strange funk got stronger the further into the cavern they went.

Carefully, the couple walked along the wall until they came to a doorway. There was no door, just a flimsy shredded fabric curtain tacked along the top opening. Inside, they found old mattresses on the floor, covered in a million years' dust.

A small table on the left held a multitude of glass jars. Some sealed with something inside, some open with dried-up, malodorous contents, and yet other's, empty. Carmen sniffed and reached for an open one and Carlos grabbed her wrist just before she made any contact. "Touch nothing. We don't know what this is."

"At least we know where the smell was coming from," said Carmen.

"I'm not so sure."

Leaving the room, they found three other similar chambers with similar forgotten remnants. In one room, they found a child's toy and clothing, and the other held syringes, empty alcohol bottles, and shredded fabric. The kind used for wound dressing. "What is this place, Carlos?"

"I'm not sure."

In the fourth and final grotto, they found pictures tacked to the mortar. Carmen immediately recognized a few of the images. "These women. There were pictures of them on the mantle in the house when I arrived. I removed the frames and put them away." She chuckled, mostly to herself, then started pulling the parchment off the walls.

"What's so funny?"

"There was a picture of you with some woman."

"And?"

Carmen started laughing again. "I kept *that* picture for safety reasons. I thought, in case you were a stalker, or...a murderer, I'd have something to identify you." The laughing started again, deep and satisfying.

Carlos held a serious expression. "Oh yeah? Well, what if I *am* a stalker or a murderer? Maybe you haven't seen that side of me yet." He waggled his eyebrows, and tried to get it out as seriously as he could, but it didn't work. The laughter was contagious. And in this place. So dark and strange, full of mysteries they haven't solved yet. It was odd to find themselves in such a jovial mood.

"Who was she Carlos?"

"The woman in the picture? You'll have to show me."

"Yeah. It's in my office. What do you think this place was?" asked Carmen.

"I'm not sure. I'll ask around. Someone must know."

The two turned to leave the chamber, still giggling, when they spot a body lying on a mattress. Carmen yelped, then covered her mouth to keep from shrieking again. "We need to call the police," said Carlos.

"Who is it?"

"I can't tell. It's too decayed and I don't want to touch anything. We should leave. Come on."

The pair walked back up the stairs and locked the eroded door behind them. Carmen called the police from her cell as her hand trembled and headed inside to wait for them to arrive.

As they made their way up the steps to the hotel, they talked about the space and the person they found. Carmen did her best to forget what she'd seen and changed the subject to her ring. "My ring is beautiful. I love it."

"I had it designed just for you."

"I can see that." Together they walked in silence toward the reception area. Carmen let Angela know the police were on their way, and that she and Carlos would be in her office and to show them back.

"I'd like to see those pictures," said Carlos. "I don't know why I didn't notice them on the mantle before."

"Because you're a guyyy," she dragged out the y's "Guys don't pay any attention to that sort of stuff. You're happy if your beer is cold and the crops are coming in." Her voice dripped with sarcasm and mockery.

Carlos laughed at her supposition. "Not all of us..." he smacked her rear.

Carmen turned and looked up at him, then grabbed his hand.

"No. Not all of you." She planted a quick kiss on his soft, warm lips.

That night, Gabby and Jose met with Pilar and Carmen. After much debate, they opted for a small wedding since they were short on time. The guest list was short, but included everyone closest to them. Carmen convinced Gabby to let one of her sous chefs come up with a menu and take care of all the details.

Gabby had a rough time letting go. She looked from one to the other, then back at Jose. She was outnumbered. "Alright. I guess I have bigger things to worry about."

"Yes. Now. We know you've already picked out a dress. Let's get it altered to fit your new frame…" began Pilar.

"Please. Don't say 'new frame.' I know. I can see my *new frame*,'" she air quoted. The corners of Gabby's mouth turned down. Her depressed demeanor worried Jose. He'd watched her fidget with just about anything she could get her hands on, even preoccupying herself with internet cat videos.

"It's our wedding, babe. Let me see a smile."

"Come on Gabs. It's only temporary. You'll be back to yourself in no time. I promise," said Carmen as she glanced over at Jose. His face puckered with worry.

Gabby was unconvinced, but she nodded anyway.

Later, Pilar and Carmen talked about post-partum depression and their concerns for their friend. "If she's already like this, what will she be like once the baby comes?" asked Pilar.

"We'll stay close. Keep an eye out. She'll be okay once the

baby arrives," Carmen assured her, though on the inside, she had the same worries. "Now. Let's get on these wedding plans. We only have four weeks."

Wednesday finally arrived and Carmen and Carlos waited on the front porch of La Mariposa de Pinar del Rio for her children to arrive. Carlos picked up on every creak, crack, and tick of Carmen's rocking chair as she rocked. Tiny fly-away hairs took to the breeze as she went forward and back, escaping from her tight ponytail.

When the large passenger van turned the corner, she stood, shielding her eyes from the ardent sun. Carmen waved as though she'd been stranded, and this was the only ship she'd seen in years. "They're here!" she fast clapped.

They'd all met Carlos on a previous trip. He smiled, took her hand, and walked with her down the steps toward the approaching vehicle. From where they stopped, they could see all her kids and grandkids waving back through the large windows. Diego drove up as close as he could before setting the van in park and unlocking the doors.

As the side curtain doors opened, bodies tumbled out, jockeying to get to Carmen. She turned to look at Carlos and grinned with a glee he hadn't seen before. Her eyes glimmered a joy only a mother who missed her kids and grandkids could possess.

He released her hand so she could greet her family. The throng of people prevented him from seeing all of her. A stark contrast to his own children's visit. Behind the crowd, her mother,

Gloria, in a hat and sunglasses, looking like one of the Golden Girls. Her straw handbag said it all. Tony's wife held her arm as she carefully climbed out of the van.

"How was the ferry?" she asked.

"So fun. We had drinks," said the oldest grandchild.

"There was dancing," said the youngest.

"The vibe was so different from last time," said her son, Tony. "Hey, Carlos," he broke from the mass and walked over, extending his hand, then a quick embrace and a mutual pat on the back. Andres followed his brother and dittoed the greeting.

"How's everything?" asked Carlos. He was all smiles at the warm acknowledgment. On the inside, he dreaded her children's reaction to their news, since his kids' reaction wasn't what he'd expected.

"What's this?" screamed Hope as she held her mother's left hand. The diamond flashed in the sunlight nearly blinding anyone close by. "Hey, Mom's engaged!" she yelled to Tony and Andres who immediately went back to their mother and hugged her while Carlos took in the scene, laughing as her grandkids gave him a quick hug hello.

Carmen's face hurt from smiling. She looked back at Carlos, her eyes spoke volumes; he was the only one who could read them.

"Wait," said Hope, and she ran to over to Carlos and congratulated him with a solid hug. "I'm so happy. When's the wedding?" Her smile hitched so wide her cheeks throbbed.

"Oh, I don't know. Ask your mother," laughed Carlos. He

jacked up one eyebrow, more of a challenge than a joke.

Carmen stopped short and looked over her shoulder at her fiancé. "We'll have to find a time when all our kids are on the island at the same time."

"Hmmm. When will that be?" Tony asked, since they'd yet to meet Carlos's family.

"We'll get settled, then we'll catch up. I want to hear the story," said Hope as they headed to their rooms.

Hope's sisters-in-law agreed; they'd ambush Carmen and Carlos about it later. The entire group headed inside for their rooms.

"What's the matter?" asked Carmen. "Aren't you happy?"

"I'm sorry. I am. Really. My kids didn't have the same reaction, and I wish they had, like yours. They were so angry. So rude and mean. That's not like them. And not the way it *should* be." Carlos's brow was a tight knot that worried Carmen.

"First, it was Frank. Everyone else seemed happy. And, it's alright. They'll come around. Just give them time." She hooked her arm through his and leaned her head on his shoulder.

That evening, as the couple sat in the study with Carmen's family, they talked about all the upcoming events. Gabby and Jose's wedding and the eminent birth of their first child.

Most of all, the women went googly-eyed at hearing about the romantic proposal and Phoenix's role. The couple held hands and smiled, happy to share the moment with her family. All the while, in the back of Carlos's mind, the unpleasant FaceTime call with Frank.

Tony stood and raised his wineglass. "To Ma and Carlos. May they have a long and happy marriage."

Hope stood next. "May you continue to find joy in the little things and stay healthy and strong."

"Always the doctor, huh Hope?" said Andres, who stood as Hope sat while crossing her eyes at her brother and shooting him a long raspberry. "To Mom and Carlos. Just don't get pregnant," and he downed his whiskey in one gulp.

The room erupted in laughter. "Leave it Andres to razz," said Tony.

Carmen looked at Carlos and widened her eyes. "My son thinks I'm still able to get pregnant? I think we have bigger problems." More raucous laughter.

"Oh. I have an idea. Carlos. Why don't you get your family down here and you guys can get married this weekend? You know how hard it is for us to all get together at the same time," said Hope. Tony and Andres nodded in agreement.

Carlos looked over at Carmen, who shrugged one shoulder. "You're okay with a shotgun wedding?"

"It's not shotgun. They're right. They're all here. We're just missing your kids. It's almost the weekend. I'm sure they'd love to come."

"I think it's the perfect time," shrugged Gloria.

He stared through her. Wondering what would happen if he

called to tell them he was getting married so quickly after announcing their engagement. Carlos also realized that whenever they *did* get married, Frank was bound to be miserable. He needed to live his life, and let his son accept his choice. After a long exhale, "Let me make a quick call."

"Me too!" said Carmen, bouncing with excitement to tell Sara, Nina, and Mary about the wedding. Her kids watched her skip out of the room with her cell and instantly knew she was calling her sister and her besties.

Once Carlos's family agreed to come in for the wedding, everyone pitched in to help. They'd settled on a casual wedding, with immediate family and friends. His family arrived on the Thursday afternoon ferry, and except for Frank, they were all thrilled and excited that Carlos found love again.

"I talked to Frank," his wife Alba told her father-in-law. "It was very difficult to get him here. I told him he has this one chance to be happy for you. This one chance to move forward without trying to make you feel bad because you lived and mom didn't."

Carlos quietly took in everything Alba was telling him. He hoped her talk with Frank was effective, but Carlos knew his son, and knew how hard he took his mother's death. It wasn't something he could fix. He tried being there for him, but Carlos's move to Cuba drove a solid wedge between father and son. Frank ignored Carlos for the better part of a year. Even forbidding Alba from calling him.

"The time he cut me out of his life was almost as painful as losing his mother. I remember lying awake all night, every night, trying to imagine what I'd done to deserve what he was putting me through. Such harsh punishment. And for what? By the time I moved here, everyone had gone back to their lives. What did he expect me to do? Wait around for the grim reaper?"

"Quite an expression there," said Alba.

"Yea, Carmen uses it, more than a little a bit," they both laughed.

"Frank promised to be supportive or say nothing at all. I know he won't disappoint me," said Alba.

Carlos hugged his daughter-in-law and thanked her for trying. The worry about his son's treatment of Carmen sat hard on his shoulders.

That next morning, Carmen and Carlos agreed to meet at Gabby's for lunch with both families. Carmen was going dress shopping with Gloria and Hope, and Carlos was taking the men to a nearby haberdashery.

As they waited at Gabby's for the rest of the family, it surprised Carmen that her mother hadn't had a single negative thing to say since she arrived. It wasn't like her. She expected some sort of argument over her choice, but it never came. "Is Abuela okay?" she asked Hope when Gloria had gone to the restroom.

Hope's medical eye looked in Gloria's direction. "She looks good. Why?"

"No. Not medically. Mentally. She hasn't complained about my choices, or had a negative thing to say since she got here. It's freaking me out."

"I think Abuela is happy that you're happy. That you found someone and you won't be...alone...when she's gone," Hope shrugged.

"Is she going somewhere that I'm not aware of?"

"No. But you know. At her age. Plus, she's old generation Cuban. 'Women need to be taken care of...' and all that crap," Hope said in a deep voice while rolling her eyes in parody.

"Oh. Yea. I forgot. Well, I hope she's not holding it all in and it blows up on me later."

"I'm sure it will be fine, Ma. Just enjoy this time. It's *your* time."

Just then, the men arrived at Gabby's for lunch.

"How did it go?" Carmen asked.

Carlos described how they were all outfitted in white guayaberas and oatmeal colored linen trousers, with tan leather loafers that had slightly contrasting stitching. He told her he'd had such a great time with them he took them all for hot shaves and trims at his favorite barber shop.

"See. I told you everything would be fine. Give him time to see how great we all are," said Carmen.

"He'd be a fool not to."

Gabby was to give her sous chef the menu, and Pilar would make the rest of the arrangements. The wedding came together fast, and everyone invited would should up in time.

The Saturday morning ferry brought Sara, Nina, and Mary. "We're so happy for you!" said Sara as she squeezed Carmen.

"I knew it the second I saw that man. This was inevitable," Nina said.

"And I suspected you liked him from the moment you met him. That night on FaceTime. You were like a giddy schoolgirl with a twist of murderous psycho," laughed Mary, her eyes ogling the group.

"Very funny. All of you. Now. Here are your room keys. I'll leave you to whatever you want to do today. The wedding starts at six. See you there!" Anticipation brought tremors to Carmen's body, making her drop the key.

Chapter 20

Feeling Parenty and What's Too Formal?

The rest of the day was a flurry of planning and questions and pressure. Finally, Carmen told Pilar to just 'follow her gut.' She didn't want to worry about anything, and she knew her friend would do the best she could with the time she had. "I don't want it to consume every breath we have. We want to get married with our family and friends attending, and I don't care if there're no flowers!" she yelled at Pilar.

Minutes later, Pilar was on the phone with Gabby. "Bridezilla is a lot right now."

"That doesn't sound like Carmen?" questioned Gabby.

"Yes. She doesn't care about flowers. What bride doesn't care about flowers? Or the menu? Or the processional? Or timing? Or any other wedding planning?"

"A bride that just wants to marry the man she loves and doesn't care about the rest. Sounds like you care more than she does." Gabby hit the nail on the head. Pilar didn't realize it; she'd been planning Carmen's wedding as if it were her own.

"Wow. Okay. I hear you. I'll reassess. Thanks Gabs," and she hung up.

Gabby thought she was feeling pretty *'parenty'* right about now. She'd addressed every crisis in a very parent-like way and could say she'd been successful. Then she thought about what she could wear to the wedding, and her thoughts went to her new frame.

Hitting the redial button, "Pilar. I have nothing to wear to Carmen's wedding. You have to help me. Nothing in my closet will fit my new frame." Her sarcasm wasn't lost on Pilar. She'd been in that same spot; pregnant, with nothing to wear to an event, and feeling like a whale in a goldfish tank.

"I think I have something," said Pilar. Even though she was drowning in a sea of wedding matter, she headed home to her closet, and dug way in the back for clothes that no longer fit her. She'd lost enough weight to buy new clothing, but true to form, she couldn't get rid of 'old Pilar.' After gathering some items Gabby could wear to Carmen's wedding, she picked up the bags of her old maternity clothes and headed for Gabby's house.

"What's all this?"

"I realize I'd brought you baby stuff, but I never thought about maternity wear. You sit on the couch and go through these bags. I'll bring in the rest."

"What rest? This is a lot…" Gabby began pulling item after item from the bag and holding it in front of her body, praying they would somehow fit, when Pilar came back and closed the door behind her. "These are too small." Resigned, she dropped them back into the bag. "Do you have any that'll fit over one of the balloons at the Thanksgiving Day parade?"

Pilar laughed hard until she realized Gabby wasn't laughing. "Come on, that was funny. What is it?"

"Look at me. And I'm seven months pregnant. I'll never be myself again."

"Yes, you will." Pilar stood, grabbed the outfit Gabby was holding, and put it in front of herself. "See. It's only temporary. I could fit two of me in this right now." Gabby remained motionless. "You'll remember this conversation after you're back to normal. If you don't, don't worry, I'll remind you."

Gabby covered her face and chuckled. "Okay. Okay. I'll try not to let my *new frame* get the better of me."

"Good. Now, let's try some of these on for size. I'm sure one will fit you. I wore these to family weddings when *I* was seven months pregnant."

Gabby took several outfits to her bedroom to try them on, then came out to the living room to model one by one for Pilar. "What do you think?"

"Oh, I like that one the best. It…fits your style."

The dress was an elegant sage polka dot chiffon. It had an empire waist that was flattering around Gabby's midsection, minimizing the growing belly. The top crisscrossed in the middle, and the pleated skirt moved with liquid grace as she swayed. Gabby turned in a circle, then looked at Pilar. "I love this one, and I know I have shoes that will work with it."

"See. Feels good to dress up, doesn't it?"

Pilar left Gabby to work out all the other items she'd brought over. All she had left to do was finish last-minute details for Carmen and Carlos's wedding, then she could get herself ready for the event. On her way back to the hotel, she called Juan for some moral support.

"Oh, wow. You're in quite a storm over there. Between the bride and the pregnant one, I don't know how you're surviving."

"I don't either. Maybe we can meet for lunch? I need a break."

Pilar and Juan met for lunch at Gabby's sandwich shop. It would be the only place she could eat something quick *and* see Juan. Pilar was already sitting when she saw his squad car pull up. Her heart fluttered as he entered, and she hoped he couldn't see it thumping through her clothes.

"Hola, mi amor," Juan bent, kissing her firmly on the lips. The touch of his hand on the back of her neck sent a shiver through her body before he sat down across from her.

"Hi yourself. I ordered our favorite sandwiches." She took his hand in both of hers. Juan could feel her adoration from across the table. Returning the intensely dreamy and faraway look she'd given him, he wrapped her hands in his. After a few moments, they released the bind, and picked up the unsweetened iced teas she'd ordered, taking a long draw through the red straws.

Pilar talked a mile a minute about her two friends and the barrage of orders that came from both in her direction. And while she told Juan all about the last couple of days in *her* world, he laughed about every bit as she described the hullabaloo.

Carmen didn't want to be involved with any of the planning. She was feeling enough pressure already. With the hotel being closed down for the week and Gabby still on bed rest, she didn't want to worry about a wedding that was merely a formality at this point. It

287

felt like it was more for their families and friends than for them.

"Mija. It's *your* wedding. Tell your friends what you envision and let them take it from there."

"I know Mami. Honestly, I don't care. I love Carlos. I just want to be with him for the rest of my life, married or not."

"Que? You have to be married! What's wrong with you? I didn't raise you like this."

"Why? Why do you need me to be married?"

Gloria gave Carmen a scowl that warned her not to question. Carmen took the warning and kept the rest of her mother's diatribe from getting to her.

Keeping with tradition, the night before the wedding, Carmen stayed in her room at the hotel while Carlos slept at their house. His sons, along with hers, all met him there for poker and drinks. Carlos invited Luis, who had a lot of stories to share about the groom. Stories the groom would have rather kept secret, and avoid the embarrassment. Still, through hysterical laughter, he told those stories. There was no slowing him down.

"…and then the mule pulled the line and Carlos didn't see the clothesline wrapped around his ankle. Damn thing pulled him, naked across the field a few hundred yards." Once Luis caught his breath, "When I looked out the window, I didn't know who it was. From head to toe, manure covered every inch." Luis's cackling was actually funnier than the story.

"What did you do?" asked Rafael.

"I had to get the hose. You stunk Carlos. The manure was everywhere. And I mean, everywhere."

The group recovered slowly. Their laughter was a genuine relief from the dreadful aura that Frank brought into every situation since arriving for the wedding.

"I thought I was too old for a bachelor party, but this is great, guys. Thank you." Carlos toasted with a shot of rum and smiled, then looked over at Frank, whose sullen expression brought down the entire gathering. "Frank?" His son looked up at him, shook his head, then slowly pushed his chair back as he stood, and headed for the back porch. "Excuse me fellas," Carlos followed.

Outside, Frank looked at his father. "Why? Why do you need to replace mom?"

"Son. Your mother is not replaceable." Carlos laid his right hand on his son's shoulder and Frank looked away. "Look at me. I will always love your mother. She gave me you and your brother."

"If you love her, how could you be with anyone else?"

"Your mother is gone. She's not coming back. I'm alive. When I'm with Carmen, I'm even more alive. I didn't realize how lost I was until I met her. The day I met her, something...I can't explain it. Something took over. Something I can't..."

"It makes me feel...bad. Like we don't matter. Like...our life when mom was alive...doesn't matter."

"I don't know why you feel that way, but it matters. It all matters. It will *always* matter. You, your brother, your families, will *always* matter. Your mom passed away over twelve years ago. It's time for you to let her go. Don't forget her, but let her rest." Carlos tilted his head and squeezed his son's shoulder.

The two stood in silence on the porch. Frank looked out toward the eastern field, at the lights that shined so brightly from the hotel. After a few minutes, Frank looked over at his father and nodded. He turned and embraced Carlos. The long hug brought Carlos the relief he needed. They returned to the poker game, already in progress in the other room, with Frank a little more relaxed.

While Carlos enjoyed his impromptu bachelor party at their house, Carmen stayed at the hotel for a fun bachelorette style sendoff with her sister, her friends, and daughter in laws, including the ones she'd gain when she married Carlos.

Outside on the hotel patio, the conversations floated from one topic to another. Carlos's family all loved the 'how we met' story, and the ladies got swept up in the 'engagement story.' But their favorite stories seemed to be the 'When Houses Attack' stories.

Carmen explained to her future daughter in laws how much work it was to bring the house up to date. When she'd met Carlos, he seemed to know exactly when she was in dire straits, injured, or in need of immediate rescue. "He would just show up. Then say I was starring on another episode of, 'When Houses Attack.' Honestly, I thought he was stalking me."

"He probably was," said Alba.

The evening had been a mix of reminiscing and 'getting to know you' stories that warmed everyone in the room. Every word

Carmen uttered fascinated her future daughters-in-law, and she was equally fascinated *by* them. It was almost as if she'd known them all along.

Sensing a moment, Pilar had an idea that once a year, the hotel would be closed for one week, where both sides of the family could visit at the same time. Carmen and Gabby thought it a perfect plan. If everyone had advance notice, then everyone could attend 'Family Week.'

Gloria opted for a quiet evening at Cristina's, catching up on the happenings in Pinar del Rio. "So. Tell me. How are things *really* going here in *New* Cuba? I think my daughter is always spinning the truth, making it all sound rosy and perfect."

"Honestly, Gloria. Why the sarcasm? I thought you wanted to catch up."

"Because my daughter has chosen to live in a place her father and I struggled to escape from." Gloria smacked the table and got up. "Because every time I watch the news back home, the reports are not new. It's the same. Always the same." She paced to the kitchen counter and turned back to Cristina, her voice rising. "These…people…who want to continue living in a Marxist society, when they know with absolute certainty that it will fail, continue to wreak havoc here, putting her in danger. And I know she's not telling me everything. So. I go home. I pray. Wish that she'd change her mind. Now, she's marrying Carlos. Don't get me wrong. I'm all for that. But why stay here?" Gloria returned to her seat at the table next to Cristina.

"I see. Do you think I should leave New Cuba as well?" Cristina gave her a sideways look and kicked up her chin. "Do you think you're safe where you live? I've seen the news about Miami. It's not all 'rosy and perfect' either."

"You're not my child. It's not the same thing."

"But I'm a human being. I'm in the same danger you claim Carmen has accepted. Why is alright for me to stay?"

"It's your choice." Gloria sat hard on the chair next to her. Cristina put her right hand over Gloria's. "Exactly. I'm an adult. This is my choice. Carmen is an adult. It's her choice. My advice? Support her no matter what her choices are. Keep your opinions to yourself."

Gloria closed her eyes and nodded, letting out a long breath, and looked up at her old friend. "Okay. Okay. Let's talk about life here. I want to hear it from you."

Cristina and Gloria spent the rest of the evening talking about the new happenings in the city. All the new stores that have opened, and the ones that returned to the island.

Cristina had quickly changed the intensity of the conversation, saving the evening from its heavy and unpleasant state. She even reported to Gloria about how successful Gabby's new restaurant had become, and how excited she and Jose were to welcome their new baby. In the end, they enjoyed their evening and were looking forward to the wedding the next day.

Five in the afternoon arrived before they knew it. Carmen dressed for her wedding in her office at the hotel. It was closest to where they'd get married; under the ceiba tree.

She wore her hair in a long braid that she wrapped in a bun on her head, revealing the delicate lace at the back of her simple off-white sheath; intricate beaded brocade made up the bodice. Baby's breath adorned the elegant braid, and a few soft curls draped delicately around her face.

As she stood in front of the mirror, that wrenching pain took hold again; her father wasn't there to walk her down the aisle. Carmen's chest went heavy, and she stared up at the ceiling, pressing down the sorrow. Her shoulders slouched, and she dropped the hand that held her bouquet to her side in surrender. Her makeup was done, and she didn't want to have to do it all over again if she let the tears run. She took several deep, cleansing breaths and shook her head.

Hope came into the room and caught the glint of an unshed tear. "What is it, mom?"

"Same thing it always is."

"I thought you said it had gotten better."

"It is. There're just moments, like these, where the void of his absence cracks everything open. Let me see your dress." Hope wore a simple dusty rose-colored dress with shirred sides. She'd gained a few pounds over the last few months, and the cut and design hid every little bulge.

Hope gave her mother a tight hug. "Abuela's on her way in. Brace yourself."

"Why…"

In walked Gloria. She wore a beaded gown with a small train

293

that looked like peacock feathers. A folding fan swung from her left wrist. The beaded feathers swooshed and scraped against the tile floor when she walked. After taking one look at Carmen, she shrugged her shoulder and twirled. "Te gusta?"

"Um. Si. It's beautiful. Mami, don't you think it's a bit too formal...for *my* wedding?" Carmen eyed Hope, praying for help.

Gloria stopped cold, and in a dark stare, "What's *too* formal? I bought this for Hope's wedding. To that asshole. And I never got to wear it. It's sat in my closet for months now. Guess what? I'm wearing it today. I don't care if it's too formal." Gloria threw her shoulders back, put one hand on her waist, and held her chin up so high her neck clicked. Then she strutted around, quite like a peacock; one hand on her waist, one in the air.

"Abuela. It's okay. Remember. *I* called off the wedding, *not* him."

"He should have tried harder, damn it," Gloria waved her fist. Like all Cuban women, they side with their own, no matter who was at fault. "Anyway, you're too good for him." Hope cracked up at her grandmother's vigor.

"But how did you get it here if it was in your closet?" asked Carmen.

"Sara."

"Oh. Okay. Have either of you seen Carlos?"

And just like that, Gloria flipped the switch on her disposition, beaming bright eyed at her daughter. "Mija, he looks so handsome. I'm so happy for you, but I won't say how I wish you weren't living in Cuba..."

"*New* Cuba. Mami." Carmen interrupted and gave her the side eye, while Hope covered her mouth to keep from laughing out loud.

"Si, I know. *New* Cuba." Gloria rolled her eyes and waved her hands like she'd been brushing crumbs off her blouse. "I won't say anything else."

The office door opened, and at once they all turned. "Sorry to interrupt. Carmen, there's an older gentleman here. He says he promised he'd stop by," said Angela.

"I can't imagine who that would be?" she looked around.

"He says his name is Pancho?"

"Oh. Yes! Send him in."

"Carmen. I'm so sorry that I stopped by unannounced." He quickly removed his hat. "I can see you're getting married today. I didn't know you were engaged," his befuddled expression troubled Carmen. She was fond of the old man and didn't want to make him feel unwelcome.

"Pancho. Hello. Yes, it was...very recent. I never had the time to tell you. Um. This is my daughter, Hope, and my mother, Gloria."

"Hola señorita, Hope. Señora Gloria." Pancho took Gloria's hand and gave it a light kiss. She turned to look at Carmen, spiraling through every shade of red and even some purples. Careful not to offend, she delicately slid her hand away like silk flowing between his fingers.

"Pancho is the Orchidist at the Orchidarium in Soroa. He gave me the ghost orchid I put on one of the trees in the garden. I invited him to stop by and see the grounds when he had a chance."

"I can see that my timing is off. I'll call and come another time." He replaced his hat, tipping it at Gloria. His green eyes, piercing in an upward gaze, met hers and she fluttered, setting her right hand on her chest. She inhaled and held a breath, then fluttered her vintage Flamenco peacock fan. The lace trimmed in iridescent lace glimmered in the overhead light.

Carmen looked over at Hope, raising her brows. "Uh, Pancho. Please stay. I'll introduce you to Carlos, afterward." Pancho nodded at Carmen and tipped his hat, looking back at Gloria.

"Si. Please stay, señor Pancho," said Hope. Gloria shot her a look that said, 'careful.'

Pancho answered shyly. "Alright. But I'm not really dressed for a wedding."

"It's a very casual affair. You'll fit in perfectly!" said Carmen.

Open-mouthed, Hope watched Gloria's moon-eyed expression when her grandmother looked back at Pancho. She'd never seen her grandmother so taken. By anyone. Seizing the opportunity, she took a big step forward, blocking the old man from walking out of the room. "Uh, Pancho, would you mind escorting my abuela to her seat?"

Pancho looked up at Hope and smiled. "It would be my honor, señora Gloria." Pedro bowed his head and hooked his arm out for Gloria to engage. She promptly glided her arm through his, and as they exited the doors, she looked back at her daughter and smiled.

"That was something," said Carmen. Hope nodded, speechless. "It was a great idea to put them together."

"Thanks. Thought of it all by myself," she teased. "You're not the only matchmaker here. And yes, Carlos told me earlier what you've been up to." The two had a hardy laugh until they heard the music start.

"I'm ready," said Carmen. Hope could feel her mother shaking when they hooked arms and headed toward the music. As the back doors opened, the sweet scent of the mariposa blooms filled the air. Carmen took a deep breath and glanced over at Hope, who was ready to walk her mother down the aisle. "Inhale."

Hope took a deep breath. "That's the most wonderful scent I've ever smelled."

Before they could walk outside, they heard screaming coming from somewhere behind them. Phoenix bolted through the open door, past them, toward the reception area. Carmen released her daughter's arm and fast walked toward the uproar.

"Mom, Angela is taking care of the hotel business. Mom...you're getting married...Carlos is waiting. What are you doing?" Hope talked a mile a minute and double timed it behind her mother. "Mom. Stop."

Carmen was reeling. She wasn't listening. She knew the voice. She knew who was at the front desk.

Chapter 21

Weather and A Surprise Visit

Gray clouds drifted over La Mariposa de Pinar del Rio. The air smelled of impending rain, and a warm breeze swept through the small gathering of wedding guests, carrying the scent of fresh cut grass and mariposa, whirling around them under the ceiba tree.

Tiny, twinkling fairy lights strung through the branches of the ancient tree, illuminating the space as darkness descended, sending a warm shiver to Carmen and Carlos's friends and family. White wood chairs arranged in a semi-circular fashion faced the altar. White tulle draped the aisle, and bunches of assorted white flowers adorned each post.

Two extra-large arrangements of white Lilys, orchids, gardenias and peonies imported from northern states created a spectacular display that framed the bower where Carmen and Carlos would tie the knot.

The white floral bouquets overflowed with snapdragons and baby's breath, and the plumeria mixed with the impending precipitation sweetened the gathering even more.

A live band played music from Cuba's golden age, as well as more progressive tunes, satisfying the older Cubans on the guest list, and the younger ones currently in residence. Pilar knew Carmen's penchant for classic rock, so she ensured the band could cover those as well during the reception.

The guests milled around on the patio enjoying the cocktail hour while waiting for the music to begin and the ceremony to start.

Cristina and Luis were feeling a surge of romance thinking about their own wedding under that very tree. "It was the most wonderful night of my life," Luis told her. Cristina smiled, swooning and fluttering her eyelashes.

"Mine as well. I carry such a terrible lament. We wasted so many years. So much time." Her eyebrows knit.

Luis grabbed her by the waist, twirling her to the sound of Gloria Estefan's, Mi Tierra. "We have now, tomorrow, and the rest of our lives. It's not something we can change. Why don't we just let that all go? Both of us."

As the song ended, they made their way to one of the high top tables, each taking a glass of red wine from a server on their way there. "It's about time these two tied the knot," said Luis.

"You're such a busy body old man. Try to mind your own business," said Cristina.

"Hello. Cristina, Luis." Gloria sauntered up to the table, holding the train of her dress in one hand, and her other arm hooked in Pancho's. "This is Pancho. He's an orchid expert friend of Carmen's."

"So nice to meet you, Pancho. That's…quite a dress, Gloria," said Cristina.

"Thank you. It was in my closet," responded Gloria, lifting her chin and looking away.

Cristina and Luis looked at each other. They weren't fond of people who 'put on airs.' "Is that so? A full length beaded gown? In your closet?" Cristina almost mocked Gloria's arrogance.

"Yes. My granddaughter was supposed to get married. It was supposed to be an enormous affair. I bought this dress, then she called off the wedding. Asi mismo!" Gloria snapped her fingers after she said, 'just like that,' and continued her address. "So I decided to wear it to Carmen's. I'm not letting it go to waste."

After that, the two couples greeted each other with pleasantries, and after a few drinks, they laughed as though they'd known each other intimately, for a long time. Given their ages, they knew more than they wanted to about the history of Cuba. The conquests, the revolutions, and the turmoil that eventually gave way to a U.S. intervention that saved the Cuban people.

Like any member of the older generations, arguing the finer points of politics always turned from a friendly exchange to a fiery argument.

Both sides agreeing about the same things in loud voices and wild arm waving, anyone who didn't know better would imagine it coming to blows at any moment.

"I support the government. Send these radical socialists to the island and let them live the way they want. Over there," said Cristina.

"That's what you think, huh? They don't belong here, in the U.S., living the good life, while trying to sabotage New Cuba's progress," said Pancho, his voice possessing that same passionate inflexion.

Gloria nodded in agreement, but kept as quiet as she could about the topic. She had no intention of moving to New Cuba. Her life was on the mainland. Pancho looked at her as if to ask, but realized the woman was not in the right frame of mind to ask her if she'd ever consider moving to New Cuba, so he remained silent.

Minutes later, the processional music played, and the four walked down the aisle, taking seats nearest the front of the space. Soon, Carlos and his sons stood in the head, waiting for the bride to make her appearance.

As Carmen and Hope reached the front desk, they found Phoenix snarling and barking madly. In her defensive crouch, she stood stiff and low to the checkered floor, with her behind in the air. Her ears pinned back while Diego held her collar, clasping her leash and keeping her close. The flowered arrangement that Pilar had assembled for her hung haphazard from her collar. A low grumble kept Miguel on notice as he stepped back and away from the dog.

"Get that mutt away from me."

"Dad?" Hope stood agape, several feet behind Carmen. The ground felt like quicksand and she couldn't move. Her feet were tingling in the worst way, so she removed her heels to get some feeling back.

Miguel looked around Carmen and exhaled. In the sweetest voice he could muster, "Hope? Sweetheart. I haven't seen you in so long. You look…" Miguel made to move closer, but she backed away and he became stoic. He snorted at her retreat.

"What are you doing here, Miguel?" asked Carmen.

"What's all this?" Miguel asked. "Who would marry *you*?"

"Um, Carmen? I was locking the door to make my way out back for the wedding, and this…man…stopped me. He was asking for you, and pushed his way in," said Angela.

The woman shook so completely; she kept dropping the pen she had in her hand. "I promise I wasn't about to interrupt your wedding over his…blustering." Behind her, Diego held the leash and waited with his arms crossed over his chest; a bouncer ready to bounce Miguel right back the way he came. Phoenix's body relaxed, and she calmed while on the leash, but her low growl remained constant.

Just then Miguel whirled on Angela. "My what? I simply asked you to fetch Carmen. You refused. Isn't that your job? Fetching." Miguel slammed his hand on the counter and spoke in a snapping, biting tone. Angela jumped back, and Phoenix hacked a slobbery growl at the sound of the loud pounding Miguel gave the front desk. Diego struggled, but held the leash steady.

Carmen's nostrils flared as she fought to keep her composure. She stepped toward her dog, petting the top of her head. "Good girl. Sit."

She looked over at Angela, whose face had contorted, horrified at the infuriated man as she strained to keep from crying. Diego took a step toward Miguel, and Carmen worried how she'd keep Diego from knocking him out.

"Yes. But I explained you were getting married today, and I wouldn't interrupt the wedding. I offered to take a message, but he wouldn't have it."

Diego had had enough and came 'round the edge of the counter, still holding on to Phoenix's leash. "Diego. It's alright." Carmen moved between Diego and Miguel and held up her free hand. "I've got this. You two go sit out back. I'll be right out. Hope. Go."

Diego took Angela by the arm, who took Hope by the arm and the three walked toward the back door, Phoenix in tow. Hope ogling back over her shoulder as Angela pulled her along.

Upon opening the door, Carmen could hear their wedding song playing, from the beginning, again, "Aquellos Ojos Verdes." Carlos selected the song as an homage to 'Those Green Eyes' of Carmen's that cast the spell on him the moment he saw her. It was an old song, originally written and performed by Adolfo Utrera in 1930, but it was exactly how Carlos felt. As the band began again, she realized she hadn't appeared when they started the first time, and Carlos might worry she won't show.

"What are you doing here Miguel?" his presence challenging Carmen's patience. Instantly, her anxiety began its regular rolling and twisting inside, tightening at every piece of flesh on her bones.

"My fiancé met with Pilar, to plan our wedding. I didn't know this was *your* hotel." His tone was different.

"And?"

"And I think you owe me." He began looking around, stuffing his hands in his pockets. "Quite the inheritance." Miguel walked over to the glass cabinet that displayed the artifacts recovered from the garden and tried the handle, then tapped on the glass.

"Yeah. It's locked. I owe you nothing. You need to leave, and find another place to have your wedding." Carmen lifted her right hand to still the fidgeting nerve at the edge of her eye, then looked at Miguel, shooting daggers.

The treacherous man spun back to face her. His lascivious eyes scanned her body while he licked his lips. "*I* think you do, and that's all that matters now, doesn't it? So here's the deal. I know you had all this while we were still married, and technically, community property..." he air quoted, "...but I'm going to let you keep my share, for now, and you'll plan our wedding yourself, Pilar can help, as a partial payment. I'll expect my deposit check returned to me."

"Get out. Get out now." Carmen set her bouquet on the counter. She pushed him and he stumbled back, catching himself before he could hit the ground. He squinted, mouth wide open. From behind Carmen came Carlos, Jose, and their sons. Hope was last, her mascara streaking over her cheeks. "Get out you, asshole," Carmen repeated as Carlos wrapped his arm around her waist, trying to hold her back.

"That was assault!" yelled Miguel, pointing at her.

"Is this Miguel?" asked Carlos.

"Yes. He was just leaving." If looks could kill, '*Miguel would already be underground,*' she thought.

"You must be the lucky man," Miguel insulted with drollery, dripping with sarcasm, and a swagger in his gait as he walked back to the group.

"Andres, Antonio. My sons," Miguel pleaded.

"Save it." Andres snapped.

The smirk was more than Carlos could take. He released Carmen and stepped in front of her, ready to crack Miguel in the jaw, when Rafael and Frank pulled him back.

"He's not worth it, dad."

"I called the police, Miguel," said Hope.

"Hope. I'm your father. How could you…?" Miguel glared at Carmen. "You did this. You turned my children against me."

Carmen stood very still. Very silent. The only thing moving was the nerve that hopped wildly next to her eye every time she was nervous.

"We're not done Carmen. I'm leaving. But we're not done," yelled Miguel as Tony and Andres escorted him out. "I'm not done with you either, lucky guy." He pointed at Carlos, heated animosity filling the space between the two.

After he left, Carmen exhaled and cried. "It's alright. He's gone. You don't have to worry. I won't let him mess with you again." Carlos wrapped her in his chest, her favorite place.

Carmen looked up at Carlos. Her hands shook as she straightened his shirt. He always knew just what to say to comfort her, and in the face of this awful development, he was no different.

Carmen was thankful that Miguel's threat didn't make Carlos run for the hills. She turned to look at her daughter, who was sobbing next to her future step brother, Rafael. He'd put his right arm around her shoulders, and she leaned her head.

"Oh mom. Why is he like this? So hateful," Hope sobbed.

"I don't know. Something in him is broken. He's always been broken. I'm so sorry, sweetie." Carmen hugged her, then Hope pulled away.

She took a deep, shaky breath and wiped the tears with her fingers. "Right. I'm going to fix my face and yours. Give me five minutes, and I'm walking you down the aisle to Carlos. You..." she pointed at Carlos, "...go wait for your bride at the end of the aisle. Rafael, Frank, take your dad and have them start the music again. Nothing is going to ruin my mom's wedding." Hope dried her tears, reapplied her and her mother's makeup, then took her mother by the arm, and headed for the opening of the carpeted walkway.

When Carmen appeared, the guests stood, smiling as they watched her glide toward the anxious groom. Carlos rocked on his heels while he covered his mouth. Hot tears stung his bloodshot eyes. Carmen saw the emotion on his face and responded in kind.

As they reached the end of the aisle, Hope gave her mother a quick peck on the cheek and handed her over to Carlos. Carmen looked into Hope's eyes, shaking. As soon as Carmen turned back to her groom, the vibration that had spread through her body subsided, and she wove her fingers through his, turning toward Pilar, the officiant.

Carlos looked deep into his bride's bright green eyes. "You are so beautiful, my love," he said.

Carmen smiled. She wanted their moment to be *just* theirs, but her insides were turning. Things were going so well, and now this prick showed up when she least expected.

"Are you alright?" Carlos asked, knowing this was a shoe she was certain would one day tumble through the sky to knock her in the head.

"Yes," she answered, hoping he couldn't read her mind, or detect the dismay in her voice. "Please, go on," she said to Pilar, who got certified to marry them just a few hours before.

Pilar began the ceremony with a short anecdotal about when Carlos and Carmen had first met. Of course, most of the guests knew the story, but Pilar wanted to point out that though their timing wasn't quite right then, the timing was perfect now, with their families and friends all gathered at the same time, in the same place.

As Carmen listened, she remembered everything that tormented her existence around that time, and counted her blessings. She wouldn't allow Miguel to menace her again. She shook it off and kept focus on her vows.

The rest of the ceremony went off without a hitch, followed by a seated dinner and dancing reception that included music from every era and every genre.

During the reception, Carmen found Frank standing alone at a high top table near the dance floor. His whiskey almost gone. "Hey. May I have this dance?" she asked with a light smile.

Frank drained the glass and set it down. He walked with Carmen to the dance floor. "Thank you for coming today. It means a lot that you're here with us."

"My wife insisted. I talked to my dad earlier, and I'm working on my…attitude. He just doesn't understand. My mom is gone. Now he's married to you. Am I supposed to call you mom or something?"

"You can call me anything you like. Listen. I know how you feel. I lost my dad. A very long time ago, in fact. And there's not a day that goes by that I don't feel this ripping pain shredding my heart out. Most days, I'm alright. I can control it. Other days, like today..." Carmen's throat closed up. Frank looked down at her as she shook her head. "Days like today. He wasn't here to walk me down the aisle. When my marriage fell apart, or I lost my business, he wasn't there. This dad that always had my back. That I could count on for even the smallest things...wasn't there."

Frank didn't know anything about Carmen. Not really. "How...?"

"Every day it gets a little easier. Then I think it's only easier because I'm adapting and getting stronger when I have to deal with it because the same pain is always there."

"In time..."

"No. There's no amount of time that can pass that will make you forget. It's not time that makes it easier. You will get stronger. You will adapt. Things won't always be as impossible as when you first lost your mom. Just know that we are family. We will be here whenever you need us."

"Us?"

"Yes. Your father *and* I will always be here."

Frank smiled down at her just before the song ended, and Carlos came over to cut in. "Here's your bride, dad." Frank smiled and bowed his head before walking away.

Carmen told Carlos all about their conversation. She felt it had gone well, and maybe gave him a glimpse into what kind of person she was. How they've both been through similar losses, they found some common ground they could stand on.

Later, the newlyweds made the rounds, visiting their guests and thanking them for attending; toasting, laughing, and telling stories about their journey to this day, this moment. And just like that, Carmen had forgotten the past that attempted to slither into her world, and the threat she was certain was empty.

The next day was Sunday. Their family and friends all headed home for the start of the new week, with the promise of participation in Family Week twice a year. The passenger van and Ubers drove them all out as the love birds waved goodbye from the front of the hotel. Carmen and Carlos turned toward each other. After a silent kiss and a passionate embrace they headed home.

Chapter 22

Too Much White and A Tinge of Purple Sky

Margot Sanchez stood on the balcony in her robe. The light breeze rippled the white silk open, revealing nothing but skin underneath. Though in her late sixties, she was proud not to be the least bit bashful. She worked out regularly, and paid top dollar for skin care, easily passing for a much younger woman.

Her exquisite home, overlooking the Viñales Valley, boasted sweeping views of the hills. Tall, wall to wall windows provided panorama views of the lush green valley from every room.

She set her vodka rocks on the wide railing and spread her arms wide, inhaling. The wind picked at her jet straight bob, and she raked her fingers through it and thought, *'It might be time for a touchup.'*

She loved her house and had spared no expense. After all, she had the money to do whatever she wanted, so she had the house built according to her specifications on one of the highest plateaus.

Gardenias filled the ground floor gardens. White lily plants intermingled with tuberose, and white climbing roses crept their way up the house's support columns. At just the right time of year, one side of the garden bloomed with white ranunculus. Even white water lilies lazed around in the pond, while tall white jasmine bushes set the green backdrop for white hyacinths, and filled the breath of wind with their sweet scent.

Inside, extra-large, white Carrera marble tile shined throughout the house, and white leather furniture blended right in with the walls. There were no paintings or photos, and much like the way she dressed and the Mercedes she drove, everywhere you looked, everything was white.

Though Margot didn't cook, she had a state-of-the-art kitchen, complete with a La Cornue custom stove. She didn't mind paying the six-figure price for it. She'd selected the range in white with details in solid walnut and accented with brass and copper to match every fixture in the house; the only items not white.

Margot continued the theme into her private bathroom. Sitting on the same marble floor was a white and gold geode bathtub with gold fixtures. Her vanity, a thick white marble, carved from one piece with an elongated, embedded sink, took up the longest wall. There were no nick-knacks or personal items visible anywhere.

The whole place had a museum feel; cold and hard. Margot liked to joke that if anyone visited, she didn't want them to have any inkling about the kind of person she was, then thought it more of a statement than a joke. She preferred a bit of mystery and enjoyed watching people not be able to guess anything about her. No one would ever know.

Without turning, she knew he was right behind her. He'd dressed and was ready to leave. "Will that be all?"

She turned to face him, and walked through the twelve-foot electric glass sliding doors. "Take off your clothes." He quickly reached for the top button of his shirt, "Slowly," she insisted. His pace slowed. Margot sipped the rest of her drink while she watched him undress. One button at a time he made his way down until he reached his pants, unbuttoning and lowering the zipper so slowly she could hear each tooth as the pull tab made its way down. After his slacks hit the floor she walked past him to her bedroom. His gaze lowered, and he followed her.

Several hours later, Margot emerged from her bathroom, leaving watery footprints in her wake.

"Ms. Sanchez. When do you think you'll be ready to help me..."

She interrupted him. "You can go now Alex."

While Carlos cleared the table, Carmen washed the last of the dishes and silverware. "Any luck on those pictures?" asked Carlos.

"No. It'll be the last place I look, though."

Carlos guffawed at her wry smile. "Why don't you turn a glass upside down?"

Carmen took the last glass she washed, looked him dead in the eye and laughed. "Okay," she plopped the glass on the counter. "I wonder when we'll find out who that person was we found in the cavern. It's so sad to see anyone's life end that way."

"I'm sure the police will let us know when they're ready." Carlos could sense her apprehension. After all, the body was found on *her* property. "That's life, baby. None of us are getting out of it alive."

"Not funny."

"It was a little funny. How about a glass of wine? There's a slight chill in the air and it feels like fall. I know how you love to sit outside in the fall."

"There's just so many things going on at the same time," Carmen worried.

"I don't think it's *all* at the same time. Hey. Do you know what Einstein once said?"

"He said a lot of things."

Carlos grabbed a bottle of Cabernet and started pulling the cork. "He said, 'The reason for time is so everything doesn't happen at any one moment.,' or something like that. And it's lucky. I don't think if the last two years happened at once, we would have survived," squeak and pop went the cork.

"That's for sure."

The couple sat on their porch as the last bit of sun dipped behind a dark cloud. Its rays shot out in every direction. A tinge of purple sky framed the glow; a magnificent display of red, orange, and yellow light in the background, and the blackened tops of royal palms lined the bottom of the picturesque skies. They toasted each other, their friends and family, and the luck they've had to be together, at this time, in this moment. The harmonic melody of the tick-tack of their rocking chairs as they swung back and forth brought tranquility to their otherwise tumultuous week.

"So. When is Mary moving down?" he asked.

"She said as soon as she clears out whatever she's got going on. I don't know how long that will be. I'm sure she'll let me know when she's ready. I told her she could have my room at the hotel until she figures out where she wants to live."

"I'm sure she'll be very happy here."

"Yes, she will." Carmen looked over at her husband. Her eyes blinked slowly, and she relaxed at the sounds of nature all around. The leaves rustling in the evening breeze. The birds chirping their goodnights, and the roosting call of chickens as they made their way into their coops. She took Carlos's hand, weaving her fingers through his, and held tight while they rocked their steady rhythm. "Everything will work itself out. Timing is everything."

Stay tuned…

Acknowledgements

Thank you to my husband.
As always, for listening and pushing me forward.
For your patience and humor, and all the little things you do.

Thank you to my family and friends
for inspiring me to keep writing.

FH Spector was a National Board Certified Teacher of the gifted and taught first through fifth grades. She was born in Cuba, and brought to the United States on her second birthday, on one of the last flights that fled the island after Batista's government was overthrown. She grew up in North Miami, and when visiting Cuba became possible, she made the journey many times. Visiting her extensive family, she was able to bring urgently needed medicine and food. Seizing the opportunity, she toured the island gathering information from her family's bottomless well of stories. She lives in Florida with her husband, and thanks her lucky stars every day.